Wild, Wild Women of the West

D1564762

Wild, Wild Women of the West

Delilah Devlin
Layla Chase
Myla Jackson

APHRODISIA
KENSINGTON BOOKS
http://www.kensingtonbooks.com

APHRODISIA BOOKS are published by

Kensington Publishing Corp.
850 Third Avenue
New York, NY 10022

All Kensington Titles, Imprints, and Distributed Lines are available at special quantity discounts for bulk purchases for sales promotions, premiums, fund-raising, and educational or institutional use.

Special book excerpts or customized printings can also be created to fit specific needs. For details, write or phone the office of the Kensington special sales manager: Kensington Publishing Corp., 850 Third Avenue, New York, NY 10022, attn: Special Sales Department, Phone: 1-800-221-2647.

Aphrodisia and the A logo Reg. U.S. Pat & TM Off.

ISBN-13: 978-0-7582-1981-7
ISBN-10: 0-7582-1981-4

First Trade Paperback Printing: June 2007

10   9   8   7   6   5   4   3   2   1

Printed in the United States of America

CONTENTS

A TASTE OF HONEY

DELILAH DEVLIN

Prologue

1880, West Texas

The wind whispered softly through the short, scrubby oak trees lining the creek, arriving at last at Honey Cafferty's back door where it tousled the hollow wooden chimes she'd hung above the stoop of the only home she'd ever known.

The sound, like half a dozen reed flutes, rose and fell with each stirring of the air, rousing her from her restless slumber. She'd opened the shutters of her windows in hopes of catching a breeze after the stifling white-hot heat of the day. As the warm air drifted over her moist skin, she sighed with relief and let herself drift back to sleep.

Then a scrape, like a footstep on sand, came from the side of her wagon. Honey jerked fully awake and snuck her fingers beneath her goose down pillow for the revolver that was never far from reach.

She eased up from her mattress, making sure she stayed away from the pools of silver moonlight that shone through her small windows, and peered around one casing, her pistol cocked and loaded, ready for whatever trouble awaited her outside.

She worried for the horses she'd tied to trees next to the shallow creek and wondered why they'd remained quiet. Someone was out there. She could feel it—and she never ignored the intuition her father had said was as much a part of her Irish heritage as her red hair, green eyes, and the touch of fey that kept her hitching her wagon to follow the stars.

A shadow passed in front of the window and another scuff sounded next to the door. She drew back, not wanting to act too quickly. The advantage would come when the intruder slammed through the back door expecting to find her groggy from sleep and unprepared.

Her eyes narrowed on the door and her arm descended, the butt of the pistol resting in one hand, a finger sliding around the trigger.

"I bring the plants you want," a raspy voice said from beside her, a round face resting on the windowsill like a disembodied head.

Honey stifled a shriek and lowered her weapon. "Señora Garza! Why didn't you call out to me? You scared me half to death."

"Girl like you shouldn't live in a wagon," the old woman groused. "You need ground beneath your feet, not wheels."

Ignoring the familiar complaint from her old friend, Honey grumbled, "I came by to see you today."

"I been walking in the hills. Found somethin' special for you."

Honey set down her pistol on the built-in dresser. "You didn't have to come all this way. You know I wouldn't leave without restocking my supplies and visiting a while."

The old woman's index finger appeared above the windowsill. "This is magic plant. Have to pluck at midnight on a full moon."

Honey tried one more time—she really did need the sleep. "It can't keep until tomorrow?"

"Gotta brew tonight. Fresh. Make very special medicine."

Honey groaned inwardly. The heat had sucked the energy right out of her, but she knew the *curandera* meant well. She believed in the magical properties of the plants she harvested. If brewing her potion by the light of the full moon kept the old woman happy, she wasn't going to complain. Señora Garza's "magic" kept them both fed and clothed.

"I build fire—you get dressed."

The *curandera* squatted in her brightly colored cotton skirt and busied herself uncovering the smoldering embers of Honey's campfire. While she blew on the coals and slowly added kindling to raise a flame, Honey slipped on a pair of wash-softened blue jeans, tucking in her shift, and tied back her hair. Although she would have liked to go barefoot to the fire, she slid on slippers, knowing scorpions might be about.

Stepping down the folding steps of her stoop, she shivered slightly at the hint of chill in the breeze—a reminder summer waned and soon she'd have to find a place to ride out the winter. Somewhere . . . needy. A quiet little town ready for a little shaking up and a whole lot of her healing potions.

"So, what's so special about this medicine?" Honey asked as she drew near the crackling fire. "What will it cure?"

Señora Garza muttered a low incantation in an incomprehensible mix of Spanish and Comanche, her graying black braids swaying as she chanted. Honey's iron stew pot sat in the middle of the flames, filled with water that slowly burped as it started to boil. When she'd finished her "spell," Señora Garza smiled a wide toothless grin and dropped gnarled bits of roots into the water. "It no cure illness. It gives *fuerza* to a man's parts."

Honey shook her head, not understanding.

The old woman rolled her eyes. "His *cojones, mija.* Makes his *pinga* strong and virile."

Honey was glad the darkness masked the heat blooming on her cheeks. "What am I supposed to do with something like that?" She whispered fiercely, although no one else was around to hear their scandalous conversation. "Won't it cure a headache or settle a stomach, too? I can't tell decent folks it makes a man's . . ." She cupped her hand and made a gesture at the juncture of her thighs that indicated a lengthening cock. ". . . his . . . thing hard!" she sputtered. "'Sides, who needs something like that?"

The old woman's shaggy eyebrows waggled and she laughed. "You tell the women what you have. They will buy."

Honey wasn't done with her tirade—the heat in her cheeks fueled a spirited anger that ripped right through her and settled as always on her tongue. "What the hell am I gonna call it?" Images of bottles labeled "Miracle Manhood Enhancer" and "Poker Potion" came to mind. *Jesus, Mary and Joseph!* She'd be run out of the next town—tarred and feathered for her licentious product.

"Easy, *mija.* Call it . . ." Señora glanced back with a wicked grin. ". . . Elixir of Love."

Honey sucked in a deep breath. It had a ring to it all right. "Elixir of Love," she repeated, liking the soft, romantic sound of it even more, now. She lifted her arms and practiced her slogan. "Cleopatra's secret weapon that captured the undying love and devotion of Caesar and Marc Antony."

The *bruja* snorted and started to cackle. "It no makes a man fall in love. Nothin' to do with the heart. Makes a man *horny.*"

"Horny?"

"Builds his juices. Makes him feel like he will die if he don't find a woman to—" She clapped her hands three times in rapid succession.

With a mortified blush heating her cheeks, Honey got

Señora Garza's meaning. However, "Elixir of Virility" was just too crass. "Elixir of Love" it would remain.

Nothing excited her like playing with her slogans. When her imagination was engaged, it seemed the sky was the limit for her ambitions. And she had big, brass-band-and-Fourth-of-July kinds of dreams. Someday, she'd have enough money saved up to build a house and get the kind of life she'd only seen from the top of her wagon seat as she rolled past the towns.

Her eyes widened with excitement. "I've got it!" She tilted back her head and raised her hands for dramatic flair. "Straight from the bazaars of Zanzibar—" That had a nice ring to it. She hoped like hell Zanzibar was somewhere near Egypt. "I bring you the very potion Cleopatra used to conquer Caesar." A very nice ring indeed!

Señora Garza's excited cackle rose like the twittering of a hoarse bird. "Only you be careful or you be the one who gets conquered, *mija*."

1

"Sheriff, you've gotta do somethin' about that woman!"

The note of exasperation in Curly Hicks' voice was one Joe Tanner had heard often in the past couple of days—at least from the unmarried men of the town. He didn't need to ask which woman he was talking about—he already knew who was responsible for Curly's agitation. Her name was on everybody's lips, although the tones with which her name was spoken varied widely.

He was curious what the normally reticent shopkeeper had to say about the lady in question. "Just what do you want me to do about her, Curly?"

"Send her packin'! She's up to somethin'. Cain't tell you 'xactly what, but ever since she came, nothin's been the same."

So, he wasn't the only one to notice. Since the day Honey Cafferty's fancy painted wagon had rolled into town, the mood around One Mule had seemed . . . expectant, like the town itself was wakening from a long slumber and suddenly discovered it was every joyful holiday all wrapped inside one bright, shining moment.

Which posed a dilemma for Joe. One Mule had elected him to keep the peace and things had been riding smooth like a Conestoga over flat land—no bumps, no bone-jarring thuds. So far, the townfolk had been pretty satisfied with their lives. It was a quiet place—the right kind of town to set down deep roots—and he intended to keep it that way.

However, Honey Cafferty had a way about her that was anything but quiet. She radiated shimmering sensuality, from her vibrant red hair and cat-like green eyes to her lushly curved lips and body. Everything about her shouted like Fourth of July fireworks and crazily spinning whirligigs, eliciting a restless hunger in him that had no place in his tidy little life.

Just looking at the woman made his teeth ache, made him want to touch the fire he sensed smoldered just below the surface of her sweet-smelling peaches 'n' cream skin.

"Whatcha gonna do, Sheriff?"

Not what he really wanted to, that was for damn sure. "Has she committed a crime?"

Curly's cheeks reddened. "You're not list'nin' to me. Amos Handy didn't open his smithy shop 'til half past noon yesterday. That ain't never happened before."

"Why do you think Miss Cafferty had something to do with that?"

"Amos' wife bought a bottle of her special *ee*-lixir the day before."

"So, you think Miss Cafferty poisoned Amos?"

"I'm not sayin' she did it on purpose, but Letty was sure lookin' happy when I came to see what was wrong. And you know that woman has the sourest disposition of any female this side of the Mississippi."

"What about Amos? Did he look like he was sickening?"

"Well, no. But he's mighty tired, he says. Said he was gonna close his shop for a couple of days—take a vacation. You ever heard such a load of horseshit in all yer born days?"

"Still don't see where Miss Cafferty fits in with all this."

"Sheriff, you need to open your eyes," Curly said, his own eyes bugging wide. "Look at all the married folk. The men are lookin' glassy-eyed and the women are hummin' like mosquitoes. I tell you, it's that woman's fault!"

"What about you, Curly? Do you have any complaints?"

"I'm plain tuckered out keepin' one step ahead of Sally. She's been tryin' to get me to stop by for her apple pie, but she has that look in her eye, again."

"Which one's that?"

"That marryin' look. The one what's got me too sceert to step outside her mama's parlor for a kiss. It might be all over for me," he said dolefully.

Joe suppressed a smile. Not that he blamed Curly for his skittishness. Despite his longing to set down roots, the thought of marriage made him itch, too. "Do you know anything about this special elixir the Cafferty woman's selling?"

"Nope. Soon as she sold her dyspepsia cures, she shooed the menfolk away for a private chat with the ladies. They sure as hell aren't talkin' about what she give 'em."

"Have you asked her straight out what she's been selling to the womenfolk?"

Curly's cheeks grew a fiery red. "I cain't do that, Sheriff," he said, his tone mournful. "I open my mouth to have my say, and all she has to do is aim those pretty green eyes my way and I'm meltin' like ice cream on a hot summer day. Before you know it, she's done sold me somethin' else I don't need!"

Joe pressed his lips into a straight line to keep from laughing. Yes siree! Looking into the woman's eyes did test the mettle of a man. If a man wasn't on guard against her charm, she'd tie his tongue in knots and swell his . . .

Best not let his mind head down that dusty trail. "Tell you what, Curly. I'll pay a visit to Miss Cafferty. See if there's anything to your story."

"Don't have to go out to her campsite. She's in the saloon, right now. That was the other thing I was gonna mention. No righteous woman like she claims to be oughta be rollin' on the floor of a saloon with Paddy Mulligan! It's just not seemly."

Joe stiffened. "She's in the saloon?" At Curly's solemn nod, he grabbed his hat and stomped out of his office onto the planked walkway, making a beeline for the Rusty Bucket. Miss Cafferty had seemed so coy, so modest, when he'd sold her the permit to solicit. She'd dressed in an outfit any Eastern-raised schoolmarm would have given the nod. He should have listened to his gut in the first place. No decent woman had ever made him so damn out of control. She was just like the rest of those independent-minded women who thought society's rules somehow didn't apply to them.

The red hair had been a bright glaring clue to her true nature—no matter that it was always neatly styled and pinned. She'd snookered him just like she had the rest of the townsfolk.

He slammed his palms against the swinging doors leading into the saloon and came to a halt. A ring of men filled the center of the room. Those on the outer perimeter stood on tiptoe to peer over the shoulders of the men standing at the center of the circle.

He elbowed his way inside and sucked a slow breath between his teeth to calm the anger that burned hot and fast as a match to gunpowder.

The sight that greeted him only raised the pressure pounding in his head another notch. The "shy and modest" Miss Cafferty straddled the barrel chest of the town drunk, her petticoats rising above her knees. Her woolen stockings hugged an expanse of ankle and calf that drew every male eye watching her wrestle the behemoth.

Paddy Mulligan groaned beneath her, sounding like a cross between a drunken bear and a man in the last throes of lust. Given his sorry state, Joe suspected his moans were due more to the heat from the woman's open legs rubbing his wide belly and her bottom bumping his private parts than the wicked set of shiny pliers she had shoved inside his mouth.

Joe's own body reacted swiftly, urgently. That was the last damn straw! "Woman, what the hell do you think you're doing?"

Honey Cafferty blew an errant curl of flaming-red hair from her eyes. "Not now," she said, not looking away from Paddy's tonsils. "Now Paddy, if you'd let me give you my special pain-killer first—"

"Smelled like skunk fart," one of the men in the circle said. "Don't blame him for refusin'."

"Shoulda just let him get drunk first," another said.

"Drinking spirits makes a man bleed faster." Honey muttered and twisted her wrist, eliciting a strangled groan from Paddy.

"Yeah, but then he wouldn't give a damn," said the bartender, who stood with his arms folded over his chest, a glower darkening his usually jovial face.

"Someone's standing in my light," Honey said and looked over her shoulder. When she caught sight of Joe, her eyes blinked and she gave him a weak smile. "If you'd just shift to your left, Sheriff, I'll be done with this extraction in just a minute."

Joe's eyes narrowed, but he moved sideways, taking a deep breath to calm the fury building inside him. He'd bide his time for now, but he and the little "lady" were gonna have a talk.

Her hand twisted again, and Paddy's eyes rolled back in his head.

"Thank the Lord, he passed right out," said the bartender, looking as pale as a ghost.

Both Honey's hands wrapped around the pliers and she leaned back. Everybody drew a deep breath and more than one man's face winced as she yanked a blackened tooth out of Paddy's mouth.

"Got it!" She raised it high for everyone to see. "When he wakes up, he'll feel so much better."

She plucked the tooth off the end of her pliers and tucked it inside Paddy's shirt pocket. Then she reached for a tapestry carpet bag lying on the floor beside her. She pulled out a small folded paper and poured a rough yellow-brown powder into her palm, then packed the powder into the bleeding hole she'd left in Paddy's gum. "That should stop the bleeding and help him some with the pain."

She wiped her hands on a bar towel, and then clambered off his chest and smoothed down her skirts, pulling her cuffs back down her forearms, cool as a cucumber, while the crowd of fascinated men watched her put herself to rights.

Joe had no doubt that every man there was reversing the process in his mind. His cock surged again against the placket of his trousers, which only made him madder.

When she finished, she flashed a bright smile. "Now, if anyone else has trouble with an aching tooth, you know who to come to."

There were a lot of heads shaking and low mutters among the men. However reluctant they might be for a visit from her plier-wielding hands, half a dozen men still reached down to pick up her bag.

"Thank you, gentlemen. I'll leave you to your business."

The crowd parted like the Red Sea for Moses, and she sailed right through, brushing past Joe with a ladylike nod.

He clamped his jaw tight and turned to follow her out the doors. On the planked sidewalk, he caught her arm. "Now, wait a minute there. You and I are gonna have us a little talk."

"Oh? Do you need a tooth pulled, too?" she said, a smile tugging the corners of her lips.

He narrowed his eyes. She wasn't wriggling her way out of this with charm. A quick glance behind them, and he realized the swinging doors were open and the men had spilled onto the walkway to watch them.

All he needed now was for a few of that beer guzzling crowd to decide a rescue was in order. "You're coming to my office."

"Anything you say," she said, her voice soft and a little breathless.

Her feminine tone had his loins tightening again, and he dropped her arm like he'd touched a red-hot poker. Hectic color rose on her cheeks and her gaze widened as she stared up at him. She was starting to look worried, which suited him just fine.

Extending his hand in front of him, he let her precede him down the walkway. She took a deep breath, lifted her chin, and glided down the sidewalk like she owned it.

A breeze caught her light rosewater scent and wafted it right under his nose. Without her gaze keeping his appropriately engaged, he was free to look his fill—and he did, his glance sliding down the slim straight line of her back to the flare of the womanly hips that twitched from side to side. It was all he could do not to reach down and adjust the front of his trousers.

They passed the front of Curly Hicks' store and several interested gazes followed. At the doorway, Mrs. Sessions, the preacher's wife, gave Honey a wide, beaming smile.

Honey shook her head and murmured, "Not now, Daisy. The sheriff wants a word with me."

Daisy Sessions' gaze landed on him and two round spots of color rose on her cheeks. "Later then, my dear."

Odd, but the woman looked flustered, almost guilty.

Finally, they reached his office and Honey breezed inside. He closed the door behind him and turned to find more faces peering through the window. He cursed under his breath and pointed to the inner room where the jailhouse was.

Her back stiffened, but she didn't demur and stepped inside. When he had her out of sight and hearing of all the interested folk of One Mule, he lifted a foot and nudged the door closed behind them.

Honey had her back to him and her slim hand lifted to smooth back her hair.

He stayed silent, deciding to let her stew for a minute. When a body got nervous, she tended to talk and Joe wanted to hear everything the little lady had to say.

At last, she cleared her throat and turned, a small, tight smile pasted on her lips. "Am I under arrest, Sheriff?"

"Should you be?"

Her breath gasped, lifting her gently rounded chest against her staid gray shirtwaist jacket. "You're angry with me."

He crossed his arms across his chest and leaned his back against the door and tried not to think too hard about the fact they were completely alone. A tantalizing prospect he'd imagined often the past couple of days.

As he watched her standing in the narrow, darkly lit room with the bars of the cell block behind her, his imaginings became disturbingly carnal. He cleared his throat and forced his mind back to business. "I sold you a license to solicit your medicines," he said, keeping his voice even although the memory of her straddling Paddy Mulligan still burned hot. "Yet I found you rolling on the floor of a saloon performing surgery."

She gave a short, strained laugh. "I wasn't rolling on the floor—Paddy's a large man and I couldn't see into his mouth when he was seated. Besides, I only pulled a tooth. I do have some expertise—"

"I'm getting complaints about possible poisonings—"

"Poison!" Her finely arched brows rose. "I don't deal in poisons, sir."

"Then explain why all the married men in town have taken to their beds."

She opened her mouth, but quickly clamped it shut. Her back straightened.

"You don't deny you're responsible?"

A blush the color of the pink roses his mama used to grow spread quickly across her cheeks and down her neck to disappear beneath her collar. "It's not what you think, Sheriff."

He wondered if the blush extended to her breasts, but didn't dare let his gaze fall below her rounded chin. "Then tell me exactly what it is."

She lifted that stubborn chin high. "I can't. That information is privileged. Meant to remain private between me and the persons I sold the medicine to, like a priest receiving confessions or a doctor—"

"You're no doctor. Those rules don't apply."

"Have you talked to these men? Have any of them made complaints against me?"

"No, but you're up to something, and I don't want any trouble." And she was trouble with a capital "T." "I'm thinking you should hitch up your wagon and head on down the road."

She blinked and, for a moment, her expression faltered. "I had hoped to winter here. Mrs. Sessions—"

"—is an innocent lady. She's not wise to your ways."

Her stillness cut him, and he felt heat warm the back of his neck and the tips of his ears. He'd crossed the line between being professional and being cruel.

Then her chin jutted higher, and her hands fisted on her hips. "You're implying I'm not . . . innocent?"

His gaze swept over her, from the tip of her red-haired head to her toes. Another insult. He couldn't seem to help himself where she was concerned. Something about her had him firing with both barrels blazing. "You travel alone—without chaperone. What's a man supposed to think about that?"

She took a step closer, her eyebrows drawing together in a fierce scowl. "Being alone in the world means I'm a whore?" she said, her voice rising.

"A decent woman," he bit out, "would set roots in a community—seek help and protection from a husband or her neighbor."

"I don't need any man to protect me or my virtue, sir."

"I'll grant you had me and most of the town fooled. But

your charm's a little too practiced, and you've got a slick tongue—"

Her mouth gaped and her cheeks went from pink to a dark red that clashed with her bright hair. "A slick tongue?"

Her anger goaded him on like a burr under a saddle. "You're a snake oil salesman, a charlatan—"

She stepped so close her chest nearly touched his, and she glared up into his face. "Now, you look here, buster!" she said, pointing a finger at his chest and giving him a nudge. "I'm a businesswoman. I sell cures people need. I haven't broken any laws, and I sure as hell haven't poisoned one damn person in this town." She paused to catch her breath . . . and that's when it happened.

Her breasts brushed his chest, and he felt a spark arc between their bodies, igniting a fire as fierce as lightning striking dry prairie grass. It filled his loins with a heavy, pulsating heat and drew his balls tight and close to his groin. His hands shot out and grasped her shoulders to pull her flush against his body, but he halted, holding her an inch away. What he wanted of her wasn't very civilized. Best not cross that line.

"Sheriff!" Her plump pink lips gasped, but her head tilted back.

Invitation enough. He slammed his mouth down onto hers even while he damned himself for being a fool.

2

Honey clung to Sheriff Tanner's broad shoulders, afraid her knees would buckle if she let go. His kiss shocked her to her toes. His mouth devoured hers—hungry, openmouthed, drawing a deeply carnal response from her that had her trembling like a leaf in a breeze.

Ever since that first day when she'd entered his office to purchase her license, she'd imagined what his kiss would be like. When he'd looked up from the rough, deeply scratched desk with the latest telegraph messages and Wanted posters spread across the surface, he'd taken her breath away.

Even seated, she could tell he was a big man. Her eyes had followed his thickly muscled shoulders and neck to his large hands with their long, thick fingers and she'd shivered at the thought of those hands gliding intimately over her flesh. Flustered by how quickly her thoughts had turned carnal in nature, she'd raised her glance.

The harsh, blunt angles of his jaw and nose had been strangely beautiful, well suited to his body. His dark eyes had glinted with interest for the barest moment, before he'd shuttered his expression and one dark brow had risen in a challenge that found an answer deep inside her core.

When her lips had opened to speak, his gaze had dipped and so had hers, until one side of his full lips had curved upward. He'd liked what he'd seen of her, and she'd thought . . . just maybe, she'd like to explore this attraction—to feel the pressure of his expressive mouth on hers.

In her romantic fantasies, she'd thought he'd gently mold her lips, slowly coaxing her to open for him before dipping inside to touch his tongue to hers. A gentleman's sweet kiss.

Never would she have imagined the depth of passion he'd unleash. He'd appeared a self-possessed man, not one prone to losing his control.

But then again, she'd never dreamed she'd enter a shouting match with him. Never mind that his voice had remained even and his words clipped, and *she'd* done most of the shouting.

No wonder he'd lost his temper. It was all her fault. She'd driven the man to resort to kissing her to shut her up. Only once he'd accomplished his goal, he seemed in no hurry to stop.

Neither was she. She opened her mouth and accepted the thrust of his tongue, shivering as he invaded, moaning softly when he rimmed her teeth and the roof of her mouth and then stroked the length of her tongue in long, scorching laps as though he had to brand her, mark this territory as his own.

Lord, she wished he'd show the same possessive heat where the rest of her body was concerned. She strained against the strong hands that kept her from snuggling close. Her nipples grew tight, hard, and irritated by the soft cotton of her chemise, and the oddest quivering pulse began between her legs, swelling her outer feminine folds, moistening the thin inner lips, until she was squeezing her thighs together to relieve the ache.

She broke the kiss and opened her eyes.

His dark brown gaze was smoking-hot, searing. Did he think she'd draw away like a frightened virgin?

Well, *literally*, she still was, but that fact didn't stop her from wanting more of his kisses and to press her body flush against his. If he was half as aroused as she was, she'd know the strength of his desire in the hardness of his cock and the fine tremors that would rack his body when she moved against him.

Could she tempt a man like this? Her pride had been wounded when he'd implied she was a whore. Had he meant it? Or was he just protecting himself from his own attraction? She wanted to know.

Not to throw his attraction back in his face because of her dented pride, but because he was the embodiment of her fantasies. Just once, she wanted to taste the desire of a decent man.

She bit her lip and watched, fascinated, as his gaze dropped to watch her mouth. Her tongue flicked out and wet her lips and his breath caught—she knew because his chest rose and lightly grazed hers. The sensation shocked her.

Slowly, she lifted on tiptoe to better align their faces, encouraged when he didn't draw away. Yet he didn't press closer either. How could she break his iron hold? She drew a ragged breath, felt the heat creep slowly over her cheeks, and trailed her fingertips up his inner thigh.

His breath gusted and his hands gripped her shoulders hard enough to bruise, but he didn't thrust her away.

Where the courage came from, she didn't want to know. She'd never acted this outrageously before, but when she scraped against the swell of his cock, she knew she was on the right track.

His thick cock jumped. Then his nostrils flared and a ruddy color filled his cheeks. His chest rose and fell more quickly, and then stilled again when she cupped him fully with her palm.

Lord, he was hard and hung like a bull! She smoothed her hand up his length and back down just to make sure.

"Know what you're doing there?" he asked, his voice sounding deliciously rusty.

She pouted her lips and raised one eyebrow, trying her best to hide her nervousness. "I think I'm just feeling my way."

"We probably have an office filled with people with their ears pressed to the door."

Her lips stretched into a wicked grin. "Then you'd better not shout," she whispered.

His lips twitched. "Why am I going to get that urge?"

Wetting her lips again, this time in anticipation, she murmured, "Because I have this damnable curiosity that has to be fed."

"Do you always follow your . . . curiosity?"

Her hand followed the hard outline of his cock, and she gave him a squeeze. "What do you think?"

He cursed under his breath and let go of her shoulders. Before she could voice her disappointment, one hand grabbed hers and pushed it away from the front of his trousers and the other reached around her and grabbed her bottom to draw her body close, at last snuggling his sex between her legs. "I think we've only got about a minute before your admirers come to the rescue."

"Who?" she asked, her mind already jumping ahead to imagine long, hot thrusts and a powerful release. "What admirers?"

His hips flexed forward, rubbing his clothed erection where she needed the friction the most. "Do I need to bring out the town census?"

Her hands wound around the back of his neck and she pressed her heavy breasts against his chest, rubbing on him like a kitten. "Why aren't you among them?" she asked, just shy of breathless.

"Who says I'm not?" he growled.

The intimate rumble of his voice did the darndest things to her body. Moisture dampened the crotch of her pantalets. "But you want me gone."

His cheek rubbed against hers, and he thrust his hips against her, grinding through her petticoats. "I want my life . . . simple."

She gathered up the front of her skirt in one hand, holding it at her waist. "I'm not simple, Sheriff."

"No, you're not." A large hand cupped the back of her neck and his thumb tipped up her chin. His lips slid down the column of her throat. "You're delicious." Another hand slipped between her legs and found the slitted opening of her underwear. Two fingers traced the moist furrow then thrust inside. "Hot. You're so damn hot!" he murmured against her hair, as a hand descended from her neck to tighten on her behind.

Honey's mouth opened, but she found she didn't have the breath to speak. Her gasp was ragged, quickly edging toward a howl. Her inner muscles clamped around his fingers and her hips rolled, trying to bring him deeper.

"Jesus, you're tight," he groaned. His fingers stroked just inside, swirling in her juices. "We don't have time to take off all these layers, sweetheart."

Honey hooked a thigh over his hips and leaned back. "What do we have time to accomplish?" she gasped.

His fingers speared deeper into her, giving her a twinge of discomfort. "Just this, I think."

"What about you?"

His jaw tightened, but one side of his mouth rose in a whimsical smile. "No time to put my clothing to rights. Let me give you this."

A man who gave without expecting his own reward? "Doesn't seem fair," she moaned, as he twisted his fingers and rubbed knuckles against the ripening nub at the top of her sex.

"Think I won't enjoy watching you unravel?"

"Does it make you feel manly?" she quipped, trying to keep the conversation light, *but damn* she needed to move.

Sheriff Tanner let go of her arse and cupped her breast through her jacket. "Makes me harder than a fencepost, but that's my problem." When she arched her back, he glided his mouth along the bottom of her jaw.

Honey circled her hips and groaned softly at the exquisite feeling of her pussy dragging away then swallowing his fingers with each little swirl. "Ummm . . . I'd like to feel that . . . fencepost."

"Bet you would," he said, a smile in his voice.

"My breasts ache."

"Wish I had time to see them," he said, giving her a squeeze through her clothing.

"Mmmm . . . What would you do? Tell me."

His mouth found hers and glanced over her lips before moving away to nibble on her ear. "I'd suck 'em till the tips spiked and your nipples got all rosy," he whispered. "Are your nipples pink?"

His fingers surged inside and withdrew, then came back, thrusting deeper. "Yes!" she whimpered. "Um . . . pink. Then what?"

"I'd pinch 'em between my fingers and tug 'til you were moaning." His thick thumb scraped her clitoris, then made another pass and another.

"Don't stop!" she said, the motion of her hips deepening, heat curling tight like a watch spring inside her belly.

"Then I'd suck on 'em again," he said, a note of urgency entering his voice that told her he knew she was close and it excited him as well. "And then when you were writhing against me . . . I'd bite. Gentle like—just enough to make you moan."

"I can feel it," she sobbed. "Jesus, don't let them come through that door. Not yet."

He circled and flicked and finally pinched the engorged knot. Honey's head fell back and her body quivered with delight. Her breath caught and she cried out, but he was there to swallow the cry, grinding his lips against hers to muffle the sound of her release.

As she grew slack in his arms, the fingers stroking her passage slowed, and his kiss softened, becoming tender caresses along her cheek and jaw that soothed her, now.

"Oh my," she sighed.

Drawing his hand from underneath her skirt, he set her away and pulled down her petticoat and skirt.

Honey swayed on her feet, but he caught her shoulders. "You'll want to keep your head down. Your lips look thoroughly kissed."

She grinned and pressed her tingling lips together. They were slightly sore and swollen, and she could only imagine what the rest of her looked like. Completely debauched? Delightfully sated?

His jaw tightened and a frown drew his dark eyebrows together. "You know it doesn't have a thing to do with how attractive you are, or how much I want you."

She shook her head to clear it. "What are you talking about?"

"Your leaving," he said, his tone flat.

As though a rug had suddenly been pulled out from under her, her heart plummeted inside her chest. "What was this all about?"

His lips tightened, and he shrugged. "My pleasuring you. It's what you asked me for."

She started to shake. Her stomach grew queasy. "I asked you for it?"

"When you touched me."

She blinked fiercely against the unexpected moisture in her eyes. "So, you were just doing me a favor?" She lifted her chin, proud of the fact her voice hadn't cracked.

"What did you think it was? Did you think I'd change my mind?"

"That isn't why . . ." She shook her head again and gave a humorless laugh. "No, you know you're right. I really should be moving on."

He raked a hand through his dark, close-cropped hair. "You can stay a couple more days."

Her heart started beating faster again as anger surged through her—anger at herself, for letting her fantasy usurp her common sense. "No. I have supplies to restock, but it's high time I kick this town's dust off my shoes." She narrowed her eyes. "I have plans, you know. Big brass band plans." She grabbed blindly for the doorknob.

"Your hair?"

"Huh?" she asked, not turning back. She never wanted to see him again.

"It's coming down."

"Oh! Well, hell. What does it matter now? The whole town knows we've been up to something in here anyway. It's not like I have a reputation to uphold."

"Honey—"

Finding it impossible to submerge her hurt and anger again, she gave him a scathing look. "Miss Cafferty to you, seeing as how we never got around to first names." She opened the door with so much force it slammed against the wall and stalked into the outer office.

Sure as hell, there stood Curly Hicks and a couple of the gentlemen from the saloon.

Honey held her head high and gave them a regal nod then

fled the office as quickly and with as much dignity as she could muster.

Tomorrow wouldn't be soon enough to leave this one-horse—No! *One-Mule* town—behind.

Honey wrote the list of supplies she'd need to pick up the following morning and slapped them on Curly Hicks' counter.

"I'll have 'em ready first thing," he said, his avid gaze watching her like she'd grown a rattler's tail.

She barely resisted the urge to flicker her tongue at the odious man. Instead, she turned her back on him without a proper farewell.

"Oh, Honey!" Daisy Sessions' voice called from behind her.

No, no, no! She'd hoped to make a clean getaway. Daisy was one of the reasons she so regretted leaving. Turning, she pasted on a smile to greet her new friend.

"Honey," Daisy said, wrapping an arm around Honey's waist. "You have to come to tea. Now!"

The warmth of another human being touching her with kindness was almost too much for Honey to bear. Drawn into an embrace against Daisy's soft, rounded body, Honey drank in the scent of lilacs and homemade bread. The woman was only slightly older than her, but she smelled like *home*—or what Honey had always imagined it might.

She pulled away and glanced up, reading compassion in Daisy's strained smile.

"Tea," Daisy said the word with a firmness that brooked no argument. "You're coming home with me."

"I need to get packed," Honey said, her chin wobbling.

Daisy squeezed her shoulder, but didn't let go as she walked her toward the door. "If you like, the ladies and I will help you pack later."

* * *

"He said that to you?" Letty Handy said in her gruff voice. Her brows drew into a single fierce line across her forehead. "Amos said Curly told him you and the sheriff were in the jail an awful long time."

Seated in a delicate chair in the rectory parlor, Honey felt a guilty flush heat her cheeks.

Something about her expression seemed to fascinate Letty and Daisy, who sat on a loveseat across from her. Their eyes widened.

"Did he take advantage of you, my dear?" Daisy asked, her voice dropping to a conspiratorial whisper.

Unable to hold their gazes, Honey nodded. "He kissed me." *Could she lie by omission in the parson's house? What the hell?* "Oh Daisy, I melted into a gooey puddle. I let him touch me under my skirts—I couldn't help myself."

Daisy blushed scarlet all the way to the roots of her ashy blond hair. "I'm sure we have all been carried away by the attentions of a handsome man."

"Speak for yourself," Letty murmured. "What happened next?"

Honey sniffed into Daisy's freshly starched handkerchief. "After . . . you know . . . he touched me, he said he was only doing me . . . a—a faaa-vor!" she wailed.

"The scoundrel!" Daisy exclaimed, a hand going to her breast. "The man thinks too highly of himself."

"He is a handsome one," Letty said, shrugging when Daisy aimed a sharp glance her way. "I may be married, but I ain't dead. The man only has to breathe and he fair takes a woman's breath away."

"Here, my dear," Daisy said, "drink this. It will fortify you."

Honey wiped her nose and accepted a small glass of port. She stared at it for a second then downed it in a single gulp. She didn't miss the raised eyebrows from the ladies gathered in

Daisy's parlor. Well, it wasn't like she had a reputation to up-hold any longer.

Daisy and Letty raised their glasses and each downed hers in a single gulp.

"Oh my, that does warm a body up," Daisy said, staring into the bottom of her now-empty glass.

"Come, Daisy," Letty said, giving Daisy a nudge of her elbow. "This is not the time for temperance."

A slow, mischievous smile stretched across Daisy's face, re-minding Honey of a child sneaking an extra licorice from a candy jar. She poured another glass for herself and topped off Letty's and Honey's. "Well, you simply must stand your ground, Honey."

"I don't want to anymore. He humiliated me."

"Nonsense," Daisy said firmly, but with kindness in her blue eyes. "I think what you're feeling has nothing whatsoever to do with embarrassment. My dear, he hurt your feelings."

"He used you and discarded you like day-old milk," Letty said, her tone flat. "That man needs to be taught a lesson."

Daisy rolled her eyes. "However crudely put, Letty is right." She reached for Honey's hands and leaned toward her. "You've taught us we don't have to accept our lots in life. We can go out there and grab for our dreams."

"All I did was sell you a 'Poker Potion'," she muttered.

"My dear, your 'Elixir of Love' placed power squarely in our hands. We rule our husbands' libidos; therefore we hold their happiness in the palms of our hands."

"Never knew how close their happiness depends on that!" Letty nodded. "Why, Amos was in such a good mood yester-day, he came to the kitchen after dinner and helped me finish cleaning up." Her cheeks bloomed with two round spots of color on her cheeks.

Daisy's eyes gleamed with understanding and humor. "In the kitchen?"

"Um, right on top of the table!"

Daisy took another sip of port and fanned herself. "Honey's problem is that the sheriff was completely in control of their . . . encounter."

"You know, Daisy, you have the right of that." Letty burped and her eyes rounded. "Pardon me. He brought Honey into the jail, no doubt for intimidation."

"He initiated the kiss and took what he wanted . . . given the time he had with her."

"Um . . . I wasn't exactly just standing there," Honey grumbled. "I may have goaded him into . . . touching me."

"Precisely what he'd like you to think," Letty said, a militant gleam in her eyes. Her stout chest rose. "Men always want to blame their lack of control on women. I'm telling you, you were a victim of his lust."

While the ladies' staunch support warmed her heart, Honey knew she was every bit as much to blame for what happened as the sheriff. "Well, it's all water under the bridge. I'm leaving in the morning."

"But you can't leave, Honey." Letty looked to Daisy, who nodded her agreement. "The weather's gonna turn any day. Like you said, you need a place to set up for the winter."

Honey took a deep breath and started to rise. "It can't be here. He's all but ordered me out of town."

Daisy stood and placed a hand on her arm. "We'll just have to change his mind."

"Oh no, Daisy, you can't talk to him on my behalf. It would be too humiliating."

Daisy and Letty shared a charged glance. "My dear, you go on back to your little wagon. Don't you dare start packing until you hear from us."

The ladies stood side by side, whether to support their swaying frames or as a show of solidarity, Honey wasn't sure. "I don't know whether I like that gleam in your eye."

"Don't you see you belong here, my dear?" Daisy said. "You've known me two days and you already have a better measure of me than my husband ever has."

Letty's bulldog expression softened. "I've known Daisy since we were kids. Never knew she was such a passionate woman. You've taught us both that."

"I'm glad I could help. My elixir worked beyond my dreams."

"So, let us return the favor," Daisy said, her expression pleading.

"But what are you going to do? You can't confront the sheriff." Lord, what would they reveal to him if they did? Especially in their slightly inebriated state.

"I won't do anything so direct. But these circumstances call for desh-perate measures." Daisy wrinkled her lips. "How odd. My lips are numb. I need another glass of port."

Honey couldn't help smiling at the tipsy woman. "Should you be drinking so much, Daisy?"

Daisy's head lifted proudly. "I need the courage for what I have in mind."

"Why do I have the feeling I'm going to be wearing tar and hen feathers before you're through?"

"Don't you worry about a thing. You head back to camp and get yourself some resht. We'll take care of everything."

Honey shook her head, sure the women would be snoring on the loveseat in minutes if they tore back into the liquor. "You two stay here. I'll let myself out."

"Good idea," Letty said, reaching for the port. "We have plans to make."

"Hear, hear." Daisy said, lifting her glass. "And a trap to shet."

Honey set off down the road to her little campsite, just beyond the second bend of the road. Whatever the women had planned wouldn't make a hill of beans' difference. Even if Sheriff Tanner came out to beg her forgiveness for his cruelty on bended knee, she still had to leave.

Sighing her relief, she reflected it was a good thing she hadn't let herself fall in love with the man. He'd already come close to breaking her heart.

3

The clopping of hooves woke Honey from her nap. Still groggy from the wine and the enervating heat, she rubbed her eyes, wondering who had come to visit and whether she would even unpack her medicines if they'd come for a cure.

Then another thought had her eyes widening, and she shot out of her bed and reached for her skirt, which was hanging from a hook beside her dresser.

Oh hell, had the ladies said something to the sheriff after all? Could it be him coming to apologize? Or worse, remind her she had to leave?

As quickly as shaking fingers would allow, she pulled on her blouse and hooked the buttons up her back, leaving the top few undone. Her hair would just have to hide her state of undress.

"Hall-ooo. Honey, you in there girl?" came a voice she'd recognize anywhere if only for its masculine gruffness.

"Letty?" she called out. She opened the door of her wagon and stepped down to the ground to find Letty with her skirts hitched high on either side of her legs, straddling a horse as wide as she was.

Only Letty wasn't looking her way; she was turned in her saddle and staring down the road.

Honey walked up beside her and followed the direction of her gaze to see Daisy and Sally Epperson seated on a buckboard wagon, waving gaily at her as they approached. What were the good ladies up to now?

Letty tapped Honey on the shoulder. "We brung you a present."

Honey's eyebrows shot up, and she turned to stare at the two women atop the wagon whose smiles couldn't have been any wider. "Letty, what the hell did you do?"

"We're just givin' you a chance to return a favor," she said with a naughty waggle of her bushy eyebrows.

Honey's heart galloped like a runaway horse. "Tell me you didn't do what I think you did." She picked up her skirts and ran to the wagon before the ladies had even pulled back the reins on the team to halt it.

As Honey ran around the back, Sally giggled. "I'd be in a hurry, too."

"Sally, you been dipping into Daisy's port, too?" Honey asked as she lowered the back gate.

"Had to make her a co-consh-pirator," Daisy said, then giggled herself.

"We couldn't have done what we did without a shot of courage," Sally said, then snorted before breaking into a gale of laughter.

The bed of the wagon was filled with loose hay. A black boot stuck out from under the straw at the end of the bed.

Fascinated, Honey gave the boot a pull, half hoping it wasn't attached to anyone's foot, but she had no such luck. She gathered handfuls of straw and started dragging it from the wagon to uncover the body of a very large man.

A very quiet large man.

With only the half of him she could reach cleared of straw,

she didn't have any trouble recognizing who it was. "Daisy, did you kill him?" she hissed.

"Now Honey," Daisy said, her normally light and musical voice pitched low with a dirty edge. "I'm a good Christian woman—thatsh what we needed Sally for."

"To kill him?" Honey asked, her breaths getting so shallow she thought she might faint.

"Sh-Shuch a suspicious mind. Although I'm almost flattered you think I could have done it."

Honey rolled her eyes, hitched up her skirts, and climbed up on the back of the bed. She shoved more hay off the back of the wagon until the sheriff's upper torso and head were cleared. Leaning close to his broad chest, Honey breathed a sigh of relief when she heard the sheriff's soft snores. He was out cold. But how?

"Did you clobber him?" she asked, as she felt the back of his head for knots.

"I already told you that was what we needed Sally for," Daisy said grumpily.

"So she could clobber him?"

Sally giggled. "No, silly. For the 'Sweet Dreams Syrup' you gave my mama."

Honey patted his cheeks. "Lord, he's out like a rock. How much did you give him?"

"I'm not quite sure. I mixed it in his coffee when he came by the café. Told him it was sweetened with honey. He's so polite he drank the whole thing, even though he made the funniest faces."

"Ya need help gettin' him inside?" Letty said, as she walked up beside the wagon, rubbing the small of her back.

"Oh no," Honey said, shaking her head at Letty. "He's not staying here."

"But we brung him just for you," Letty said, disappointment making her face look as drawn as a basset hound's.

"Well, you can take him right on back." Panic made her voice a little shrill. "What were you ladies thinking? You kidnapped the sheriff!"

"We sure did," Letty said with a wide grin. "He fell asleep sitting on the stool, and I had to lean real close to him to keep him from sliding to the floor until we could chase Amos out of the restaurant."

"He's a big man. How the hell'd you get him out of the café and into the cart?"

"I'm a blacksmith's wife," Letty said, hitching up the waistband of her skirt. "I've helped Amos around the smithy so long, I can pert near carry a horse on my back."

"Doesn't matter," Honey said, shaking her head. "Ladies, I appreciate that you went to all this trouble for me, but what am I supposed to do with him? He's going to blame me when he wakes up. I'll end up in jail for real this time."

Letty slapped a hand on Honey's shoulder, her smile widening. "He won't press no charges. Think he'll want the whole town to know that a bunch of women kidnapped him, stripped him nekkid, and tied him to your bed?"

Honey's mouth gaped open. "That's your plan?"

"Ain't it brilliant? The stripped nekkid part was my idea. You can compromise him right back for what he did to you."

"Compromise him?"

"Yup." Daisy's nod almost unbalanced her, and Sally grabbed for her shoulder to keep her sitting straight. "Euphimischt-ically speaking.

"Eupha-what?" Sally asked.

"Close your ears, Sally," Letty said, then leaned close to Honey to whisper loudly, "Honey-girl, you kin have your wicked way with him."

"I don't believe you just said that," Honey said, wishing the ground would just open up and swallow her whole.

"No time to be mishish-missish," Daisy said and stuck out

her tongue, staring at it cross-eyed. "Why isn't it working anymore?"

Letty gave Honey a fearsome scowl. "Don't you remember he told you he was doing you a favor?"

Honey remembered those were her words, but his reply had been spoken so coldly he had made her feel dirty and ashamed. She gave him a kick.

"That's the shpirit," Daisy said.

"Just think," Letty whispered. "All that prime-grade male, just lying there. Think you might need some help?"

"Help?" Honey asked.

"Letty, for shame!" Daisy said, but her lips twitched. "But we do need to strip him, since we're the married ladies in the group."

Honey shook her head again, wondering when everyone had taken a crazy pill. "And I thought this was a nice, quiet little town."

"Can't I help?" Sally asked, her pretty face blushing. "I could keep my eyes closed and just feel my way."

Honey blushed scarlet at the familiar phrase. "Ladies, we can't do this."

"Too late to back out now," Letty said. "If he wakes up in the wagon, he's gonna arrest us all. Have to get him compromised first. That way he won't say a word."

Honey closed her eyes and wished she'd already packed and left. "I don't believe this."

Letty hopped into the back of the wagon, surprisingly spry for a woman of her proportions. "Someone get his legs," she said, as she lifted up his shoulders.

"I want a leg," Sally said, jumping from the wagon seat.

"Just don't think you can pull on him like a wishbone," Letty said. "We want him fully functioning when he wakes up."

Honey rushed to help Daisy from the wagon seat. The woman swayed and put a hand to her mouth.

"You gonna be all right?" Honey asked. A crash from the back of the wagon had her rushing around to find the sheriff sprawled on the ground. "Oh Lord, you're gonna kill him for sure. Then where will I be?"

"We'll help ya hide the body," Letty said.

"The point is I don't want him dead. I don't even want him hurt."

"Then why'd you kick him?"

Frustrated now, and wondering why she was the only one sober in the group, Honey picked up a heavy leg. "Come on, ladies. Since we're already criminals, we might as well make the man comfortable."

Sally, Letty, and Honey wrestled with his dead weight, managing nicely until they reached Honey's narrow stairs.

With the weather already stifling, by the time they had him at the foot of the stairs, sweat plastered Honey's forehead and her shirt was wet beneath her arms. The other ladies weren't in much better condition.

Honey gently lowered the leg she'd carried to the ground and wiped sweat from her forehead. "So how are we going to get him up those stairs?"

"Maybe we could just make him a pallet here under the trees," Daisy said.

Exasperation sharpened Honey's words. "For anyone to see who might come by? I don't think so."

"Get a blanket," Letty said. "We'll lay him on it and slide him up the stairs."

Honey found her oldest threadbare blanket, and they rolled him onto it. Then Letty took position at the top of the steps, squatting with her legs spread wide. She gathered the end of the blanket and began to pull.

The sounds of stitches popping had Honey rushing to pull on the sides and help ease the sheriff up the steps. His head hit the steps with each pull.

"Lordy, that man's gonna have a headache," Letty said. "Deserves every knot, too."

"If the overdose of the potion doesn't kill him," Honey mumbled, her breath rasping with exertion. "I'll be hung for bludgeoning him to death."

"Don't be such a sourpuss," Letty said. "Wait until we get him nekkid—you'll be happier then."

Honey shook her head forlornly. She'd be the one left to explain why he was in her bed with goose eggs on the top of his head and bruises over every other inch of his skin. Tar and hen feathers were looking pretty good, now.

Daisy and Letty settled him onto her narrow mattress. Because it had been her father's bunk before his death, the sheriff's feet stretched to the very end of the mattress with only an inch to spare.

"Let's make him comfortable and get the hell out of here before he wakes up," Letty said.

"Getting nervous now? Need a little more port?" Honey asked, acid in her voice.

"You got a mean streak. Never noticed that before."

When Daisy started unbuttoning his shirt, Letty reached eagerly for the waist of his trousers.

"Letty," Daisy said, her tone holding a warning. "The man is incapacitated. Remember, you are a Christian lady—*and married.*"

"Doesn't mean I can't look."

"Just be quick about it. We shouldn't take any joy in this."

Daisy had managed to strip away the shirt and Letty had the placket of his trousers unbuttoned when Sally sighed. "My word," she said breathlessly as the pants opened to reveal the sheriff's substantial cock.

Even resting, it was a beautiful sight to behold—at least to Honey.

Sally's eyes widened, and she looked more than a little frightened.

"Sally, you go step outside," Daisy said. "We'll have a talk about the birds and the bees on the way back to town."

Sally fled without a backward glance.

Letty seemed to take her sweet time dragging his trousers and drawers down his long legs.

"What are you going to do if he opens his eyes and sees who's strippin' him bare-naked?" Daisy asked.

Letty's lips curved downward. "Spoilsport. Only ever saw one man nekkid. Just wanted to peek."

"Don't you think Amos would mind you ogling another man's privates?"

"It's just natural," Letty said, her eyes never straying from his sex. "What God gave him."

"You are not communing with nature. You're ogling a defenshless man."

Letty's hand hovered over him, and Honey's eyes widened.

"Letty!" Daisy hissed.

"It's all curled up like a giant clam. I just wanted to see how big—"

"Honey can tell us later."

When the boots and trousers dropped to the floor, both church ladies gave him one last head-to-foot glance. "Just want to make sure he's not too badly bruised," Daisy murmured.

"I think you've done enough, ladies," Honey said, gritting her teeth. She loved them both, but they'd landed her in a pile of manure without a shovel to dig her way out.

"Wait!" Letty dug into the pockets at the sides of her wide skirts. She pulled out two short pieces of rope and quickly tied his hands to the bed posts. When she was done, she shook her head. "Gives a woman ideas."

Daisy gave Honey a quick hug. "Follow your heart," she whispered, then tugged on Letty's sleeve.

Letty gave her a bone-crunching hug. "And if your heart's not in it—remember there's always revenge."

The ladies piled onto horses and wagons and waved happily at Honey as they headed back down the road.

Honey took a deep breath and turned around to face the man who'd haunted her dreams since she'd arrived.

What to do with him, now? Should she try to revive him, beg him for mercy and hope he didn't arrest her on the spot? Or should she just let him sleep it off? She honestly didn't know if her libido could take the torment. She'd never been presented such a ripe temptation in her whole life.

Gazing at his loins, she quickly came to the conclusion she was a weak-willed woman and she'd burn in hell for all the lewd possibilities flashing through her dirty little mind.

Well, first she had to look her fill or she'd get a headache trying not to. Not that she needed much convincing.

His body was a beautiful thing. So large he sprawled over the length and width of the narrow mattress, his size alone made her belly ache with need. She stepped closer and marveled at how well God had arranged all his . . . parts.

Everything in proportion.

Nearly everything lightly furred with dark curling hair that looked shiny and silky-soft. She didn't resist the urge to touch him and combed her fingers through the hair on his chest.

Just as she'd thought—soft—and curling around her fingertips, like it was trying to trap her hand against his skin.

Her fingertips grazed a small flat nipple and she paused to circle it, amazed when a small nub rose at its center. Were his nipples as sensitive as hers? Just looking at his naked body had her nipples poking at the front of her blouse. She circled the pad of one finger on the tiny tip.

Then his "giant clam" pulsed and began to unfurl, drawing

her fascinated glance back to the part of him she really had no business exploring. Her sense of fair play was stretched to its limit—snapping like a rubber band. Naked and restrained, the man was truly at the mercy of her discretion.

Still manipulating his little nipple, Honey held her breath and watched as his cock slowly straightened until it nearly reached his belly button. Her cheeks grew warm and her belly tightened. Familiar now with the signs of desire, she knew she should just throw a blanket over him. He'd made his feelings clear where she was concerned. While he might be aroused by her, her unconventional lifestyle put her beyond the pale in his eyes. He'd all but said he considered her a whore.

But the temptation his naked form embodied was just too hard to ignore. That he was unconscious only seemed to sweeten the lure, and the devil whispering in her ear reminded her she had a score to settle.

Yet, she feared he'd waken while she took advantage of his helpless state. How would she explain herself? Could she live down the humiliation?

She leaned close to his face. "Sheriff," she said softly, but he didn't move. Not an eyelash blinked. His eyelashes were dark and thick, and when she ruffled them with a finger, they felt like soft bristles. Again, he didn't react.

Her hand cupped his cheek and she felt the coarse whiskers that shadowed his strong, square jaw. Leaning closer, she rubbed her cheek against his and felt the friction that excited her all the more. Her true fascination lay in all the ways their bodies differed. The most prominent being the thick, ridged cock that lay against his belly.

Darker, ruddier in color than the rest of his skin, his sex was capped with a blunt, rounded cap that was surprisingly spongy to the touch—which she discovered when she gave it a timid poke of her finger.

Beneath the ridged crown, his shaft was anything but soft.

She lightly scraped a fingernail along his shaft, all the while scolding herself for her wicked curiosity.

His cock jerked, which made her gasp, and she felt her own sex tighten and pulse. How odd they seemed so in tune.

Another sweeping glance and she noted the powerful swells of his chest muscles and the tapering of his narrow waist. She skipped over his sex and followed the curves of his massive thighs and calves all the way down to his large feet and toes.

Was there a part of him she didn't want to touch?

The ladies had made sure she could have her "wicked way" with him—if she had the courage to try.

A light, warm breeze wafted through the wagon, reminding her the door was wide open and anyone who might approach her camp would have a helluva view inside, despite the waning daylight.

She closed the wooden door and leaned her back against it, biting her lip as she fought with her conscience . . . and lost.

He'd touched her intimately. Made her feel things a woman only wants to feel with a man she truly cares about.

That he couldn't be that man didn't matter now. She'd had years of loneliness to imagine what lying with a man might be like. Now she had one at her disposal to explore all the wicked wanton things she'd dreamed of sitting on her wagon seat, watching the homes she passed and daydreaming about the couples who lived inside.

Only once before had she let herself be fooled that she could have that normal life, but the man who'd first turned her head had taken from her—just like this one had. That her first lover hadn't fully consummated the act didn't make her feel any better about herself.

She'd been desperate for the feel of strong arms around her, a broad shoulder to rest her head upon. That Sheriff Tanner had seemed to be a decent sort of man and had indicated interest in her had once again turned her head.

"Fool me once, shame on you," she whispered. "Fool me twice, shame on me."

Well, if there was already shame to spread around, why go only halves. Staring at his wakening cock, she reached behind her and unbuttoned her blouse and hung it on a hook. Then she stepped out of her skirt. Dressed only in her chemise, she decided she didn't look nearly wanton enough.

She dug through her dresser for her favorite corset—a black confection of lace and satin with bright red lacings up the front. She tore off her chemise and donned the corset, lacing it up tight so her breasts spilled over the top.

Then she did the wickedest thing she could imagine, she shucked her pantalets and drew thin stockings up her bare legs, fastening them with frilly black garters.

She didn't particularly care what he'd think when he first spied her, standing nearly naked in front of him. This was all about how she felt.

Wanton. Free. A little scared, but determined she'd have him—if only to satisfy herself for once. When this night was over, there wouldn't be a craving she hadn't tried to feed or a part of her body that didn't know his touch.

4

Joe awoke slowly, drifting between clouds that sifted away one layer at a time, until at last he felt as though he lay trapped halfway between heaven and hell.

The hell was his head hurt and his mouth was so dry it seemed stuffed with cotton balls. Worse, his wrists burned and his legs were wedged tight between something warm and soft.

The heaven was the sensation engulfing his cock. A moist, humid heat surrounded then deserted his sex, sucking relentlessly, wringing a dark delight that had his hips tensing as he attempted to lift them and follow the upward pulls rather than lose the warm, wet cocoon.

A soft murmur—feminine, guttural—came from further down his body and vibrated along his shaft. A woman then. A woman was sucking his cock.

His eyes shot open and pain lanced through his head at the sight of the lantern hanging from a hook in the ceiling. His gaze dropped to candles lining a dresser a short space away. Another quick glance around, and he realized he was either in a very small bedroom—or in the back of Honey Cafferty's wagon.

Despite the pain that lanced through his head, he lifted it to confirm the source of his torment.

Light glinted gold on the cloud of red hair surrounding his loins, and Joe couldn't help the leap of fierce joy that filled his chest, creating an aching warmth that left him deeply moved.

Until he remembered all the reasons this woman was all wrong for him.

He remembered the first day she'd stopped her colorful wooden wagon in front of the mercantile. He'd marveled at the design—it looked rather like a giant oak barrel on wheels, a completely enclosed living space, painted with primitive pictures of Indian villages, churches, and saloons with a trail that stretched all along its length to tell the story of its travels.

When Honey had stepped down from beneath the eave that kept the sun and rain from the wagon seat, she'd lowered the gate that stretched along one side of the wagon and quickly set out colorful bottles, their labels decorated with drawings of pyramids and castles.

When she'd started to call to the people gawking at her odd conveyance, he'd stood in the shadows, smiling at how easily she'd drawn them in with her charm and radiant smiles. He'd been drawn as well, stepping off the walkway to stand at the edge of the gathering crowd, just to listen to her voice, which was flavored with a hint of brogue and Texas twang. He'd been captivated like everyone else.

Only when she'd come to purchase her license had he seen the hint of fire that simmered just beneath the prim clothing— much more in keeping with the eccentric wagon and her odd profession.

Honey Cafferty was stardust and moonbeams—fleeting as the wanderlust in her blood—while he needed a steady partner, someone who'd weather good times and bad.

Another incredible pull of her lips and he gritted his teeth. Sweat broke on his forehead and upper lip. Peeking at her beneath his lashes, he watched while she drew off and stared, seeming to take pride in the erection she'd nurtured. She wrapped her hands around him, squeezing to see whether her fingers met. Then she twisted her hands and glided them up and down his shaft. She lapped at the crown, swallowing it and sliding down to meet her hands.

He'd never known a woman so eager to experiment with a man's cock—or one who'd found the knack for torturing him so sweetly. She hadn't seemed to notice he'd woken up, and he considered pretending a little longer just to see what she'd do next, but he needed to move—needed to spear upward into her hot mouth. All her sucking, pulling, and twisting had made his balls heavy and tight as stones and his cock so hard he could have hammered a nail into solid wood. One good thrust and he'd spill his seed deep into her throat. And wouldn't she be surprised?

The thought of filling her mouth, seeing his pearly cum on her lips, had him biting back a groan. He didn't want to spoil her pleasure or miss a moment watching her expressive face as she worked on him. Her curiosity lit her eyes; her natural sultriness pouted her pink lips.

Her lips! Damn, her mouth was opening again, taking him deep while her tongue swirled around his crown and licked over the sides. She was killing him by inches.

Needing something else to ponder so he could control the urge to explode, he thought about how he'd come to be here and wondered what magical spell she'd cast on sweet Sally Epperson to convince her to doctor his coffee. Then he wondered how the hell the two women had managed to move him here, so far out of town. And for what purpose?

For Honey to have a little revenge for the hurt he'd caused her? Or simply for her own pleasure? That thought brought him squarely back to the urgent need to come and Honey's hot little mouth.

Just looking at her wildly curling red hair and bare shoulders was enough to tempt him over the edge. What else wasn't she wearing? The sides of her thighs, encased in sheer black stockings, were visible beyond her shoulders, but not much else was. Her knees, which straddled either side of his legs, sank deep into a red satin comforter that covered a very soft feather bed. The thought of rolling her beneath him, sinking into all that softness. . . .

Again, Honey's mouth dove onto his cock, driving it along her tongue until it bumped the back of her throat. A soft hand scooped up his balls and squeezed. His eyes rolled back and he sucked air deep into his lungs, fighting the need to shout.

Only when she rose, did he remember how to breathe, and he opened his eyes.

She'd lifted her head, affording him a delicious view of the tops of her creamy breasts as light glanced on the mounds and darkness added depth to her cleavage. "So, you're finally awake, Sheriff," she said, her voice low and husky.

His cock thrust upward inside her squeezing palms. "Joe," he said, his voice sounding rusty and thick. "Call me Joe since it looks like we've been introduced."

A slight smile curved the corners of her lips, then she bent and stuck out her tongue to lick the head of his cock, taking a bead of pearly excitement from the tip, her gaze locking with his all the while.

He watched her pink tongue lap him like she was licking ice cream, curving under the ridge, delving into the little eyelet hole. *Goddamn*, he wanted to fuck that mouth. Would she climb between his legs and give him leverage to plow into her mouth? Could she take him deep, like he was dying to go?

Her lips glided over his head, and then she lifted her face again. "Bet you're wondering why you're here."

Lord have mercy! Just the sexy velvet voice made every muscle in his body tense. "Haven't been able to hold a single thought since I woke up with my cock in your mouth," he drawled.

Despite the blush staining her cheeks, she raised one dark eyebrow in an unspoken challenge. "Can I convince you not to think for a little while longer?" She pumped her hands down and up his cock.

He swallowed hard, feeling his gut tighten, priming for release. "Guess it depends."

She gave him a slow spiraling twist and smiled when he groaned. "Depends on what?"

He gritted his teeth and bit out, "On whether there's going to be a posse with shotguns sitting outside your door in the morning."

Her smile held a wicked warning, but she circled her cheek on the head of his cock. "This is just between you and me, Joe," she said softly and released him. "Besides, it's been pointed out to me that the virtue of a woman who travels alone is suspect. No one's gonna come storming my doors demanding you do right by me."

Drawing a deep breath of equal parts relief and regret, he said, "I'm sorry about what I said, Honey."

She shrugged—a movement that lifted her breasts and drew his gaze down again. "I'm not. At least I know where I stand. Now, I don't have to worry about holding anything back or wondering if you'll still respect me in the morning."

He tugged the ropes around his wrists—more for something to spend his frustration—but he felt a slight slackening. His heartbeat thudded slowly, pounding in his ears when he realized he could free himself. Turn the tables on her and have her completely at his mercy.

Honey had thrown down the gauntlet, giving him the right to have her when she'd taken him and tempted him with her sweet little mouth.

She hadn't thought to tie his feet—big mistake. "What do you have planned for me?"

Her gaze was direct. "No plans. I'm just feeling my way."

She'd said that before when she'd shyly caressed his cock in the jailhouse. He wondered how experienced she really was. First, he'd give her one last chance to keep this on equal footing. "Wouldn't this work better if you untied my hands?"

"Not until we're well past the point of no return. I don't want you hauling back on the reins while I'm still raring to go." She sat up, letting him see exactly what she wasn't wearing beneath her corset.

Air hissed between his teeth, and his whole body tightened. The corset reached only to the notches of her hips: below stretched another creamy expanse of bare flesh and a triangle of dark reddish hair.

"Just so you know. I didn't dress this way for you," she whispered.

His gaze lifted to her face and he saw a hint of vulnerability in the stubborn tilt of her chin. "Then why?" he asked, his voice rough as sandpaper.

"I have my own fantasies. Things I want to learn. I figured since the ladies were so kind to give me this gift, I'd take my fill."

Clawing need settled in his loins. He strained against the ropes, and they gave a little more. If he had his hands on her now, he'd flip her on her back and crawl right inside her. He'd show her how well he'd fill her pretty little cunt.

He drew a deep breath, seeking to calm his galloping heart. Inside, his whole body was well past primed for fucking. He was so hard, his cock so packed full, he ached.

He'd have her now, make her just as hot and hurting—make her beg for release before he'd work himself inside her body, stroking her inner walls, tunneling so deep, thrusting so hard she'd be a wild thing in his arms.

Only he didn't think he'd last that long the first time. He needed to come now, needed his mind free of his own painful need before he saw to building hers.

Could he talk her into stroking him to completion? "Honey, I don't suppose your fantasies included watching a man come?"

She blinked and then her gaze dropped back down to his cock. "Why would I want to waste this watching you . . . spend yourself?"

"Don't you think I can get it up again?"

"You can do that?" Her surprise seemed genuine.

What kind of men had she been with before? "I promise I can. And I'll be more cooperative, see to your needs, if you'll just help me out here, first." As she hesitated, he added, "Have you ever seen a man explode?"

She shook her head, but he could see he'd sparked her curiosity. Her eyes narrowed, and she bit one side of her lip. "How would you like me to proceed?"

"You were doing just fine before, but I need to lift my hips and push into your mouth."

"I see." But she didn't move.

"If you'll slip your knees between my legs, I can dig my heels into the mattress for leverage."

"Oh!" She quickly shifted to the side so he could move apart his legs. Then she settled in between.

The space relieved the pressure on his balls, and he sighed. "One more thing." His glance dipped to her corset. "I need to see you naked. A man likes to look."

Her hands shook as first she stripped off the stockings and garter, then unlaced the corset and slowly peeled it away, revealing her breasts and a narrow waist.

Her breasts were so lovely his mouth went dry. Perfectly formed, just the right size to overfill his mouth and hands. Large pink areolas with hard little buttons at the center.

"Touch yourself," he rasped. "Pretend it's my hands, my fingers."

This time she didn't hesitate. She tossed back her red hair and cupped her breasts, lifting them, staring down at herself as she squeezed them, her soft belly quivering with her quickening breaths.

"Your nipples," he gritted out. "Pretend it's my fingers pleasuring them."

Her thumbs circled and toggled her nipples. Then she pinched them between her fingertips and her lips opened around a moan, and he couldn't stand it any longer.

"Jesus, I need to fuck your mouth."

Swiftly, she bent over him and gripped his cock between her hands and sank her hot, wet mouth over him, murmuring as she drew him inside.

He couldn't hold back another second and flexed his hips upward, spearing into her like he'd imagined, stroking past her tongue to the back of her throat.

She gagged slightly, and then opened her jaws, taking him deeper, her moans vibrating along his shaft.

Groaning, he lowered his hips and lifted again, driving upward while her mouth sucked and her tongue stroked his length.

Over and over, he thrust inside her, groaning, shuddering, as she worked him with her mouth and hands, bringing him quickly to the brink. "Back off me, now, baby. I'm gonna come."

But she murmured a protest and tightened her grip around his shaft, forcing him deeper into her throat. He roared, growling, cursing, thrusting upward, his balls emptying, forcing liquid through his cock in an endless stream.

Honey swallowed, her throat clasping and opening as she drank, wringing every last drop until he shuddered one last time and let his hips drop to the mattress. Still, she sucked and licked, soothing him now. When at last she raised her head and let his cock slip from between her swollen lips, she gave him a look filled with wonderment.

Joe closed his eyes and drew in ragged breaths, waiting for his body to calm and his scattered thoughts to return. He'd never been pleasured so well, so completely, by a woman. Never wanted to drag her body against his and burrow his head against her breasts, then suckle her softly while he forgot about the world outside her embrace.

With Honey, he was afraid he'd discover other joys he'd miss when she was gone.

"So, how long will it take?"

He opened his eyes and found her staring at his cock again. The woman did have a one-track mind and a list of fantasies to be fulfilled. He'd better get to work. "Not long, I think, by the way you're licking your lips."

She flushed, but a wide, proud grin stretched across her face.

"In fact," he drawled, already plotting her downfall, "we could hurry it along, if you let me pleasure you."

Her eyes narrowed. "I'm not setting you free."

"You don't have to. I can use my mouth."

Her breath caught and her creamy bosom lifted with an in-drawn breath.

"Have you ever had a man pleasure you like that?"

She shook her head, blushing to her roots.

"It's a lot like what you did for me. You don't even have to untie my hands. Just straddle me backward—"

Her eyes widened, and she shook her head. "I can't do that."

"Tell me, Honey," he said, pitching his voice low. "Was I a mouthful? Did your lips stretch around me?"

Her nod was a sharp, reluctant dip.

"I don't want you hurting yourself when you take me. Let me prepare you."

"You've . . . prepared a woman before?"

"A time or two."

She looked away, sucking her lower lip between her teeth.

Knowing she was close to caving, he counted slowly to ten, keeping his breaths even and his expression shuttered.

"I don't know . . . it's too embarrassing. You'll see everything."

"Do you think a man wouldn't find that view attractive?" he growled. She scowled and he nearly laughed. "Well, you're wrong, sweetheart. Tonight's supposed to be about your needs. I promise, you'll like this."

"I just turn around . . . ?"

"And bring your pussy to my mouth."

She shuddered and closed her eyes. "Say that again."

"What? Pussy?" At the quickening rise of her chest, he grinned. "Like that word?"

"It's nasty."

"But you like it."

She opened her eyes, heat blazing in her eyes. "Yes."

"Put your pussy on my mouth," he said more firmly, growing more confident by the moment he'd bend her to his will.

Finally, Honey shifted on the mattress, moving so slowly, his control felt stretched to the limit by the time she faced away and straddled his belly. Moisture from her slick sex seeped onto his skin, and he gritted his teeth.

Jesus, he wanted to taste it, wanted to slide his tongue deep as it could reach and drink her cream. "Get up on your knees and back up to me."

"This was definitely not one of my fantasies. I can't believe I'm going to do this."

"Don't think. Just do it."

Her bottom rose in front of his face and her cunt hovered just above his mouth. The musky aroma of her arousal had his mouth watering. He blew a stream of air at the moisture clinging to her nether lips, and her thighs and bottom quivered.

"Come closer, sweetheart."

When her cunt touched his lips, she hissed air between her teeth, and her sex tightened.

He kissed her pretty lips. "Good girl, easy now." He wished he could have used his fingers to spread her. Instead he rubbed her cunt with his mouth and bristly chin, working her side to side to open her. The outer lips of her sex were plump, engorged, and he sucked on them one at a time until she squirmed and gasped. Knowing how aroused and frustrated she was becoming, he took his time—sucking, then licking between, fluttering his tongue on the thin edges of her inner lips, dipping into her entrance to take the cream that seeped from her pulsing cunt.

The salty-musky flavor of her desire exploded on his tongue, and he fought the ropes binding his wrists, needing to touch her, needing to plunge fingers, tongue, and cock inside her.

When he felt a slackening in one of his bonds, he quickly slipped his hand free and reached across to untie the other, all the while continuing to suckle and lick her ripening sex.

Free now, he gripped her arse hard, ignoring her shocked gasp, and forced her forward, wrestling her squirming body to the mattress until he had her pinned with his weight.

He nudged her bottom with his hardening cock. "My turn," he growled.

"You made me do that just so you could take advantage," she said, her voice tight.

"Think I didn't like it?" Her silence firmed his jaw. He'd show her how much he'd liked it. He'd hold her down and pleasure every inch of her luscious body. He worked a hand between their bodies and slid two fingers between her buttocks, gliding lower, thrusting straight into her wet pussy. "I'm going to eat your sweet cunt."

She gasped and shivered, but he knew she liked the naughty words.

"I'm going to fuck you with my tongue, suck your pussy lips until you're begging me for release."

"I won't beg you for a damn thing, bastard." Her voice was harsh, but her body quivered with excitement like a nervous filly.

He leaned close and sucked her earlobe between his lips, then gave it a gentle nibble. "Guess what else I'm gonna bite?"

5

Her deep groan elicited a satisfied smile, which he was glad she couldn't see. He wanted her worried, maybe even a little scared.

He wanted her anticipating his next moves, then surprising her, even shocking her, as he eased her toward an arousal she couldn't control, couldn't tamp down no matter how much she might want to thwart him. Honey's fiery way of doing battle only inflamed his passion and spurred him to conquer her.

Eager to begin the steady climb again, he straddled her, rising on his knees to roll her body over between his legs. He wanted her breasts and cunt beneath his hands—wanted to watch her eyes spark with fury when he dominated her. When she flailed her arms, aiming half-hearted punches at his shoulders, he grabbed her hands and pulled them high above her head, securing them firmly within one hand. She squirmed and wriggled, and finally bucked her hips, trying to unseat him, which only excited them both. He could see it in her tight, spiked nipples and heightened color. Not all that heat was fury. Her desire perfumed the air around them.

Content to let her wear herself out, he kept his expression

shuttered, unwilling to let her see even a glimpse of his amusement.

As her struggles waned, the taut set of her chin softened, becoming less belligerent. Her mouth trembled as she drew soft, ragged gasps. Her eyes blinked at tears of frustration.

Not a speck of guilt dented his determination to wrest control of her silken reins. She'd set this wagon rolling when she'd plotted to bring him here. If the consequences weren't exactly what she'd expected, well, tough.

While she settled, quivering beneath him, he felt his own body responding to her distress. He wasn't exactly proud of the fact his loins filled rapidly, seeming to feed off her surrender, one shiver, one sobbing breath at a time.

He wasn't feeling very civilized. He couldn't be tender. He'd take her hard, fuck her raw—make her howl and cry and thrash until she didn't have anything left for him to plunder. When she finally lay quivering and acquiescent beneath him, he'd take her again, just to make sure she knew she was his to do with as he pleased.

She must have read some of the savagery roiling through his veins because her eyes closed tight. "Please," she whispered.

He dropped his chest fully onto hers, snuggled his lengthening cock against her soft belly—surrounding her, reminding her who was bigger, stronger—before he placed his mouth just above hers. "Please, what?"

"Take me."

Because it was the only response he could trust himself to give without sounding like a ravening beast, he softly kissed her lips, drinking in her sigh as she rubbed her mouth on his, straining upward to deepen the kiss.

Releasing her hands, he lifted his torso off her body. Her eyes blinked open and their gazes locked. "We'll do this my way," he said, his voice rough and harsh. "You won't deny me anything I want."

Her breath was jagged, and her breasts jerked against his chest. She wet her lips with the tip of her pink tongue. "I won't deny you anything."

Joe released her ankles where he'd trapped them with his feet and forced a thigh between them. "Spread your legs wide and bend your knees."

She did so quickly, her hips tilting up to grind against his balls. God, this was going to be so good.

He reared back and knelt between her legs, smoothing his hand from her knee to her pussy, stopping when he grazed her outer lips. "Wider," he said, not looking away from her sex, watching closely as her little hole gaped when she complied with his command. He pressed a thumb into her center, noting the moisture instantly surrounding him. Then holding her gaze, he brought his thumb to his mouth and licked away her juices.

Honey whimpered and the sound went straight to his cock, hardening him further. Her nipples spiked, red and full, and his mouth watered to know their taste and texture.

He reached for a pillow and held it out to her. "Put this under your head. I don't want you to miss anything." His hands cupped the backs of her thighs and lifted them, spreading them wider still, until he changed his grip and pushed them high enough to see everything in the lantern's light—all of her pretty, pink cunt, clothed in wisps of red fur, and her rosy arsehole.

Sweet Jesus, she'd promised he could take what he wanted. And he damn well wanted it all.

Honey panted as he pressed her legs higher.

"Hold them," he commanded, then waited while she caught the backs of her thighs with shaking hands, freeing his to plunder her.

From the determined set of his chin, he intended to do just that. Since it was exactly what she wanted too, she stayed silent, letting him look his fill. Watching the changes his body and face underwent as he stared at her . . . pussy.

His gaze narrowed, his nostrils flared, and he breathed deeply as though catching the scent of her arousal. That animalistic little action tightened her belly and her sex—which resulted in a deepening growl that rumbled from his throat.

Which taught her a very important lesson. While he might be calling the shots, commanding her cooperation, she was definitely the one in charge. A powerful, heady sensuality filled her. She'd let him be in charge because she wanted the benefit of his experience and didn't want the responsibility of owning up later to whatever debauchery he had planned. With that acknowledgment, she felt no less nervous about what was to come.

He'd said he'd make her beg, and she'd start right now if she thought it would get him to the riding part any sooner, but she figured he was hell-bent for leather to do things his way.

With his thumbs resting on either side of her sex, he bent over her. She sucked in a deep breath before his lips ever touched her, then moaned when they glided softly up the length of one nether lip and down the other. His tongue quickly followed the same path, licking her over and over, and she knew he loved it, loved the way she tasted, by how often he came back for more.

Thick fingers plucked her outer lips, spreading them, and he sucked her thin, tender inner folds between his lips, fluttering his tongue along their sensitive edges.

Honey mewled, not recognizing the sounds tearing from her throat. She wanted to release her legs and thrust her fingers into his hair, guide his mouth over one sensitive spot to the next, but he seemed to find them all by himself and she didn't want to lose the unimpeded view.

Watching a man make love to her, delighting in her flavors as he sucked and licked her sex, was astounding. The sight caused her chest to tighten, and she knew she was falling deeper in love by the minute, but she couldn't stop, couldn't think about to-morrow.

When he licked lower, grazing the forbidden tiny hole, she froze. He couldn't have meant to do that! But he came back for more, lapping over it, teasing it with the tip of his tongue while shock and nervous excitement stiffened her whole body.

Then he pointed his tongue and spread her pink pussy—and oh! *He fucked her!* Just like he'd promised, plunging as far as he could reach into her pussy, his tongue acting like a miniature cock to stroke inside her.

Her *pussy* spasmed—clasping, opening. Christ, she could think that word now without hesitating! Watching him love her, seeing how her body responded to his attention, fascinated her, even as the feelings of excitement and the curling, burning need escalated.

She forgot how to breathe, struggling for each breath, as she strained her thighs against her own hands' fierce grip. Her release was rising up to strangle her, pitching her toward heaven. It was too much!

She must have gasped that last thought out loud, because Joe sat back and stared, removing his glorious tongue from her opening.

"No!" she cried out, then sobbed when he gave her a wicked little smile and licked upward, finding the hard, rounded bead at the top of her pussy, the one she'd used often to get herself excited when she couldn't stand being alone.

"Too much!" she moaned, again, quivering and melting as he plied her with teasing licks and flutters. She couldn't look anymore and squeezed her eyes tight, thrashing her head on the pillow, as he swirled his tongue around and around, building a tension she didn't think her heart would survive. When he sucked her clitoris with his lips, her whole body trembled.

When he bit it, she screamed and pitched headlong over the edge.

* * *

Joe watched her come apart as he chewed gently on her "love button." Lord, she was beautiful, lost in her release. Her pretty tits dimpled and quivered, her soft belly vibrated. Her rosy, swollen lips opened wide around her moans, and he craved to cram his cock into her mouth to feel those keening cries all along his shaft. Instead, he watched and plied her with his tongue and teeth, knowing his turn was coming and he wanted her well-satisfied and compliant when the time came.

Honey's breaths were ragged, whimpering sobs. When her head stopped rocking back and forth on the pillow, he pried her hands from her thighs and eased her legs to the mattress. Then he scooted up her body, intent on exploring the parts he'd never touched.

With his cock drilling into the mattress between her sprawled legs, he cupped a creamy breast and bent to glide his lips over the soft underside, marveling at the baby-soft texture of her skin, and then slid upward to capture a ripe nipple between his lips.

Her moan was thin, almost reedy. Her hands smoothed over his shoulders, soft caresses that made him shiver with delight. When her fingers sank into his hair and held him to her breast, he smiled. She didn't give him a gentle tug. Her fingers dug in and pulled hard.

He sucked her nipple between his teeth and bit.

"Ouch!"

"Did that hurt?" he asked, lifting his head to look into her slackened face.

"You know it didn't," she said, her lips pouting. "It just surprised me."

"Is that the only surprise I've given you?"

Her fingers loosened their fierce grip on his hair and her expression grew solemn. "I was amazed at the care you took to make this special for me."

Her praise warmed him, but he deflected the unwanted feeling. "Don't you think I treat all the ladies like this?"

Her eyes narrowed. "I'd like to think I inspired you. Let me dream, hmmm?"

"You do inspire me," he said softly and kissed the tip of her nipple. "But, baby, I'm so hard now, I'm not sure I can concentrate any more on you."

She stilled for a moment. "Are you going to fuck me now?"

She spoke so simply, without inflection, she might have been asking him directions to the livery. He'd done that—rocked her past embarrassment and modesty. He nodded slowly, the heat and urgency in his loins spurring faster and higher as her features lost their love-softened drowsiness, and her gaze sharpened with excitement.

"What are you waiting for?" she asked, her tone sharpening, tightening.

"For you to feel the same way, too."

"You think I don't?" She inhaled, pausing, and then whispered, "My . . . pussy's seeping cream."

His eyelids dipped. He felt like a stalking mountain lion sighting a quivering jackrabbit in the underbrush. "You do like dirty talk."

"You inspire me, too."

He mouthed her breast once and kissed her nipple before locking gazes with her again. He let her see the heat he'd banked, let her see how raw he felt. "No more play. No more preparation."

Her heartbeat thumped beneath his hand. "Just come inside me. I'm dying to know how well you fill me."

Joe scooted higher up her body and she eagerly parted her legs, making room for him. Without asking, she raised her knees on either side of his hips, tilting her cunt upward. He rested on his elbows, determined to take her slowly—at least for the first little while. He leaned in for a kiss, and she rose up to meet him, her mouth opening, her tongue ready to feel his answering thrust.

Slow. He had to take it slow. Make it good for her, no matter what he'd said.

But when he lifted his hips back and centered his cock between her swollen pussy lips, her moist heat greeted him, coating his head, inviting him to sink hard and fast. And suddenly he was poised on his hands above her and tunneling inward, cramming himself into the tightest, hottest little cunt he'd ever had.

He pulled out and flexed forward again a few hot inches, packing himself tighter and farther inside, caught up in the sensations surrounding his cock. Her walls closed around him, massaging his shaft, scalding wet heat coating him as he crammed deeper, working her cunt forward and back to ease deeper still.

God, she couldn't be this tight, couldn't be this small. She squeezed around him, gloving him closer than any clenched fist, and he came unglued. He groaned and growled, circling his hips to screw deeper.

Her whimpers finally broke through the haze of desire that clouded his mind and told him something wasn't right. He paused above her, his chest squeezing like a blacksmith's billows, and looked down at her face.

Her eyes were shut tight and her bottom lip was between her teeth.

"Honey? Baby, look at me."

She opened her eyes, but pressed her lips together.

"Was I wrong thinking you had at least a little experience?"

"I've done this before." She bit her lip and winced. "Sort of."

He wanted to howl, wanted to fuck deep into her—she'd given him permission, engineered his seduction for just this objective.

However, her opening was tiny, untried. He'd tear her tender tissues unnecessarily if he took her the way his body was primed. Jesus, she was killing him.

He was there—inside her at last, but he couldn't move. He'd felt her stretch to accommodate him, felt the resistance of her tight channel and the little piece of inner flesh that guarded her portal.

"There's no in betweens here," he growled. "You've been with a man or you haven't."

Still gasping, her hands clenched in spasms on his shoulders. "I had one man, a preacher's son, but he came as soon as he started slipping inside me."

"He never came all the way into you?"

She shook her head. "Say this doesn't change anything."

It did, but not the way she was thinking. "I'm almost there, sweetheart. I can't stop now. I'm going to take your maidenhead, and I need you to hold on to me. Hold me tight."

She wrapped her arms and legs around him, clinging to his body the same way her gaze clung to his face—with trust he wouldn't hurt her.

Joe leaned his forehead against hers and closed his eyes, trying not to focus on the quivering, clasping flesh that caressed every inch of cock he'd managed to push inside her.

If he were a better man, he'd pull out now, let her save herself for the right man. But he was too far gone, nearly sick with the need to fuck deep into her body, stake his claim where no man had ever gone before.

As though she'd read his mind, she whispered, "Please. I want it to be you."

He leaned to the side on one elbow and slipped two fingers into her mouth. "Wet these." She sucked him, like she'd done his cock, and once again, the feral heat rose in him, pounding a drumbeat in his ears.

Raising his hips to make a space, he slid his hand between their bodies, pressing between her cunt lips, and drew up the hood that protected the center of her desire. When his fingers touched her clitoris and circled on it, she cried out, her hips slamming upward, trying to capture him, trying to drive him deeper, but he held himself away, only letting her go so far.

Only when her legs quivered and squeezed around his back to draw him closer and her cries grew ragged again, only then did he roll fully over her and stroke deep into her cunt—tearing away the thin membrane, making her his forever.

Honey's cries grew hoarse and she swallowed, trying to clear her head enough to register every stroke, every thrust of his thick cock. She wanted to remember how it felt to be filled by him.

He'd crammed her channel tight with his sex, crowded her inner tissues, scraping them raw until the friction had drawn a scalding hot trickle of juice from deep within her that moistened and lubricated and helped her finally accommodate his girth within her body. He filled her exquisitely.

Her whole body felt rubbed raw, her breasts tingled, and she wanted to wrap her arms and legs tightly around him and keep these feelings building inside her forever, but he was slowing the tempo of his thrusts, grunting softly until his hips stilled.

He leaned down and kissed her, squeezing his eyes tight for a moment, seeming to steel himself, if the bunched muscles of his shoulders and arms were any indication. When he locked his gaze with hers again, he said, "How are you doing?"

How could he get words past his throat? Hers was so tight, so strained, she was afraid she'd squeal like a rusty hinge, but she dragged in a deep breath. "Fine, I'm fine. Why'd you stop?" She couldn't help the petulant edge to her voice.

One side of his mouth tipped up in a strained smile. "Can you take more?"

"You mean you're not all the way inside me?"

"Not quite."

Her hands squeezed his shoulders, her body tensed. "I can take it. Finish it, please."

He snorted and dipped down to kiss the corner of her mouth. "I doubt it, but I'm busting. Can't hold back any more."

If this had been him holding back, she was in trouble. She already felt stretched, split up the middle by his huge cock, but dear God, she needed him to move. "Fuck me, Joe. Jesus, fuck me hard."

His lips pulled back in a savage snarl and his arms trembled and tensed. When he unleashed himself, all Honey could do was hold on tight and ride out the storm. Joe bucked and thrust, tunneling so deeply she thought she should taste him at the back of her throat.

Too breathless to cry out, instead she grunted, unable to restrain the harsh gusts he forced from her body with his powerful thrusts. He hammered her womb, hard and fast, his thighs and buttocks delivering powerful strokes so fast, so hard, his cock shoved her up the bed.

He followed, crowding closer, bumping the backs of her thighs as he hammered her up the mattress until she had to let go of him and press hard against the wall at the end of the bed to brace herself against his powerful strokes.

He was harsh, brutal—but she loved it, took all of it. His reddened face drew into taut harsh lines above her, his lips curled back in a frightening grimace. His gaze was feral, wild—his wildness set her free.

Her hips slammed upward, out of rhythm with his strokes, but she couldn't find it, couldn't match his speed. But she had to answer his thrusts, had to take him deep as she could. She wanted it all, the painful fullness, the scalding heat, the power that crushed and battered her body so incredibly.

She sobbed, tears threatening to overspill her eyes, and then she exploded like Fourth of July fireworks, falling like a shimmering waterfall of aftershocks to rest against the sheets.

Joe shouted, the muscles of his belly and thighs bunching hard as steel as he pounded faster, delivering sharp slaps of flesh to flesh, his balls slamming at her arsehole until a second, softer explosion took her.

When the hot streams of his seed flooded her channel, her tears slid into her hair and her arms and legs melted to the mattress. She hadn't the strength to move, didn't have the heart left to think about what happened next.

Joe came down on top of her and scooted lower, withdrawing his cock from her swollen channel with a reluctant groan, and rested his head between her breasts.

As their breaths slowed, Honey thought the sweetest feeling she'd ever known was Joe suckling softly at her breast as she fell asleep.

6

Joe awoke surrounded by softness—a downy mattress beneath him, Honey's breast pressed against the side of his chest, and her small hand cupping his balls.

A man could get used to this.

He stretched his toes against the footboard and yawned, and then reached down to cover her hand and give it and himself a squeeze. A smile tugged the corners of his lips. "You sore?"

Her gaze shot up, and she wrinkled her nose. "That's not the first thing I wanted to hear this morning," she said grumpily.

He rolled over her, bringing her under him on the narrow bed, pressing her deep into the downy mattress. He could get used to covering her, having all her parts crushed beneath him. At his mercy.

He kneed apart her legs and settled his cock in between. "What did you want to hear?" He thought he knew, but he wanted to hear her admit it.

Even in the gray light of dawn, her many vivid colors were a beacon—her red hair shimmered, her creamy cheeks glowed, her pink swollen mouth. . . .

Damn, just looking at that mouth had him getting harder. He nudged between her folds, but stopped there. She wanted to talk. Wanted him to say something, but he wasn't ready for those three words. Not yet.

Should he comment on her beauty? Making love suited her, made her lips and nipples rosy and her face soft, but he knew she didn't want to hear that either.

Her green gaze narrowed, and her lips pressed into a stubborn line. "Maybe I was just waiting for a good morning."

She was so easy to rile—and when she riled up, she got as horny as he did. Feeling light-hearted, he decided to tease her a little, to see how far he could push before her passion exploded all over him. "I think you want to hear how good it was last night—you and me."

Her eyebrows shot up. Outrage reddened her complexion all the way down to the tops of her breasts. "I'm sure that wasn't it," she bit out, her tone frosty. "You can let me up, now."

"Maybe you want me to say how pretty you are—how hot and pink your—"

"Nope—not it either. And if you don't get off me now I'm gonna make you a gelding!"

He bent to kiss her lips, but she turned her face, so he sucked on her earlobe. "But those weren't any of the things I wanted to say," he said softly.

She lay so still beneath him he could feel her heart beating against his chest, speeding to keep up with the quickness of her breaths.

He snaked an arm beneath her shoulders and a hand beneath her bottom, holding her close, waiting for her to meet his gaze.

When she did, that heavy ache inside his chest was back and he recognized it for what it was.

Her eyes welled with tears and her lips trembled. She was scared and as vulnerable as she'd ever allowed herself to be with a man. He knew it, welcomed it. Hoped it meant she felt as raw and vulnerable as he did.

"Wh-what were you going to say?" she whispered.

"That I want you to stay. Here. With me." That was as much as he was willing to admit. They'd known each other just a few days. Maybe it was too soon for her. He didn't want to spook her into fleeing.

"Why? Because of this? You want to fuck me some more?"

Her words were harsh, but her tone wasn't nearly as brittle, and her voice held quaver.

"I'd like that," he said honestly, "and I'd like to spend time with you. Learn all about you. Have you learn all about me."

"How long? A few days?"

"How about through the winter, and we'll see how it goes?" Should be long enough to plant a babe in her belly and give her a lifetime of reasons to stay with him. And damn, making that baby would sure light a fire on those cold winter nights.

Her gaze slid away. "I don't know. I have places to go. You know, I'm a businesswoman—I have to mind my business."

He bent his head and this time she didn't turn away. He kissed her, sliding his lips over hers. They'd talked enough. If he said anything more, he'd mess it up. He drew a whisper away from her mouth and said, "Think about it. Think about this." Then he flexed his hips, thrusting into her snug channel.

She grimaced and sucked air between her teeth.

He didn't like that he'd hurt her, but at the same time he felt a deep, masculine satisfaction that her discomfort was due solely to the wild ride he'd given her. "I did ask," he growled. "Want to stop?"

Her cunt tightened around him, rejecting his invasion. "Um . . . I think we just need to take it a little slow."

Relieved he'd have her anyway, he pulled out and rolled again, stopping when she lay stretched on top of his body. He placed his palm on her cheek, and rubbed his thumb over her pouting bottom lip. "Straddle me. Take me inside you."

Her eyelids dipped and, when she met his gaze again, fresh sensual excitement lit her features. With her hands braced against his chest, she rose up, watching as he spread her swollen folds. He licked his fingers to wet them, then rubbed the moisture all around her entrance. She surprised him when she licked her own fingers and rubbed the tip of his cock.

When he gave her clitoris a sensual slide of his calloused thumb, she pressed down, blowing out a breath, then halted after accepting only a few inches of his cock and rose again.

He kept his hands off her, knowing he'd bruise her delicate skin if he put his hands where he wanted—on her hips to force her to move faster. Instead, he fisted his hands in the bedding beside her knees.

She took him so slowly he gritted his teeth and counted, reaching thirty before she sank far enough to suit him even a little. Hard as a railroad spike, he knew his girth caused her pain. Still, Honey rose and fell with her thighs quivering and her eyes squeezed tight. Her head canted and her hair trailed down one shoulder, her curls capturing a nipple.

The sight of the soft tangle tugging at her breast was more than he could stand. He couldn't take another minute of not touching her and reached up to brush away her hair, then cupped her, squeezing her breasts, thumbing her nipples while she pushed a little deeper.

A little dry at first, her cunt juiced up fast, aiding her movements so she glided up and down faster, pushing down on him, taking more of his length, packing him harder into her narrow passage.

Her mouth opened on a ragged sob, and he tried to soothe her, knowing she was quickly being overcome by all the emotions, all the sensations swamping her now.

Did she know this was special? That any other man wouldn't affect her this way, wouldn't fill her like this, wouldn't love her with the same intensity? Joe knew he'd never have the likes of her again.

Joe came up on his elbows and rooted at her breast, taking as much as he could into his mouth, suckling as she pumped up and down.

It was almost enough. His balls felt heavy and full and had drawn up close to his groin. His cock was ready to burst, but he needed to lift his hips and stroke her walls, needed to move against her and feel her surge against him as he crammed deep inside her.

"Please," she keened, shuddering over him, her cunt rippling all along his shaft.

The plea was the answer to his prayer, and he lay down and bent his knees, planting his feet firmly in the mattress. When he grabbed her hips, her eyes flew open and her gaze locked with his. He speared upward, the stroke hard and sharp, and at the same time forced her hips down.

She yelped, but didn't fight the next lunge, letting him guide her, letting him pull her down his shaft to fuck his cock with enough force to slap their groins together. Hard enough to jar him, hard enough to make her shout and cry as she exploded, hard enough to make him come in a furious flurry of thrusts that jiggled her belly and breasts. When he exploded, his shout sounded incredibly loud inside the close confines of her wagon.

When he slowed, he ground against her, scraping her clitoris with the base of his cock while she moaned and gasped. He tried to make her release last, but needed to rest because his heart pounded inside his chest and he couldn't catch a breath.

As she collapsed over him, he wound his arms around her back and held her hips close, not letting her slip off his cock. He wanted to stay like this, surrounded by her, overwhelmed with her passion.

"I think you killed me," she said, gasping against his sweaty skin.

"Murder by fucking?" He closed his eyes and grinned. "Think they'd hang me?"

"They'd probably pin a medal on your cock."

He thrust his fingers in her hair and pulled her head back. All he had to do was stare at her mouth and she leaned forward and kissed him hard, framing his face in her hands as their kiss deepened.

"Think they're done?" came a gruff whisper from just outside the window.

Honey jerked back, her eyes rounding. "It's Letty!" she whispered frantically.

His lips twitched. Letty must have had her ear to the wagon wall. He wondered whether she'd even had a peek inside. He wouldn't put anything past the rascally woman.

"They can't find us like this," Honey said, trying to push his hand off her bottom.

He captured her hands and pressed her palms flat against her bottom, enjoying the sight of her jiggling breasts and the feel of her pussy wriggling on his cock as she tried to free herself. "Would it be so bad?"

"Joe! This isn't a joke. You have to let me up!"

Her expression went from shocked fury to mortification with a single blush and he relented. "One kiss, then I'll let you up."

"Joe!"

"A kiss," he commanded, wiping his face free of any amusement.

When she leaned over him, he reached up and captured her mouth in one lusty caress. "It's gonna be all right, sweetheart. Trust me."

Then he let go of her hands and she scrambled off the bed, jerking her clothing off the hooks to dress in a hurry. He liked that she didn't bother with the pantalets. The thought of her greeting whomever waited outside with his release drying on her thighs gave him a primitive satisfaction.

"Letty? Are you out there?" she called out, holding up a mirror as she tore at her tangled hair with a brush.

"She must have heard us," came another gruff whisper.

"She must have heard *you!*" came a hissed response.

Joe pressed his lips together to suppress a grin. Embarrassing though the next few minutes would certainly prove, he had no regrets. The women could have flung open the door while Honey rode him so sweetly, and he'd have been happy to prove up his claim.

With her hand on the door knob, Honey tossed a frantic glance over her shoulder. "Get dressed! And for goodness' sake, cover yourself!"

Honey stepped down to the ground and right into a passel of trouble. The number of riders, most of the men with shotguns in their crossed arms, made her stomach lurch.

Letty stood in front of the group, a floppy hat pulled down so low her eyes were shadowed. Daisy flanked her, her expression pained.

Honey scanned the riders, trepidation rising when she noted Reverend Sessions wearing his white collar and Amos Handy's beefy fist holding a shotgun like it was a fly swatter. Even Curly Hicks rode with the gang, looking oddly happy.

Honey cleared her throat. Maybe they were on the trail of outlaws and their appearance here didn't have a thing to do with the sinful goings on inside her wagon. "What can I do for you folks?"

"Now, Honey-girl," Letty began, her tone holding more than a hint of regret, "You know why we're here."

Mortification, of a deep, soul-crushing sort, heated her

cheeks, made her hands shake and her stomach roil. "Letty, why'd you bring all these folks here?" she asked softly.

"It was all part of our plan," Daisy said, her smile strained.

Anger, swift and blazing hot, took the edge off her embarrassment. "You mean besides the kidnapping and stripping him naked part?" she asked, her voice rising. It would have been one thing for the women to accidentally let slip and mention what had occurred, but to set a deliberate trap?

Letty winced. "Well, it seemed like a good plan. At the time, anyways. And could ya keep yer voice down?"

"Why?" Honey said, scowling. "You have a headache?"

"Damn, she gets ornery when she's riled."

"I suspect she's simply embarrassed," Daisy said, her expression apologetic. "And a little worried about the sheriff, aren't you, my dear?"

"If it helps, yers won't be the only weddin' today."

Honey fisted her hands on her hips, not ready to be sidetracked from her anger, but she was curious. "There's gonna be another wedding? Whose?"

"Sally's," Letty said, a little smile curling her lips. "Curly finally ate that apple pie."

"Pie?" Honey shook her head, not understanding, and then her mouth gaped. "Letty? Did you give her some of your elixir?"

"Some things call for desperate measures and that man was as skittish as a colt when it come to marrying the girl. He just needed a little shove. Doesn't look unhappy about it now, does he?"

Honey leaned to the side and stared at Curly. Sure enough, his grin stretched so wide she could see every one of his pearly white teeth.

"So how much elixir did you have to give the sheriff?" Letty whispered. "Must a been a whole bottle, since you two were still frisky this morning."

"Letty!" Daisy exclaimed, shoving her elbow into Letty's side. "I swear, Honey, we just arrived—"

"'Bout half an hour ago. With all the noise we had to take a peek to make sure he wasn't killin' you." At Honey's shocked expression, Letty added, "It was just a quick peek. I swear we didn't see . . . much."

Judging by the blushes both women wore, it had been more than a peek. But it didn't matter. This had gone far enough. "I didn't ply him with any potion. I'd never trick a man into marrying me. And while I'm happy for Sally, there will be only one wedding today."

Daisy reached across to touch Honey's shoulder. "But you have to let the sheriff do right by you. Your reputation will be in shreds—"

"And it's so much worse," Letty interrupted, "'cause he wasn't even under the influence of your potion."

"He took advantage of you."

"I have no reputation to lose," Honey shouted to be heard above the women's chatter.

"But what about mine?" The low rumbling voice brought everyone to silence.

Honey closed her eyes for a moment and then looked over her shoulder. Joe stood in her doorway, his shirt only partially buttoned, exposing most of his naked chest. And he was bootless. Anyone looking at him knew, by his state of undress and the thick stubble shadowing his jaw, he'd been up to no good. His expression didn't give much away, but his gaze was piercing, maybe a little possessive, when it landed on her.

Honey melted. This proud, handsome man stood on her stoop, looking so well-pleasured and debauched—and she was responsible for that. She didn't much care what anyone else thought; she felt pride in the fact she'd held his interest all through the night, that she'd sparked his passion and taken all of his rough loving.

In fact, she didn't much care if she followed him back inside and started all over again. They could all damn well watch and listen!

"What about my reputation, Honey?" he asked, stepping barefoot to the ground. "Won't you do right by me?"

"You mean marry you?" she asked faintly. Oh, she wanted to, but not at his expense. She straightened her shoulders. "I thought a man's reputation was only enhanced by his conquests."

"Only a bastard thinks like that," he said, walking toward her.

"Still, none of this is your fault." Could he see how sorry she was? "You were entrapped."

"You think I couldn't have walked away if I'd wanted to? I could have had my hands out of those ropes at any time. Someone used slip knots."

"Sonuvabitch," Letty muttered.

"Joe, I'm not blaming you for taking what I offered. I gave freely, no strings *or ropes* attached."

His hand came up and cupped her cheek. "And if I don't want to be set free?"

The temptation to lean into his hand and accept his comfort was so strong tears welled in her eyes. "What are you saying?"

"What I've been trying to say to you since I woke up with you snuggled up next to me, woman."

Sighs from the women standing next to her couldn't draw her gaze from Joe's fierce scowl. He was going to say it.

"I love you," he said, loud enough for everyone to hear.

Feeling as though the rest of the world had faded away, she stared at him while her heart felt full to bursting. If he could be that brave, so could she. "I love you, too."

"Whoo-ee, we got us a double wedding, Daisy," Letty said. "And you just got yourself out of a spanking."

Daisy turned scarlet and glanced back at her husband, who

gave her a wink. "Letty, remind me never to confide in you again."

Letty slapped Joe's back. "Saddle up, cowboy."

Joe's gaze stayed on Honey. "Miss Cafferty and I both need to clean up. How about we follow you in a little while?"

"Don't make me come lookin' for you. I might forget to knock."

Joe pulled Honey flush with the front of his body and encircled her in his arms.

Honey shook her head. Her head still reeled from his declaration. "Do I get any say in this?"

"Of course you do," he said, grinning, "so long as the words are 'I do.'"

She narrowed her eyes, just to make sure he knew she wouldn't always be this easy to herd. "You think you're always going to boss me around?"

"Only when you want me to."

Her lips parted on a sigh. "I'm not wearing any underwear," she whispered.

"I heard that," Letty said. "Think she whispers about as well as I do."

"Letty," Honey said, giving her friend a killing glare, "I wanted to make sure you knew that it's time for you to head on down the road."

"Let's leave them alone to 'clean up,'" Daisy said, leading Letty away by the arm.

Honey's body burned everywhere Joe's pressed close. His rigid cock nudged her belly. "Think we have time?"

He bent and whispered in her ear. "You too sore?"

Gazing up into his handsome face, she licked her lips and said, "I was thinking about stretchin' my lips . . ."

His gaze narrowed, dropping to follow her tongue. "I'm thinking you have a nasty little mind."

She pouted her lips, teasing him. "You made it that way."

"I've got no regrets."

His solemn gaze stole her breath. "You promise?"

"I promise. Forever. No regrets." Then he ducked and shoved his shoulder into her belly, draping her over his shoulder like a shirt.

Honey guessed that meant he was done talking. Before she could catch her breath, he'd lowered her to the bed and had her skirt shoved up to her waist. "Will you always be this eager?"

"Just pout those lips . . ." His hands disappeared from view beneath her rucked up skirt.

She gasped when his fingers rimmed her opening. "I thought I was the one who was going to do all the work."

"I don't want you changing your mind."

"You do want to marry me."

"Do you think I'm this eager with every woman I've bedded?"

"How am I supposed to know?"

With his fingers swirling, encouraging her cunt to melt and moisten, he leaned over her and brought his face over hers. "That's not your fault. This is happening too fast. I know I'm not going to change my mind, but I don't want you pining for the road, someday."

That surprised her and she canted her head. "You think I want to live like this?"

"Don't you? You have everything you need," he said, his forehead wrinkling with the beginnings of another fierce frown. "This wagon's a comfortable little nest. You have exciting places to go, new people to meet."

"Joe, all I've ever wanted was what everyone else has. A real home."

"We can give that to each other. Home's not a house, it's family."

"It's love?" she asked, wanting to make sure she understood. "You don't think it's too soon? To know, I mean."

"Do you?"

He gave a slow shake of his head. "I've never felt this way about another woman. I don't want to lose this or you—"

"I fell in love with you that first day when you smiled from the edge of the crowd—"

"I watched you thinking I was looking at stardust and moonbeams and didn't think I could ever hold you—"

"I'm not leaving," Honey said. "I'll be yours."

Joe's gaze dropped between them and his fingers stroked deeper. "To do with as I please?"

She rolled her hips to take him deeper. "I like what pleases you."

He closed his eyes for a moment. "Thank God." Then he gave her another of those fierce scowls that made her melt into a puddle. "Now, about stretchin' those lips . . ."

Honey grinned and rolled with him, coming over him and scooting low. She trailed a fingernail down his shaft and watched it jump. "I don't think he needs any old elixir to encourage him," she murmured.

"There's only one elixir of love this man needs," Joe growled.

As she bent over him, she wondered if Señora Garza had cast a spell over more than her bottled potions. Somehow, all her dreams had come true. In this one man lay all her big-brass-band kind of dreams.

"You're thinking too much."

She arched an eyebrow. "Getting nervous?"

"Getting thirsty. I haven't had anything to drink since your sweet cream."

"Funny, I was thinking the same thing."

"We are well matched."

Honey was through playing. "I want you inside me."

"I want your tits in my mouth."

She crawled back up his body and into his arms. When she'd filled the ache between her legs with his strong cock, she leaned over him. "Give me fireworks."

"Sweetheart, I'll give you the whole damn Fourth of July."

QUEEN OF HEARTS

LAYLA CHASE

1

1880, Mississippi Delta

Lissa Tayte's gaze circled the eager male faces surrounding her, scrutinizing each individual, looking for a giveaway sign. Nothing besides lusty masculine interest, and she'd become immune to that. She ran the tip of her tongue along the inside of her upper lip. "I'll take three."

Almost as one body, the men sucked in their breaths and shifted in their wooden seats. From across the crowded saloon filtered the sounds of the piano player banging out a raucous tune and the rise and fall of several conversations. Smoke from tobacco and candles hung in a wispy cloud below the chandeliers.

Arthur Lansing, the town doctor, snapped three cards onto the table and shoved them in her direction.

Lissa drew the cards across the gouged pine table and added them to the two she held. Damn! Nothing to better the pair of nines. She forced her eyes to widen and let a corner of her mouth quirk before quickly pressing her lips together and drawing down her brows. Let the others think she'd drawn something of value.

She eyed her stack of gold coins, comparing it to the stacks in front of the other players. Hers was still taller than most. Luck and the right cards had been hers again tonight, so why not take a chance? No one ever won big without a risk.

A thrill tingled her stomach. "I'll bet these." She laid her cards facedown on the table and pushed the majority of her coins forward, keeping back enough to stake a few more hands.

The mustachioed man on her left jerked, his chair legs screeching on the plank flooring. "What? That must be pert near fifty dollars."

She arched an eyebrow and turned her head, dipping her chin to smile over her raised shoulder. "Why, sir, I understood this particular table had no limits on bets." For good measure, she batted her eyelashes as she scanned the faces of the other players. "Was I wrong?"

Several men shook their heads. "No, ma'am."

"The bet's forty-two dollars to you, Johnson," Dr. Lansing said as he finished counting the coins. "Are you in?"

Lissa held her breath, hoping her bold move hadn't knocked everyone out of this round of betting. Wouldn't do to scare away players she'd been beating for the past couple hours. Her thoughts strayed to the darling feathered hat she'd spotted in the milliner's window this afternoon.

Her anticipated reward for an evening's winnings.

"I fold." Johnson slammed down his cards. "Can't believe this dame's luck."

"Johnson, watch your mouth." Dr. Lansing connected with Lissa's gaze and dipped his chin. "Sorry, ma'am. I wish I had the cards to see your raise, Mrs. Tayte. But I fold."

The next two players tossed down their cards, shaking their heads and mumbling about their rotten luck. The remaining man stared hard, first at his hand, then at her face, and the skin around his eyes crinkled.

Lissa vowed to hold his scowling gaze.

"Nobody's as lucky as this da—, um, lady. She's gotta be bluffing." The red-bearded man to her right pushed his coins to the middle of the table. "That's forty, and . . ." He stood to dig in his trouser pocket, then tossed a coin onto the heaped pile in the middle of the table. "Here's the other ten."

The coin bounced against the others in the pile with a loud clink and then settled.

At the display of his bravado, she sucked in a breath. Maybe she'd misjudged her luck.

"Okay, Bergstrom met your bet, Mrs. Tayte. Let's see your cards."

Displaying a big smile, Lissa separated out the pair and laid them on the table. "A pair of nines." She picked out a single card from the remaining three and set it next to those on the table. "With an ace high."

"Damn it all!" Shaking his head, Bergstrom tossed his cards onto the pile of coins. "I was holdin' nines, too, but had only a queen kicker." He took a deep breath and extended his hand. "Well played, ma'am."

From behind a demure smile, Lissa released her breath and accepted his brief handshake. "Thank you, sir." She rose off the chair just far enough to scoop the coins from the middle of the table toward her seat, well aware the men enjoyed a generous display of her décolletage.

Any and all weapons were fair at the gaming tables.

With practiced moves, she grabbed a handful of coins and slid them into the velvet reticule lying in her lap and then stacked the rest in neat piles.

A couple players excused themselves from the game, but others quickly grabbed the seats.

Ah, new challenges. She batted her eyelashes and smiled in the new arrivals' direction. "Welcome, gentlemen."

"Howdy, ma'am."

Aah, these opponents were still young enough to blush when she turned her special smile their way. The perfect type to be susceptible to all her attributes.

A prickly feeling running along the skin of her neck told her she was being watched, and she fought off a shiver. Rather than give away her suspicions, she reached into her reticule and pulled out a floral fan. With a snap of her wrist, she spread it and waved it near her chin.

"Warm in here, tonight." She turned to the man on her left and leaned close. "Don't you think so?"

Looking over this man's shoulder, her gaze touched on shiny black boots under the impeccably tailored pants of a long-legged man near the entry. Red silk vest, creamy white shirt, fitted black waistcoat. If she wasn't mistaken, the cuffs on those arrogantly crossed arms held gold cufflinks. The gentleman chose quality clothing. A habit they had in common.

Her gaze traveled past a silk string tie to a resolute jaw darkened by a day's growth of whiskers. A stray lock of brown hair fell over his forehead. Handsome . . . and compelling. From this distance, she couldn't tell the color of his eyes under the dark slashes of his brows.

The idea of getting close enough to determine the shade floated around her thoughts. Tonight was her last opportunity for a frolic before fulfilling a business obligation. Why not have it with that handsome stranger? A man she'd surely never see again.

At her lascivious thoughts, her smile widened and her cheeks flushed. An unusual reaction for her, and she quickened the movements of her fan. The heat of anticipation spread through her body, making her squirm a bit in her chair.

The evening had just become more exciting.

Now, she had to figure out how to entice the handsome stranger over to this table.

The doctor cleared his throat. "Ma'am, you going to ante up?"

With a swallow against a dry throat, she forced her attention back to the table. Every player's face wrinkled with a frown at her delay of the game. The tall man had distracted her from her game and that made him dangerous.

From his location near the swinging doors of The Cotton Palace saloon, Roark Sheridan spotted the table with the saucy blonde his deckhands Malloy and Linden warned him about. In a minute, he'd investigate their assessment that a woman got prettier as her winnings grew.

Right now, he needed to get his bearings. Smoke hung in a vaporous cloud around the chandeliers. The sharp scents of cheap whiskey and the yeasty tang of beer teased his nostrils. He drew in a deep breath and felt the tension of the day leave his shoulders.

Here was a world he knew.

Here he was in control of the next few hours.

Here no one expected him to know the answers to questions about whiskey storage, curtain mending, and produce deliveries. All the pesky details of operating a riverboat that he'd had to learn over the past two weeks—since that fateful poker game.

Why in hell had he challenged the captain that Saturday night? Lady Luck had been on his shoulder to deal him that last queen, the sweet one that filled out an inside straight. Had he known what headaches winning that hand and his riverboat would be, he might have folded those cards.

Thinking about that moment, he shook his head. A concession like that was not in his nature.

After tomorrow's launch, he'd have no easy escape from his new position as owner/captain of the Queen of Hearts, paddle-wheel showboat and gambling saloon of the Mississippi Delta.

Rooms like this had been his most common surroundings for the latter half of his 30-year life. Gambling, high stakes, and beautiful women. What man could want more? Roark's fingers itched for the feel of stiff cards in his hands and the sound of coins clinking into stacks within his reach.

The blonde beauty's gaze started at his feet and traveled up his body until it connected with his eyes and held. Did the lady betray an interest? A smile twitched at the corners of his lips, and then she suddenly looked back to the game.

Easing from the wall, he headed toward the table ringed with spectators at the side of the saloon. He weaved across the crowded room, scanning the players' faces at the gaming tables for a familiar one who may bear a grudge over a game that went against him.

A man who made his livelihood on the losses of others couldn't let down his guard.

As he joined the circle, a roar of laughter burst out. A sweet, throaty sound rose above the others. His gaze sought the woman who belonged to that voice. When he spotted her up close, his breath lodged in his chest. Linden and Malloy hadn't been grand enough in their description.

More than the combination of creamy skin offset by golden curls and sky-blue eyes, the woman was high-class. From the perfect fit of her rose-colored silk dress with low-cut bodice to the sparkle of jewels at her neck to the glittering combs in her shining hair. Right down to the sheer lace gloves she wore.

A broad-shouldered man slammed his hands on the table and stood, his chair toppling backwards. He swept his hand at the cards faceup on the table and the lopsided pile of coins and bills. "Who in hell stays in with a lousy pair of sixes? That loot could have been mine with the pair of jacks I tossed away."

Conversations at the nearby tables hushed, as if everyone held their collective breath.

Roark tensed, memories of similar disputes that ended badly tumbling through his mind.

A throaty laugh sounded and its owner's gloved hand closed over the man's beefy one. She cocked her head to the side and smiled from under her lashes at the irritated man. "Next time, sir, be daring. Believing in a hand like that might win you the prize."

The burly man cleared his throat and swept his hat off his head. "Why, thank you, ma'am. I'll consider that for another time."

Like a wave rippling away from the table, conversations resumed and the sounds of gaming—the shuffle of cards, clink of coins, and murmur of betting—spread throughout the room.

Roark let out the breath he'd been holding in his tight chest. The change in the man's attitude amazed him. From angry to appreciative in less than five seconds. This woman possessed a talent he'd not often seen. And he wanted to learn more about her skills.

2

Roark remained at the back of the crowd, observing, as several more hands were played. Not his usual habit. Normally he pressed his way forward until he was close enough to claim the first vacant chair.

Tonight, he was content to hang back and study every movement the saucy blonde made. Over the years and through many a card game, he'd learned a person who enjoyed her kind of luck often wasn't playing by the rules. Several times their gazes met and held, and she was always the one who looked away.

In particular, he studied her hands, looking for any flicks or twists that gave away a hidden card. The fact she wore gloves and kept her hands in constant motion made him more watchful. His concentration was interrupted by each sassy toss of her chin that brought her profile into view.

Or the sound of her laughter. A deep throaty laugh that lifted her creamy skin to the lacy neckline of her gown, pressing rounded mounds—. He shifted his stance and shot sideways glances at the men around him. No worry about being caught gawking—every other man within twenty feet stared at the same woman.

He hoped the others weren't experiencing the same tightening in their guts as he had. What had been an impersonal review of her abilities now became a burning need to know.

Was the woman as accomplished a player as she appeared?

Suddenly he had to be part of that game, to judge her skills at close range.

"Drink, mister?" A barmaid brushed her hip against his leg, her cheap cologne stinging his nostrils.

He glanced at the woman whose full figure almost burst out of her low-cut dress. A worn-around-the-edges smile flickered on her overly rouged lips and interest glinted in her muddy brown eyes. On another night, he might have shared time and a quiet drink at a secluded table. Possibly even paid for an hour of sport in a second-floor bed.

Not tonight. Not when a woman more to his liking was in sight.

"Not now." He let a grin slide over his lips. "But as soon as I'm seated at that poker table, bring me a bottle of your best wine. Champagne would be better, if it's in stock." For good measure, he gave her a wink before focusing his attention back on the game.

With a wide swing in her step, she sashayed toward the next man in the crowd.

A check of the coins stacked in front of the players indicated the one most likely to exit next. With unobtrusive movements, Roark eased his way through the crowd until he stood three feet from the losing player. Positioned to the woman's right, he could watch her moves from this new angle.

Or catch a glimpse of her cards. A hint of another's strategy was a valuable weapon in a smart player's arsenal.

"How many cards, ma'am?"

Roark concentrated on the lay of the table. Of the six players, two had already tossed in their hands.

The lady tapped a fingertip on the top of her fanned cards. "Just a moment more, sir. Should I hold this bitty card . . ." She ran a finger along the length of the card.

A man shifted to his left, reaching to accept a beer from the barmaid.

She looked across the table, straight at the dealer. "Or this one?"

Roark slid his foot left and pressed forward until he had an unobstructed view of the table. And an excellent view over the lady's shoulder—straight down her cleavage. At the sight of her jiggling breasts, his cock strained against the buttons of his trousers. An inconvenient reaction.

He forced his gaze up to scan the cards she held. Two jacks, a six, a seven, and a nine—not suited. An easy choice. Keep the jacks and dump the rest, hope for another pair.

With the tips of two fingers, she pulled the jacks from her hand. "I want two, please."

What the hell kind of strategy was that? Nobody dumped a pair of face cards. . . .

He stilled and his gaze ran around the circle of players. Unless she knew something better was coming her way. Could she be teamed with the dealer? Was a stacked deck being played?

His gaze lingered on the face of Doc Lansing, a man he'd lost about thirty dollars to on his first day in town. Average player, no obvious tells, seemed honest enough. Through painful experience, he'd learned those were the ones to watch the closest.

Requested cards moved from the deck to individual hands and bets were laid down.

Although the movements were small, unobtrusive to anyone not watching her, the lady's head kept turning toward the exit. Once she leaned to the side, as if trying to see through the crowd.

He rolled around the thought that she was looking for him. Could be, especially after that sultry first glance. He watched her face for signals going to another player but couldn't catch any. The next thing he knew, the play was finished without him knowing the order of players tossing in their cards or even who'd won the pot.

Too much time spent watching the flash of candlelight in the lady's blue eyes and the turns of her graceful neck.

"Count me out." The chair to his immediate right scraped on the floor.

Exactly the player he'd anticipated would leave. He grabbed the wooden back, staking his claim, and slid into the seat. Behind him, he heard a man's muttered curse.

The lady fiddled with her stack of coins, lifting a couple and letting them drop back in place.

The metallic sound of coins hitting each other was always satisfying. He leaned toward her, intoxicated by the scent of expensive perfume—citrus with a hint of herbs or sandalwood. "Evening, ma'am. Well-played hand."

She turned toward him and jerked, eyes widening at seeing him. In a flash, her eyelids dipped and she tilted her chin. "Good evening, sir. Thank you."

Her manner was coy, but practiced. He'd seen a few like her, but none had twisted his gut the way this one did. "I've not had the pleasure of an introduction."

"So you're joining our little game? Feeling lucky tonight?"

The lady had no idea who she was up against. "Always. Name's Sheridan, Ro—"

"Mr. Sheridan, I like keeping to last names only. Less personal. For the sake of the game." She extended her hand. "I'm Mrs. Tayte."

Roark reached out, clasped her hand, and had raised it

halfway to his mouth before the impact of her words sunk in. Missus? For only a second, he hesitated, then lifted her hand and brushed a kiss across the gloved ridge of her knuckles. Her scent filled his nostrils and he fought back the stirring in his groin.

She was married? "Enchanté, madam."

Damn, he hadn't counted on that. His seduction plan went up in smoke.

"What's your buy-in, Sheridan?"

Her hand slid from his, and for an instant he wanted to grab it back. From inside his jacket pocket, he withdrew his leather wallet. Normally, he carried between five and six hundred dollars in preparation of staking himself at any level table.

But this morning, he'd had to pay for a load of coal and a supply of firewood. The first of many, he'd been told. Another pesky detail. Had he remembered to enter those sums in the ledger?

He rifled through the remaining bills and thought of what other expenses might occur before they sailed. A curtailment on his gambling enjoyment he hadn't anticipated. "I'll take two, no, one hundred fifty."

Stacks of coins were counted and shoved to his side of the table.

A quick inhalation of breath next to him revealed Mrs. Tayte's surprise. So, she was impressed, and she recognized a man with a promising business future.

He glanced at the woman beside him, particularly at her left hand. No evidence of a ring bulged underneath her gloves. She wouldn't be the first woman to adopt the guise of widowhood for the freedoms it provided.

He couldn't worry about that now. He had to get his thoughts centered on the game. "What's the ante? Any limits on bets?"

"Two-dollar ante." The dealer shuffled the cards. "No limits."

"Any table rules I need to know? Wild cards? Blazes?"

Roark watched the middle-aged man's hands as he shuffled and stacked the cards. Nothing out of place.

"Why, Mr. Sheridan, you sound like a man who likes risks." Mrs. Tayte tapped two one-dollar pieces on her stack before tossing them into the center. A metallic clink sounded.

Roark turned to see her wide smile, almost a flirtatious one, and started to answer.

"Sir, you're in luck." The round barmaid leaned a breast against his shoulder as she placed a frosty bottle in front of him. "We had the champagne you requested in the spring house."

One of his favorite gestures that always scored big with the ladies.

"Oh, I dearly love champagne." Mrs. Tayte turned and rested her hand on his forearm. "What a treat this is."

Her eyes danced with delight and his skin burned under her touch. He gritted his teeth against the increase in his heart rate. A treat? More like a waste of money!

"Thanks for the prompt service." He forced a thin smile and tossed a ten-dollar gold piece onto her tray. "Keep the change."

The barmaid clamped a hand on his shoulder. "Thank you, sir. How many glasses do you need?"

While easing from under her heavy touch, Roark waved a hand at the other players. "Glasses all 'round. We'll start our first hand with a toast." With a carefree grin plastered on his face, he stood and uncorked the bottle with a resounding pop while waiting for the barmaid to return with the glasses. When she did, he poured each glass half full.

Let them all think he'd intended this generosity.

When the other players raised their glasses and looked to him, he proclaimed, "To luck and to success."

His words were repeated, as were the multiple glasses tapping together among players.

Beside him, Mrs. Tayte murmured, "May they go together and may they be mine."

Competitive . . . he liked that. His first sip of the bubbly liquid bit at his tongue. By the third swallow, all the rough edges had smoothed out. Let the games begin.

Roark's strategy was to act nonchalant about winning, at first. The early hands were used for judging the opponent and checking out the physical signs, the tells each player made that indicated how the cards in their hand rated. In the first half-dozen hands, he tossed away about forty dollars.

That's all he intended to lose.

"Hot damn, this one's mine." A sandy-haired cowhand immediately lifted his hat and dipped his chin. "Excuse my language, ma'am. But that's the first pot I've won all night."

Time to get serious.

Tells for four of the players were known, but he hadn't spotted one for the lady. Yet. A professional? If so, why wasn't her name familiar?

He recrossed his legs under the table and his left leg bumped something. Strange . . . this type of table didn't normally have a center post. Staring at his cards, he shifted in his chair and pulled back his leg.

The bet to him was four dollars. He held a chance at a decent full house—with a pair of tens and another of queens. One last check of the other players before he tossed in his coins. Nobody held his gaze, which probably meant they held bad cards. "I'll see your bet and raise five dollars."

A pressure ran from the top of his boot, up his calf, and circled behind his knee. What the—? He cut a look to his left.

Mrs. Tayte squinted at her cards, appearing to be planning her next move. A gloved finger rhythmically tapped the tops of the cards.

From the corner of his eye, he spotted the rounded bosom of the barmaid as she hovered near his chair.

Which woman had touched him?

"Mr. Sheridan has made this hand a bit more interesting. So . . .

that's seven to me?" Mrs. Tayte fluttered her eyelashes and gazed at the other men, careful not to turn in his direction.

Roark bit back a laugh. These other men were sods if they believed her innocent act. "Seven is just to stay in the game. You could raise the bet, madam."

"A challenge, Mr. Sheridan?"

"Only if you're up to it, Mrs. Tayte."

Her gaze shuttered, darkening her eyes for just a moment, then she smiled. "Always." She grabbed a stack of coins, letting each drop onto the pile. "Here's the seven and one, two, three more for good measure."

The next three players tossed in their hands. The fourth man, the cowhand, grumbled but tossed in his money. Scowling, he grabbed the deck of cards. "Cards, Sheridan?"

"Just one." He set down his throwaway card and three dollars to match her bet, and drew his new card into his hand.

"Uh-oh, should I be worried, Mr. Sheridan?"

He bestowed a wide grin and a wink in her direction. Let the woman stew.

3

"**P**ot's yours again, Sheridan."

By this hour, Lissa had grown tired of hearing those particular words. Her lucky run of the early evening had definitely ended. Over the last several hands, her glorious pile of coins had dwindled to less than ten dollars. Not even enough to play a respectable hand. And she refused to dip into the amount already in her handbag—her personal policy for staying ahead.

She faked a yawn and tapped a gloved hand over her mouth. "So sorry, gentlemen, but I'm calling it a night." With a smooth movement, she scooped the remaining coins into her reticule.

Mr. Sheridan stopped stacking his coins impossibly high and shot her a soulful gaze. "But you'll be depriving us of your lovely company."

Not to mention the rest of my winnings. She bit her lip to keep from speaking aloud her thoughts. Instead, she smiled at the well-dressed gentleman whose scent was a curious mixture of tobacco and wood smoke. A man whose attraction had probably caused her downfall in this night's gaming. How was she expected to keep her mind on the cards when such a fine phys-

ical specimen sat within arm's reach? "I have an early engagement tomorrow, and I really must get my beauty sleep."

"No need to improve on perfection." He quirked an eyebrow and looked around at the other players. "Am I right,
gents?"

A chorus of male rumbling echoed agreement.

Ooo, she could get used to his flattering talk. "You are just
too sweet to say so." Her gaze linked with his and heated. The
man all to pieces intrigued her, and she regretted losing an op-
portunity to see what sparks they could create.

Maybe one last chance existed. . . .

"But I truly know my own constitution." She gathered her
skirts to stand and pushed her fan onto the floor between their
chairs. Pausing a second, she waited until Mr. Sheridan leaned
over the side of his chair. "Oh, my fan."

Ducking her head below the table's edge, she inhaled close
to his body. Maybe a hint of bay rum in his hair. "Interested in
a private game, sir?"

With his hand wrapped around her fan, he tilted his head,
eyes squinted. "Games always interest me."

"Room nine, left at the landing, second door." She held out
her hand, wiggling her fingers.

His brows lowered into a frown. "Room nine?"

The confused look on his face threw her. Hadn't he understood her invitation? She reached for her fan and trailed her
fingertips along his hand. "Why, thank you, Mr. Sheridan. Tomorrow morning, I would have wondered where this had disappeared."

She winked and straightened, holding up the fan. "I bid you
gentlemen adieu." Her gaze touched on each of the players at
the gaming table, ending with Mr. Sheridan. "I really must get
my sleep, my *nine* hours of sleep. Upstairs . . . in my room."

At her back, someone pulled out her chair. With a handful of
her skirt held high, she turned to leave the table, brushing her

knee along Mr. Sheridan's leg. If he didn't get the hint after all that, then he didn't deserve entry into her boudoir. She smiled and murmured, "Good evening," to several men she recognized from earlier games as she wound her way through the crowd of gaming tables.

At the top of the stairs, she turned for one last look, her heavy reticule clinking against her knee. Her intention was to grace them all with one last wave. With a shock, she saw the game continued and all the men sat concentrating on the cards in their hands.

Two hollow knocks sounded on the door.

She whirled, her breath caught in her throat. He'd interpreted her message. Had he accepted her challenge? With a couple of pats to smooth her hair back from her face, she grabbed the robe ties and cinched them at her waist. A slow count to three preceded her crossing the room, then she stopped, hand on doorknob.

Wouldn't do to appear too eager. "Who's there?"

"A fellow player."

Her heart rate accelerated at his words. The confident tone of Mr. Sheridan's deep voice. Clever . . . not willing to give too much away. She turned the porcelain knob and eased open the door several inches. Best not to flash the fact she was admitting a man to her room in her state of dishabille.

She glanced through the opening and spotted the impeccably dressed man leaning a shoulder against the wall. Ah, how she loved a well-tailored suit of expensive wool. And a man with the physique to properly fill it. "Good evening, Mr. Sheridan."

He dipped his chin, a hint of a smile teasing his sculpted lips, but he didn't speak.

Worry churned in her stomach and she plastered on a smile. Downstairs, he'd let her know he was interested. Those heated glances, comments made in an intimate tone. Now he acted reserved. Certainly she hadn't read him wrong. "How did you fare after I left?"

"Won a few hands. But with your departure, the spark of the game was lost and the others drifted to different tables."

His backhanded compliment warmed her heart. The players had missed her company. Too bad she couldn't translate that into ticket sales for her performances. "Tell me, Mr. Sheridan, did you miss me?"

"Answer this first." His gaze narrowed. "Won't Mr. Tayte mind my presence here?"

Of course, that misunderstood detail explained his cautious attitude. She hesitated about revealing her true state, because once revealed, the protection was gone. "No, we won't be bothered."

"Not an answer." His brow rose and he remained with one shoulder pressed to the doorjamb.

She blew out an exasperated breath. "I'm a widow. No husband will be interfering tonight."

"That's good news." He stepped inside and kicked the door closed.

Following the door slam, the room closed in and his presence filled the space. She edged backwards until her hip nudged the table she'd set up earlier. "I left the table downstairs feeling a bit . . . unsatisfied." And decidedly poorer than was comfortable.

"Interesting choice of words."

With an idle motion, she fingered the lace that ran along the neckline of her gown, hoping to draw his gaze. But his jade eyes remained locked with hers. "Our card playing seemed better matched than that of the others. Don't you agree?"

He lifted a shoulder nonchalantly. "Could be I was having an off night."

Her first impulse was to tell him she'd been doing a lot better before his appearance. Without him there, her distracting those buffoons with a little bust shimmying and a few eyelash flutterings had kept the winning pots coming her way. An admission that would reveal way too much. "Maybe your night just got better."

His gaze ran down to her satin slippers and back, skimming on her full bust and how the gown clung to her hips without the padding of bustles, hoops, and petticoats. "The view has definitely improved."

Her skin heated as he looked his fill. She imagined his hands making the same journey his gaze had and her blood thrummed. Flashing him a seductive smile, she gestured toward the chairs, the table set with refreshments, and the deck of cards. "I have sherry, but if you'd like whiskey, that can be arranged. What would you say to a private game?"

"I'm always up for a game."

Her heart jumped at his words, and a tingle ran over her skin. So he *had* gotten her message downstairs. "Really?"

He rubbed his hands together, then rested them on the back of a chair. "An uninterrupted game. My favorite kind."

Poker! Disappointment filled her but she refused to let it show. She smiled and gathered the deck of cards from the top of the bureau. "Let's sit and get started then." She nodded at his act of pulling out her chair. "Any preferences on the limits?"

"Your invitation, your limits." He angled back his chair and sat.

With a sideways glance, she watched the easy way his body moved, trouser wool pulling taut around muscled legs. Why not let him see her interest? "My limits? Well, Mr. Sheridan, I'm not sure you've bargained for what I'm prepared to wager."

"Ma'am, I've been a wagering man for a long time."

She rested an elbow on the table and leaned toward him, knowing her gaping gown displayed her generous breasts to full advantage. "What if the stakes are more personal than most games?"

"Personal, huh?" Heat flared in his green gaze. He started to lean forward but instead grabbed the cards and shuffled them. "I'm listening."

Slowly, she placed her hand over his to still his movements and then trailed a finger along the ridge of his knuckles. "What if the loser of each hand grants a favor?"

His thumb captured her pinky finger. "A favor, like carrying your bags?"

Her eyelids drifted shut and she shook her head. She'd heard about incredibly handsome men who weren't interested in women. Had she been unlucky enough to invite one such man to her room on the last night for a long time of having a private room? His touch strengthened and her hand was tugged sideways. Her eyelids flew open.

Roark watched the confusion in her blue eyes quickly warm to speculation. He was intrigued with how her body movements revealed her emotions, an openness not on display at the gaming table downstairs. Watching her increasing disappointment at his misdirection convinced him he wanted to see more. "Or a favor like a kiss?" Unable to resist teasing her, he leaned forward until his lips brushed across hers, intending a carefree gesture.

To test her limits.

She tested right back. While gazing into his eyes, she responded with a nibbling pressure, tugging at his lower lip.

The unexpected movements of her warm lips sent his blood racing. Surprise forced him to inhale and the fragrance of roses mixed with spices filled his nose. He eased back and blinked, his cock stiffening with anticipation.

What had just happened here?

From under lowered lashes, her eyes flashed. "Exactly." Her tongue ran along first her upper lip, then the lush lower one as if seeking every bit of his taste. She rested her chin on both fists and smiled.

Rather than risk getting his face slapped by making assumptions, he hesitated, wanting confirmation from her next statement.

She reached out a hand and trailed her fingers along the cuff of his sleeve. "At least, for starters."

Roark watched her delicate fingers, knowing if she moved them to bare skin, he'd have his answer about her intentions.

"Am I being too subtle?" A finger moved inside his sleeve to the sensitive skin on his wrist. "I was hoping I wouldn't have to rub my body against yours like the barmaid did."

So she'd been watching him that early in the evening? He captured her hand, entwining their fingers and caressing his thumb across her beating pulse point. He let his gaze linger on her breasts before raising it to tangle with hers. "Question becomes do we bother with cards at all?"

She sucked in a breath and her other hand rose to cup his jaw. "I say no cards, gambling man."

At her touch, Roark shoved back his chair and stood, pulling her up and against his frame, their clasped hands caught between their bodies. "Agreed, widow lady." He bent his head and captured her mouth.

She snuggled close and her hand snaked around his neck to tangle in his hair.

Her soft body melted against his and he wrapped an arm across her back to keep her close. His lips parted to taste her plump lips and his tongue pressed into her warmth, stroking first her lips then the edge of her teeth.

She moaned, her own tongue fighting for entrance to his mouth.

He had a tigress in his arms and he aimed to enjoy her. Uncurling his fingers from their clasped hands, he stretched them across the soft skin of her chest. Moving in small circles, he edged lower until the silky fabric of her gown tickled his knuckles.

She tugged his hair and rocked her hips against his cock, increasing the tempo of her thrusting tongue.

The press of her body jolted pleasure through him. He sucked in a deep breath, and his hand rested on the upper swell of her breast.

She broke the kiss and trailed kisses along his jaw, a warm hand pressing on his chest. "Don't stop yet."

Not shy about open invitations, Roark eased his hand around her breast, centering the nipple on his palm, and squeezed. The steady beat of his heart kicked up.

"Oh, yes." She arched, pressing harder against his hand, and sighed. "Since I first spotted you across that saloon, I wondered how your touch would feel."

Seemed the attraction had been mutual from the first moment. "You have, darlin'?"

"You bet I did." Her hand trailed from his neck to his chest and her fingers tugged at the buttons of his shirt. "We're two of a kind. I recognized that right off."

He got distracted by the graze of her fingers against his chest. His muscles twitched in response. "Two of a kind?"

Her fingers ran through the hair on his chest and she looked up. "Yeah, gamblers, thrill seekers, people who live for the moment."

Two weeks ago, that description fit him perfectly. He had been exactly that type of person for the past fifteen years. Since taking on the responsibility of the Queen of Hearts, he'd forced himself to be more practical and to plan ahead.

But tonight was different. Tonight he wasn't the captain of a riverboat. Instead, he was a gambling man taking a chance on a couple hours with a delightful and willing woman. "Right, we're well matched. No more talking, Mrs. Tayte."

"Finally." Her eyes sparkled with mischief before she pressed moist lips to his chest. She trailed her tongue along his flesh until she reached the nipple buried in coarse hair and circled the flat disk.

His entire body tensed, his cock pressing against the confines of his trousers. A glorious tension that really should be shared.

At some point, her gown tie had loosened enough for him to push her chemise's fabric to the side, exposing her breast with its berry-red nipple. He rubbed the peak with the pad of his thumb.

She grabbed his forearms and tossed back her head. "More." A stance that pressed her abdomen tighter against him.

He couldn't resist a slow slide of his bulging fly across her belly, enjoying the rasp of her quickened breathing. As he watched, her other nipple poked against the creamy silk of her gown. He bent his head to capture it in his mouth, teasing it to a harder peak with his teeth, and then sucking it deep into his mouth.

Her leg clamped around his and she rubbed her mound against his thigh. A throaty moan filled the air.

They were definitely wearing too many clothes. While still lavishing attention on her nipple, he tugged the gown down her arms, and then reached to lower the straps of her chemise down to her elbows. Everywhere he touched was soft, smooth skin and his fingers lingered.

She loosened her grip, letting her arms dangle at her sides. Dazed blue eyes met his gaze. "You've entrapped me."

Her words echoed his feelings, touching something deep inside. Although he should have headed for the closest exit, he looked his fill. From tousled honey blond hair to her dressing gown and chemise hanging halfway down her arms to one delicious breast exposed, the other with a hardened peak in the middle of a darker circle on the creamy silk. She leaned backward and tried to rotate her shoulders to slip out of the gown but the damp fabric clung to her breast.

This woman set his blood on fire. He had to have her. Now. With a groan, he reached for the front of his trousers.

She stepped forward and rested her hands on his. "What's your hurry? I wanted to do that." She stretched up and pressed her parted lips against his, teasing him with a playful tongue. "First, help me out of the gown."

The fabric slid under his fingers as he eased it over her elbows and down her arms. At the sight of both uncovered breasts, he stopped and inhaled. If he didn't slow down, he'd embarrass himself. Right here and right now.

Once her arms were free, she shook off the gown, and then pushed at the lingerie. A wiggle of her hips, and the silky fabric pooled at her slippered feet.

Roark watched her graceful movements with a hungry gaze. He enjoyed the jiggle of her breasts and the sway of her wavy hair. A feeling of intimacy with her grew.

She stepped close and her hands returned to the buttons on his trousers. Two fingers snaked under the waistband to hold the fly steady, the backs of her knuckles grazing his abdomen.

He sucked in his stomach and clenched his fists. The woman was driving him crazy.

The lower her hands moved, the harder his cock grew until he stepped back. "Let me." He cleared his throat. "I'll do the rest and meet you in the bed."

She smiled and held his gaze, then winked and turned. Her walk to the far side of the bed was slow, her hips swaying with each step.

He scrambled to remove his clothes and draped them over a nearby chair. The bobbing of his rigid cock as he walked made the distance to the bed feel longer.

With the bed sheet raised, she waited, her gaze watching every movement of his approach. A wide smile graced her kiss-swollen lips.

If possible, his cock grew more rigid. He glimpsed the tantalizing length of her slender body, zeroing in on the tufts of blond curls above her sex for only a second before sliding under the sheet. A more thorough inspection would have to wait. He scooped her into an embrace and dragged her body next to his.

She sighed and cuddled close, her fingers toying with the stubborn hair that fell over his forehead.

Soft, smooth skin met lean, hard muscle and something inside his chest tightened.

The need to claim her was strong. His hand captured her breast and he rolled her nipple between his thumb and finger. His cock pressed against her thigh and he groaned. His lips moved along the column of her neck, searching for secret sensitivities.

And to give him a minute to regain his control.

4

Lissa relished the feel of this man's hard muscles pressed against her length. But he was taking much too long. Didn't he recognize the signs of a willing partner? She moved her hands to the sides of his face, kissing him long and hard, then kicked a leg over his hips and straddled him.

His head came up off the pillow. "Hey."

"My game, my rules, remember? And I say this one needs a kick in the butt." She grinned and rubbed the tips of her breasts on his chest. The tingles that ran through her set her hips rocking. Creamy dew seeped along the edge of her nether curls and she traced the slippery juices along the length of his cock.

His hands gripped her buttocks and he flexed his hips, his cock probing for entrance.

She shook her head and settled her butt lower on his thighs. Her hands caressed his ribs, her thumbs tracing the outline of each hard bump on his abdomen. "I decide when, gambling man."

The dark brows lowered and his green eyes narrowed but he

didn't argue. Instead, he raised his arms to adjust a pillow higher behind his head. "Yes, ma'am."

She splayed her hands across his stomach and chest, enjoying the jump of his muscles under her fingers. So, the man wasn't as relaxed as he appeared. Holding on to his broad shoulders, she drew her mons up his hardness, hesitated, and then wiggled her way down again.

His breath hissed between his teeth and the bed jerked when he grabbed for her thighs.

The abrasive movement sent thrills through her and she wondered who was losing control faster. Did that matter?

Pushing herself to her knees, she waited to connect with his gaze. The longer his gaze lingered on her curls, then her waist, then her breasts, the hotter she got. Her pussy flooded with cream and she clenched her inner walls tight.

Finally, his green eyes looked into hers and his sculpted lips quirked into a crooked smile.

She lowered herself until her moist folds touched the velvety tip of his cock. With a slow circling, she inched down his shaft until her thighs rested on his. The sensation of being totally filled satisfied her. But only for a moment.

He flexed and surged deeper inside, but his hands remained on her thighs.

Why had she told him she made the rules? Her nipples ached to be touched, and she wanted to be fucked hard and fast. She trailed a hand from his shoulder, drew circles on his chest, and then flicked a fingernail across his nipple.

"Ahh." His upper body surged off the bed and he grabbed her hips, his thumbs running along her hipbones. With a rocking motion, he stroked inside.

"Harder." She pressed against his movements, creating the friction she needed. Expectation spiraled deep within her womb.

He thrust upward, holding her hips in place, his breaths rasping in his throat.

"Faster." Her body rocked in opposition to his, and the wave twisted within.

"I know how to fuck, lady. Stop giving me orders." His hand smacked her rump then caressed the very same spot.

"Hey!" The sting of his slap mixed with her rising arousal made her womb clench hard and her nipples ache. Her pussy gushed with cream. "Oh . . ."

The grin widened. "Like that?" When she didn't answer, his thrusts slowed. "Two can play at being in control."

"Yeah, right." She planted her hands on the mattress next to his shoulders and moved her body against his but the friction wasn't the same. Settling back on her knees, she skimmed her hands from her knees to her stomach to her breasts, cupping them and squeezing.

His hands tightened on her hips for a moment, and then relaxed.

So, he liked to watch. She raised her thumbs to her mouth, licked them both and then rolled her nipples between her fingers. At the tingle that went straight to her swollen bud, a moan escaped her lips. She threw back her head, enjoying the tickle of her silky hair cascading down her back.

Beneath her, his hips flexed and the strokes renewed, deep and strong.

This time, she let him set the pace, but matched her body's rhythm to his.

A flush darkened his cheeks and he hissed out a breath.

She tweaked her nipples and moaned, the fullness in her womb almost ready to burst.

In rapid synchronization, he surged deep inside and smacked her rump three times, and then grunted as he climaxed.

At the first slap, she cried out, long, high, and loud. The wave of completion overtook her and she slumped onto his chest, breathing hard. Every part of her body tingled. The earthy scents of their lust mixed with roses, tobacco, and a hint of bath soap surrounded her. She huffed out a breath and watched his chest hair ruffle.

He jerked. "Trying to arouse me again?"

"No, just catching my breath."

With gentle movements, he eased her off his lap and snuggled her against his side. "That's better." A finger pressed against her chin, angling up her head. "Now I can do this." He leaned over and kissed her, slow and gentle.

Lissa cuddled her cheek against his shoulder and closed her eyes. This moment was just about perfect. "You were right, gambling man."

"About what?" His hand smoothed her hair along her shoulder and back.

Her breathing deepened and she mumbled, "You most certainly don't need directions."

A shaft of moonlight hit him in the face and Roark shifted positions to avoid it. And rolled right into a soft, warm body.

The night came back to him in a flash. The uncertainty of commanding the riverboat, seeking out a poker table, an invitation to a private game, then a surprising, but enticing, seduction.

He rose onto one elbow and watched the mystery lady sleep, her golden hair spread across her pillow and onto his. If they'd crossed paths two weeks ago, he'd roll her over for another hour of tussling in the sheets. But a sense of duty called him back to the riverboat. He slipped out of bed and tucked the covers around her slender back.

As he buttoned his shirt, he stood where he could see her, wanting to store away the details of her face in his memory. A quick brush of his lips across her cheek and he slipped out the door, making sure the hall was empty before he headed down the back stairs and outside. Judging by the light gray at the horizon, he'd have plenty to do when he reached the Queen.

Away from The Cotton Palace he strode, each step separating him from the memory of the previous evening's entertainment.

The sky was a clear blue and the morning air was tolerable. Years of living along the Mississippi told Lissa that by late afternoon, the heat and humidity would be oppressive. A lingering thought went to Mr. Sheridan, who was her last night of frolic for a while. She would have liked one last kiss before he disappeared from her life forever.

Lissa looked at the riverboat moored at the base of the dock. The familiar outline of the proud 175-foot long paddle steamer warmed her heart. Although her father and siblings might be nosy and bossy, they were her family. This annual trek up the Mississippi allowed her enough time for a reconciliation visit but not too much for them to get on each other's nerves.

She turned to the porter who'd accompanied her from The Cotton Palace. "I'll go on board and send someone back here to help you with the luggage. You'll be taking it to the Blue Dahlia stateroom."

"Yes, ma'am." The porter nodded and leaned against the trunk containing her costumes.

Expectation fueled her steps as she walked down the ramp from the shore and stepped onto the front deck. Normally, the deck would be bustling with the loading and stacking of cotton bundles, performed by a row of workers. Maybe the cargo was already loaded.

She ran a hand along the smooth wood railing and a sense of homecoming welled inside, surprising her. The ornate latticework adorning the column supports. White cane-bottom chairs lining the side guard. Familiar details that meant she was home. She looked closer. Why on earth would Papa have painted the guard deck ceilings red? Her steps slowed as she gazed at the Queen of Hearts, noting small changes here and there.

Where was the calliope? Papa was so proud of having that

instrument aboard. He loved the fact the clear tones could be heard for miles up and down the river.

A burly man exited the back door of the boiler deck and moved aft.

"Chauncey? Hello, I'm back." The man had been Papa's mechanic for years, and Lissa moved toward him with quick steps.

The man turned, dark brows drawn low and his stance rigid.

Her footsteps stopped and she grabbed the railing. This bearded man was a stranger. "Oh! Who are you?"

He hitched up the sides of his trousers. "Name's Tug. Who're you?"

"I'm Lissa, the daughter of the captain."

The man scrutinized her from head to toe and then shrugged. "Don't think so." He turned and ambled away.

"Hey, what do you mean? I need answers." Hands on hips, she waited but he disappeared below deck. What was going on here? She leaned over the railing and read the boat's name. This was the correct boat.

With brisk steps, she crossed the deck and opened the door to the main gallery and called out for her family. "Papa, Forrest, Marigold, Magnolia. I've arrived."

A young woman scrambled to her feet from where she'd been scrubbing the floor. "Boat's not ready for passengers, miss."

Lissa glanced at the wide-eyed woman but didn't recognize her. Papa must have hired some new maids. "I'm not a passenger, I'm family."

"So sorry, miss." She fidgeted with her apron. "I didn't know the captain was expecting family."

Lissa headed toward the steps leading to the Texas deck. Where was everyone? Why weren't any of the entertainment acts rehearsing? "Papa?" The hallway was empty and she debated whether to search for him in the pilothouse or his cabin. As she walked down the hall, she heard the murmur of male voices from behind his cabin door.

Finally, she'd found someone. Two taps on the door and she flung it open, stepping inside with arms open wide. "Papa, I'm here."

Several men leaning over a map spread on the table glanced in her direction. A buzzing sounded in her ears as she realized all were strangers, except the dark-haired one seated at the head of the table.

Him. Her mystery man from last night's frolic in The Cotton Palace. Her heart raced and dread dropped heavy into her stomach. Today he wore a dark green jacket that brought out the color of his eyes.

Their gazes tangled. Heat raced over her skin, and she remembered the breadth of his naked shoulders, the whorls of hair on his chest, and the way his—

Her arms dropped to her sides like anchors and her stomach churned. "What are you doing in this cabin? Where's my father?"

Mr. Sheridan stood, a surprised grin lighting his face. "Uh, Mrs. Tayte, how nice to see you." He started around the end of the plank table.

She held up a hand to stop him. In close proximity, this man's charm was lethal and she needed answers. "Stay right there and answer me. What have you done with my father? Who are these men?"

All the heads swung back in his direction.

His expression darkening, he glanced at them and then at her. "I'm sure we can discuss this calmly."

She stalked across the room, narrowing a hardened gaze on this tall man. "Calmly? You're in my father's cabin on my family's boat, and I want to know why."

"Your father is . . . ?"

She jammed her hands on her hips. "Hiram Springer, the owner of this boat."

His gaze softened, and he cleared his throat. "Hiram Springer is the previous owner."

"What?" Her stomach churned. What had Papa done now? She turned to the men standing awkwardly by the table and searched their faces for confirmation. "Is he correct?"

None could hold her gaze.

Mr. Sheridan edged closer. "As of two weeks ago, I'm the registered owner of the Queen of Hearts."

"My papa would never have sold this boat." She gasped and a hand rose to cover her mouth. "Oh gracious, is he hurt? Sick?"

She paced to the door and back. "I know I should have written more frequently, but I was busy and June was coming. I knew we'd be together on our annual trip. Where are my brother and my sisters?" She approached Mr. Sheridan and rested a hand on his forearm. "Please tell me what's happened."

"All I know is he tossed the boat's ownership certificate into the middle of a poker table, and I won." He gripped her hand and shook his head. "Besides that, I have no information."

"Papa bet the boat? Give me a chance, and I'll win it back." Her skin tingled at his touch but she fought her reaction. "Oh, how could he? This is their home . . ." She swallowed hard, blinking to fight back tears. "This was my home."

Mr. Sheridan turned to the men. "Could you excuse us, gentlemen? I'd like to speak with the young lady in private."

"Captain, we need to—"

Mr. Sheridan swept his hand toward the door. "I understand, Guthrie. Ten minutes is all I'll need to take care of this matter."

Lissa seethed while the men filed out. Take care of this matter. As if she was an annoyance to be dealt with and forgotten.

He turned from the door and gestured to the table and benches. "Please sit."

She steeled herself against the compassionate note in his voice. "Tell me what you know." If Papa no longer owned the Queen, what were her family members doing for a livelihood? What happened to the family's belongings? Five years of living in one place accumulated things. What about the items in her stateroom?

"I told you everything."

"There has to be more. Was the game on board?"

Scowling, he shook his head. "On the Bayou Belle while it was docked just north of New Orleans."

"After he lost, he just walked away? You didn't talk to him?" She fought to keep a quiver from her voice.

"Listen to what you're saying." He ran a hand through his hair. "You know how poker games go. Bets fly, cards are laid down, and someone walks away with less than he had. If a man isn't prepared to lose, he shouldn't buy into a game."

"You're right, of course." She slumped onto a bench and buried her head in her hands. "This is my worry talking."

Footsteps approached and she felt his large hand caress her shoulder.

"I'm glad to see you, widow lady." His breath tickled her neck.

At the sound of his pet name, she swayed back, for one moment wanting to be swept up in his embrace.

Until their true circumstances hit her.

"No." She shot to her feet and crossed the cabin. Mr. Sheridan was her new employer. Getting involved with a boss was the surest way to get put ashore at the next boat landing. "We can't."

"But we did. And so well, I might add." His eyes gleamed in challenge. "Or have you forgotten?"

She gasped, and her traitorous body responded to the glint

in his gaze. Her nipples peaking against her corset with delicious friction, she exhaled slowly. "Under the new management, will my contract be honored?"

His gaze narrowed. "What contract?"

"June is the month I come aboard every year as part of the boat's entertainment."

He shoved a hand through his hair and paced to the door and back. "The boat's entertainment? First I've heard of this."

"Surely you've been on boats that include shows of singing and dancing acts." Her gaze followed his movements as he paced, and her heart beat faster. The man sure did fill out a suit well.

But as her boss, he was off limits.

"Some did. Tell me, what talent do you perform in public?"

One look at his eyes and she remembered how they'd flashed like jade in the heat of passion. She squared her shoulders and forced a smile. "My stage name is Miss Alyssum, and I've been singing on riverboats and showboats for years. Popular music, ballads, light opera, some hymns if requested."

"Years, huh?" His gaze narrowed, and his lips twitched at one corner. "You older than you look?"

"I started performing on the Kansas Belle when I was five." She shrugged, hesitant to reveal too much of her history. "Family business. Papa's been operating," her voice faltered, "um, operated showboats on the Ohio River for almost thirty years."

At the mention of Papa, a stab of pain went through her. She'd find out what happened, but she'd be damned if she relinquished her spot on the Queen. A plan was forming and she knew she couldn't leave the boat without trying to win it back. Somehow. "Will you honor the previous arrangement, Captain Sheridan?"

"After last night, don't you think we could use our first names?" He lifted his gaze and smiled. "Mine's Roark."

Roark Sheridan. It fit him—strong and confident. She shook

herself. "Precisely because of last night, I think we should stick to our full names. I don't want our . . ." She rolled her hand in the air, waiting for him to provide the proper label. When he just stared, she continued, ". . . our familiarities to be a problem for our professional relationship. Believe me, I know it happens."

She clamped her lips tight before divulging her past mistakes. No need for Roark, um, Captain Sheridan to learn of her embarrassing situation on the Mississippi Steamer two years earlier. She would be forever grateful the boat sank and Jed Hopkins moved back to the family's Virginia plantation.

"Are you saying we'll be living on this boat together for weeks and pretending we don't, that we haven't . . ." Roark's hands clamped onto his hips, and he glared. "Impossible."

After a worried glance at the closed door, she stepped to his side and whispered, "Now you see the problem."

"Yeah, I do." He reached out and grabbed her shoulders, hauling her close.

She stiffened. "What?"

"Problem is I have to taste you." His lips crushed hers, his tongue taking advantage of her surprise.

For a split second, his passion was impossible to resist and she met the erotic dance of his invading tongue with twirls and dips of her own. Then she stiffened and pushed him away. "We can't do this. I don't want the others to think I'm getting special treatment."

He chuckled, his hand running up and down her arm. "I assure you I'm not like this with my mechanic Tug or First Mate Jimmy."

"Not the crew, the rest of the entertainment troupe. Performers get jealous over the smallest detail, like who has top billing on the posters."

His brows drew into a frown. "Troupe? Performers? Posters?"

A hollowness settled in her stomach and she crossed her

arms over her stomach. "The other performers." From the confusion on Roark's face, she guessed the answer to the question she was about to ask but felt the need to fill the silence. "I must have a small band play during my performances."

He shrugged. "Haven't seen a band."

Panic threatened to overtake her. She glanced at his mantel clock. Two hours remained before the boat's scheduled departure. "Dancers?"

Wrinkles invaded his forehead and he shook his head.

"An illusionist? A raconteur?"

His mouth hardened into a tight line and he glared.

"Actors? A ventriloquist?"

A hand ran through his hair. "What's that?"

Her shoulders sagged. If he didn't know, then one wasn't booked. "A performer skilled at throwing his voice so people believe his puppet can talk."

A hand ran over his jaw. "I'd like to see that."

"Roark, please say someone besides me will be on stage." Her hopes of winning back the boat faded.

"Hey, you used my name. Sounds nice coming from your mouth." His gaze focused on her lips and he took a step closer.

No distractions! She stepped back, hand held up to ward him off. "There must be others. Maybe they will show. A riverboat like this needs entertainment."

He scowled and drew his hands into fists at his sides. "Not all riverboats are operated the same."

"Entertainers need an audience." Desperation fueled her temper. She slapped her reticule onto the table and paced. "Where's the calliope? Did you send an advance man to distribute handbills in the next town upstream? How do you expect to draw customers to your gaming tables?" She thought back to the few furnishings in the boat's gallery and whirled to face him. "There *will* be gaming?"

"Gaming is the draw." He squared his shoulders. "We're

prepared for this. The faro tables are in good shape, and the roulette wheel has been cleaned. I've planned for poker tables with various betting limits."

"Who will be gambling?"

His brow creased into a frown. "Passengers, I suppose."

"How many on the boat's manifest?"

"Manifest?"

"You don't know what that is." She shook her head and dropped onto the bench next to the table. "Your steward has the list of everyone with paid reservations. I'm guessing you won't have more than a hundred. Not nearly enough."

"Who the hell are you to be telling me my business?" He dropped onto the bench opposite her, his fists slamming on the table. A narrowed gaze zeroed in on her face. "Look, Mrs. T—, Miss Alyssum, hell, I don't know what to call you."

On some level, the frustrated note in his voice got to her. "Call me Lissa."

He acknowledged that with a dip of his chin and flattened his hands onto the table. "Lissa, because I'm new to being captain doesn't mean I haven't been around riverboats for years. I told you I won the Queen only two weeks ago." With an angry swipe, he flicked back an errant lock of hair. "Seemed like a good idea at the time. I finally have a roof—"

A knock sounded on the door. "Captain?"

Lissa wanted to shout "go away" to the man outside the door. Roark had been about to reveal something important, something personal.

His breath whooshed from tightened lips and he gazed at the ceiling. "What is it, Jimmy?"

"Thomas requests your presence on deck, sir."

Roark's expression grew impassive. "Duty calls. We'll talk later." He stood, crossed the cabin, and opened the door. "Please show Miss Alyssum to the Queen High Flush stateroom."

To where? Lissa stood, her gaze lingering on Roark as he left the room. The man was easy on the eyes and a crack poker player, but he obviously knew little about running a successful boat. If she expected to accomplish her goal, she'd have to take matters into her own hands. Decision made, she turned an engaging smile on the young man. "I can find my own room. Tell me, are any of the previous crew still here?"

5

As he strode through the gallery, Roark couldn't believe this new situation. When he'd slipped out of The Cotton Palace before dawn, he'd been reluctant to leave the blond beauty in the bed they'd shared. He'd never have guessed she'd turn up on his boat.

Or that she'd be telling him how to run it.

Worse, she was his employee. His stride slowed. Not that he'd had much experience, but he figured a proper business owner ought to keep business and personal relationships separate. If he hadn't been amazed at seeing her again, he might have listened closer when Lissa mentioned that very fact.

He'd spent a night challenged by a feisty woman who shared his love of gaming, enjoyed romping between the sheets, and, by that kiss, was still interested in getting physical. If he could get around this boss/employee situation.

Planning ahead was not his strong suit. He'd think about it later.

Stepping onto the deck, he blinked against the rays of the late afternoon sun and sought out Thomas.

"Ah, Captain." Thomas stood at the lectern near the back of the boat. "I have a group here who isn't on the manifest. But they are asking for Springer."

Roark glanced at the three men sitting on strangely shaped cases and satchels. He took a chance. "I'm Captain Sheridan. Does one of you have a contract signed by Hiram Springer? And are you musicians?"

The thin man with a small goatee stood and reached into his jacket pocket. "I do, and we're The Bayou Trio."

"Welcome aboard, men." Okay, one problem solved. "Thomas, find berths for these gentlemen and anyone else who presents a contract to provide entertainment. I'm learning the previous owner didn't divulge all of the boat's benefits." He forced a smile and turned away, confident his steward could handle the bookings.

Before he took half a dozen steps, his chest grew tight. Each performer who showed up with a contract would expect payment. Problem was, he had no idea what kind of money was involved.

The responsibility of being captain weighed on him. He eyed the wooden dock leading to the shoreline and a dirt path that disappeared under the cypresses. A wistful, but fleeting, thought of escape crossed his mind. But he was no coward. This riverboat was his chance at a legitimate business, and he'd figure the way to make it profitable.

He'd spun on his heel and started back into the gallery when Jimmy stopped him. "Problem in the kitchen, sir."

"Can you handle this one, Jimmy?"

"Nah, Floyd says his answer has to come from you."

In the heat of the afternoon, Lissa reclined on her bed, wearing only underclothes and using her fan to cool herself. The open skylight transom let in a breeze that kept the room's temperature from being unbearable. Only a couple hours to go before her scheduled performance. After discovering Floyd Hermann had remained as cook, her worst fears were allayed. Her family was working in a small resort hotel near Lake Ponchatrain. Musicians had arrived and she'd talked with several crew members to learn about a dance duo and one other performer.

Floyd had told her about other crew members who'd worked on the Queen or her family's previous boat, the Kansas Belle. Ones with experience at acting in Papa's productions containing parts for everyone. Tonight's performance was set. Tomorrow she'd work on a plan for promoting the Queen. Determination to win back this boat for her father was lodged deep inside.

She rolled over to one side and waved her fan before her face. The gentle rocking motion of the boat was making her drowsy. Maybe her tiredness was because of the previous night's frolicking. Once that thought entered her head, all she thought of was Roark—that stray lock that hung over his forehead, his green eyes that lit with laughter or darkened with passion, and that splendid chest with tight muscles.

A knock sounded on her door and she gasped. "Who's there?"

"Your captain."

Almost as if she'd conjured him. She stood and crossed to the door, leaning her cheek against the cool wood. "Why are you here?"

"No one can overhear us. I wanted you to know a band has boarded." His voice was pitched low. "You won't be singing alone."

She turned and leaned the back of her head on the door, her hands clasped on her chest. How sweet, he didn't want her to worry. "I appreciate hearing that."

A boot shuffled at the base of the door. "Will I see you at supper, Lissa?"

Could the two of them become more than just one night? Her breath caught in her throat, but she quashed the thought. The boss was off-limits. "I never eat before a performance."

"Oh. Maybe—"

"Thank you for the information, Captain." She pressed an ear to the door and heard a muffled curse before the clumping of boots on wood receded. A pent-up breath escaped. Keeping Roark at a distance would be difficult. Thinking about Captain Jed should help her remember. If things went badly, and her attachments always did, she'd learn the hard way that singing contracts ranked lower on a captain's priorities than his own peace of mind.

Not a mistake she'd make twice.

A few minutes before the appointed hour, Lissa left her stateroom, sheet music in hand, and headed for the back door of the stage Jimmy had pointed out earlier. The sweet strings of a violin guided her steps until she reached the curtained dressing area behind the stage.

When the trio took a rest, she stepped forward. "My name's Miss Alyssum and I was told you'd be my backup."

"I'm Rolly." The saxophonist stood, and then pointed at the other two. "That's Jeremiah on piano and Charles cradling the violin."

"Here are the songs for tonight's set. See any problem ones?" She watched their expressions as they conferred. Later in the week and as they learned each other's capabilities, they could add or subtract songs.

Rolly mopped his forehead with a handkerchief and winked. "You ready?"

She took a deep breath and nodded.

The plump saxophonist stepped onto the stage, followed by the other musicians. "Folks, I want to hear a real southern welcome for our next performer, Miss Alyssum."

To the sound of applause, Lissa smoothed the front of her

rose calico-and-lace dress and stepped onto the lit stage. Within seconds, she was swept up in her performance. During the third song, she recognized Roark's silhouette at the back of the crowd, his face shadowed, backlit by an overhead chandelier. Inexplicably, her stomach tightened with nerves, and she relied on years of training to stay in her professional character.

To her disappointment, only half the available seats were filled. Since her arrangement had always been sharing in the entertainers' fifty-percent of the performance tickets sold, she knew she'd have to work hard on promotion. Maybe a parade. As she finished her performance, she asked if the audience had any requests.

A woman with a feathered hat raised her hand. "I have one. Do you know *Sweethearts* by Gilbert and Sullivan?"

A love ballad? Her favorite type. Lissa turned to the band and whispered, "Do you know it?"

"Sure do, miss." Rolly grinned and wet his lips before blowing the first note in a lower key.

Following his lead, she sang alto while imagining how she'd feel if she and Roark were separated by life events for thirty years before meeting again. With eyes closed, she infused her voice with poignancy. When she finished, she noticed a few women dabbing handkerchiefs at their eyes.

That had never happened before. Her first thought was to share it with someone, and she searched the back of the crowd for Roark but he'd gone.

Too restless to stay in her room, she strolled the deck, enjoying the cooler night air. The sky was studded with bright stars and the river gently lapped at the side of the boat. Her stroll took her past the main gallery, where the gaming tables were in full action. Her fingers itched to feel the stiff cards.

Long ago, Papa had taught her the importance of maintaining her performer's image throughout her contract. And Miss Alyssum didn't play poker. Now, roulette was a different matter. No one looked down on women who played that game. She dashed back to her room for her money and found a single magnolia blossom lying on her bed. She lifted it to her nose and sniffed its citrusy vanilla aroma, her heart warming at Roark's nice gesture.

As she hurried back toward the gaming salon, she reminded herself she wasn't going there just to see him. That she was simply too agitated to be in her stateroom. With the closed door at her back, she scanned the room, squinting against the tobacco smoke drifting in the candlelit chandeliers.

He wasn't at a table. In fact, she didn't see him there at all. Disappointment filled her and she wandered slowly through the maze of tables, soaking in the play at each one by lingering as long as she thought proper. After several frowning looks, she moved away. Most players were uncomfortable with a woman dressed like a preacher's wife anywhere near their table.

She approached the roulette table and watched the play for several spins before buying chips from the croupier. A man with a thick Yankee accent was winning; each of his chips stacks were several inches high.

Within a few moments, the hair on her neck tingled. She inhaled and caught the unique scent of tobacco, bay rum, and fine clothes. Roark was close. Again, her nipples hardened. She started to turn but felt pressure on her left shoe.

"Ah, Miss Alyssum." His cajoling voice rumbled. "Allow me to extend my compliments on your performance this evening."

So, he was keeping their conversation on a professional level. A little part of her was disappointed.

With a sideways glance, she granted him a polite smile. Her gaze took in every aspect of his appearance. Tonight, the jacket he wore was midnight black with red threads running through the lapel. "Thank you, Captain. I hope others share your opinion."

He waved a hand at the table. "Are you a gaming woman?"

What was he up to? "On occasion, to pass the time."

"A gambler and singer of sweet songs—an odd mixture."

She placed a chip on the black diamond and another on black twenty-six—she always bet her age—before answering. "People with a variety of talents and pastimes are more interesting. Don't you agree?"

The ball bounced, and then rattled to a stop.

"Winner is black twenty-six. The lady in pink wins," the croupier intoned as he pushed stacks of chips toward her. "New bets down."

Roark raised an eyebrow. "Luck is with you tonight."

Lissa placed three chips on red fourteen, her birth date, and shifted two chips to the red diamond. The beginning of a routine of family birthdays and special days she always ran, and usually she came out ahead. "This is nothing. I'll have tripled this by the end of the evening."

His eyes widened. "Bragging a bit, Lissa?"

"Winner is red fourteen. The lady in pink wins again."

"I'm not bragging." She turned to Roark, spotted the tension in his jaw, and fluttered her eyelashes. "Stick around and watch." Half the winnings went into her reticule and the rest went to red seven—for Papa's birthday.

Ten minutes later, she'd run through her special numbers and continued placing bets on instinct alone.

With each winning bet, Roark grew quieter, his body tenser. Finally, he slipped his hand around her elbow and leaned close. "Can I interest you in a game of poker?"

Her skin tingled at his touch and she pressed her elbow to her side, for only a second. "Oh, I never play card games when I'm on board as Miss Alyssum."

His gaze raked her body. "That explains your dress. All prim and prissy. And your hair tucked up tighter than a—" An impatient hand waved at her figure, and he shook his head.

Ignoring his snide comments, she focused on his earlier

question. "You wouldn't mind if I played poker?" This could fit right into her plan. Her winning potential was definitely bigger at the gaming tables.

"Frankly, I'd prefer it. Go win someone else's money." He urged her back from the table. "If you're worried about your appearance, put on something like you wore last night." He raised his eyebrows. "The men in The Cotton Palace enjoyed it well enough."

Roark tossed in his rotten hand and glanced at the staircase from the Texas deck—again. Lissa Tayte had gotten under his skin and he was determined to figure out why. Given enough time, he could charm her into forgetting the obstacle of him owning her family's boat. A flash of red caught his eye and he leaned back on the chair legs to appreciate her entrance.

Dressed in red silk accented with black lace, her figure was cinched into this concoction so her curves were displayed to advantage. His hands itched to smooth along those curves, the sensuous ones he'd enjoyed the previous night. Forget the charm, maybe they'd just fuck to the point of exhaustion.

At her approach, he stood and grabbed a chair from a nearby table. "Welcome to the table, Miss—"

"Call me Lissa." Her wide smile radiated around the table. "Nice seeing y'all this evening."

What happened to knowing only last names? He coughed to avoid scoffing at her behavior. Her seduction of the other players had begun.

Her head whipped toward him at his sound, and he spotted the magnolia blossom pinned in her hair. She'd acknowledged his gift.

When they were settled, John Hobbs dealt the cards and the play started.

Roark arranged his cards in order. A pair of jacks, a ten, a seven, and a six. He'd be content to win back about half of what the roulette table had put into Lissa's hands. If he hadn't hand-picked the croupier Louie himself, he'd have suspected the pair of working together to drain his bank.

He glanced around the table to catch any obvious reactions to the cards just dealt. His mind had been filled with the image of a saucy blonde and he hadn't watched these players for their tells. Probably why he'd been losing while he waited.

"Captain Sheridan, are these chips I won at your roulette table good to play here? Or do I need coins?" Lissa's eyelashes fluttered and she looked at him with her chin resting on her shoulder.

The bodacious flirt. His groin tightened at the throaty purr in her tone. "Chip or coins, they play the same." Irritated at his body's reaction, he glanced around the table. "Who bets first?"

"I'll open with two bucks." A scruffy cowboy tossed in his money.

Lissa ran her finger along the top edges of her cards and looked around. "I'll see that and raise three."

Was this her strategy? Double up on the first bet. Not a bad idea. He tossed in a ten-dollar gold piece. "I'll double that." He listened to her gasp from his right and remembered a similar sound from the previous night. His cock stiffened and he shifted in his chair.

"Too rich, Captain." The next player tossed in his hand.

Hobbs pushed his bet into the middle. "Who needs cards?"

Three hands later, Roark was down thirty-five dollars and almost every one had gone into her stacks. He hadn't yet figured out her methods, but her manner was so smooth that he almost didn't mind losing. Almost.

Every move she made reminded him of the previous night. His body was wound as tight as a hog chain bracing his boat's hull. Maybe if he shared a bit of what he was feeling, the distraction might hinder her game. He angled a leg to the side and pushed his boot along the edge of her shoe.

She jerked, cards almost dropping from her hand, and leveled a challenging glance at him. "Captain, I compliment you on the smooth ride of your boat. The cargo must be well balanced."

Cargo? Why would his boat carry cargo? This was a riverboat. "Thank you, ma'am. At the trip's end, please put your comments in writing. The crew would be right proud to hang your commendation in the pilot house." He played by rote, his senses too aware of the woman at his side.

"I assure you, Captain, I know the importance of giving praise where praise is due." Lissa started dealing the next hand. "Tell me, gents, did any of you hear my performance earlier?"

Throats cleared and a chair or two scuffed on the wooden floor.

"Don't be shy." She placed cards on each stack, holding each player's gaze as she dealt the last card. "If you didn't, then tell me why." Her wide blue-eyed gaze turned to him. "The captain and I wish to present a show that folks want to hear."

Roark cut her a look. He'd figured she'd been fishing for compliments on her voice. Why had she included him?

Hobbs tipped back in his chair. "I don't like them opery songs. Too screechy." His eyes bugged out. "Not that yer voice were like that."

"So you like more popular tunes?" She waited for his nod, then looked directly across the table. "And you, sir? Any opinions?"

The tip of a shoe pressed along his leg and Roark fisted his hand, fighting to keep from jumping off his chair and dragging her behind him to his cabin.

The cowboy glanced between Lissa and the captain. "I'm partial to rousing songs about the sea. My pappy was a sailor and he always sang of ships battling storms and pirates."

"I know several of those songs. Thank you, gentlemen. I'm

always interested in the tastes of my audience." She smiled and then reached to pluck coins off a stack. "Has everyone anted?"

Now what in hell was that about? Roark slid in his coins and looked at his cards, wondering at her reasons for asking their song preferences. If she stepped on stage with her curves cinched in and enough bare skin showing, those men would listen to a recitation of nursery rhymes.

An hour later, a grumbling undercurrent had begun to pass around the table. The other players grew more irritated after each hand she won. From her chatty manner, Lissa appeared unaware of their displeasure.

Not smart for business. He eyed the tall stacks of chips before her and wondered whether he could get her to cash in for the night. Maybe with a bit of distraction. As carefully as he could, he slipped his hand under the table and onto the voluminous skirts covering her thigh.

She laughed at a comment by another player before cutting him a questioning look.

Now he had her attention. He loaded his gaze with heated promise and cupped her knee.

Her leg stiffened, and then she responded by trailing a finger along his thigh. When she turned toward the banker, her fingers moved to the inside of Roark's leg and grazed his balls. "I'll take two."

6

Roark stood with a jolt and stepped behind his chair, hoping it hid enough of his physical response to avoid embarrassment. He stretched over the chair, grabbed his small stack of coins, and shoved them into his trouser pocket. "Lissa, may I have the honor of buying you a refreshment at the bar?"

From beneath her lashes, she glanced up and shook her head. "That's sweet but no thanks."

With steady pressure, he eased back her chair. "Captain's privilege, ma'am." He glanced past her to one of his floor bosses and crooked a finger. "Templeton, take charge of Mrs. Tayte's winnings and issue a credit in her name."

Lissa rose, eyebrows drawn into a scowl. "But I don't want—Mike Templeton? Hey, I'm glad to see you again." She squealed and embraced the floor boss.

"Miss Alyssum, ain't you looking mighty fine?" Mike scooped her up in his arms, lifting her off her feet.

Her throaty laugh sounded.

At the sight of her slender body in another man's arms,

Roark's blood beat a staccato in his eardrums and his grip on the chair tightened until his fingers hurt.

The poker players tensed in their chairs.

Roark cleared his throat, aware of a sudden tightness in his chest. Jealousy? Not him.

Mike's head twisted toward Roark and his eyes widened. "Nice seeing you, ma'am." He set her down and stepped back.

A jerk of his head and a glare at his employee sent the man toward completion of his task. Roark linked his arm with Lissa's and rested his other hand on top, effectively trapping her hand. "Excuse us, gentlemen." He stepped away from the table, pulling her beside him.

"Good night." Lissa wiggled the fingers of her free hand at the players and followed. "I enjoyed our game."

When they were halfway down the main gallery, she hissed, "I told you I didn't want a drink."

Frustration fueled his pace. "Fine. We'll stroll on the outside deck." His pace increased and he was vaguely aware she struggled to match his strides. When he reached the end of the cabin, he twisted the knob, threw open the door, and strode out onto the deck.

A cool evening breeze tugged at his hair but did nothing to ease the raging inferno inside. A few steps to the side and they were out of the shaft of light shining through the windows.

"Why are you taking me outside?"

He spun her against the cabin wall and leaned a thigh between hers, holding her captive. "So I can do this." Before another second passed, his lips crashed down on hers and his arms circled her shoulders.

At first, she stiffened and tried to free her legs.

He cupped her cheek and skimmed her chin with caressing strokes of his thumb. Such smooth skin. The same skin he wanted to feel rubbing on his bare body. The spicy scent of the magnolia blossom in her hair filled his nostrils, imprinting her fragrance on his mind.

Her movements along his thigh changed from forceful to sensual. Then her body relaxed and her hands crept inside his jacket, grabbing handfuls of his shirt.

His tongue slipped along her lips and he sucked at her lower lip until she granted him entry. An exploration of the hot cavern of her mouth only made him hungry for more, for deeper places he wanted to be. He rocked his hips, pressing his engorged cock against her abdomen, and groaned into her mouth at the exquisite pressure.

Her body answered with a sideways slide and she sucked at his tongue.

That reaction put him over the edge. He dropped his hand to her waist and his thumb drew circles on her corseted stomach, stretching upwards with each move. His palm itched to cup her bosom again, to fill his hand with the weight of her plump breast. He ran his thumb along the underside of her breast but held back from the final action that could create embarrassment if they were discovered.

He broke from her mouth, brushing kisses along her temple, and then drew in a deep breath. "Tell me you want this." He cut off his sentence before revealing the rest of what he felt—"as much as I do."

"I shouldn't." She rubbed her cheek on his chest, then leaned back and met his gaze, her crystal blue eyes brimming with unshed tears. "I can't forget you took my father's boat."

"Not took, Lissa, won." A muscle in his tightened jaw jumped, and he forced his voice to a softer tone. "I *won* the boat. A world of difference separates those actions."

She dropped her arms and ducked her head.

He swallowed hard against the dryness at the back of his throat. Damn, the woman was so deep in his blood, he thought for a moment in that kiss that their heart beat as one. The same exasperating woman who couldn't see the event that might be the best change in his life, a windfall that represented security to a footloose gambler, as anything but an act of thievery.

How could he change her mind? His hands dropped to his sides and he turned to grab the railing, dreading the sounds of her footsteps retreating to the safety of the main gallery. He forced his attention away from the deck. Dim moonlight filtered through the trees overhanging the river and danced on the water's surface. High, wispy clouds obscured most of the stars.

"Roark?"

The hesitancy in her soft voice startled him, but he didn't trust himself to speak yet. "Mmm?"

"Maybe if you explained about the game . . ."

He looked over his shoulder, debating what to say. "A one-time explanation. That game on the Bayou Belle was an honest one." He straightened and turned, then braced his stance by leaning back with hands on the railing. A grip that was necessary to keep from pulling her back into his arms.

"Any player sitting at a high-stakes table has to acknowledge the likelihood of walking away empty-handed. Otherwise, that player has no business pulling out a chair in the first place. About two hours into this game, Springer started betting heavy on his hand, doubling and tripling up."

Her brows drew into a frown. "Was he drinking?"

"Some, we all were. Not enough to impair his playing." He connected with her gaze and held it, needing to watch her face as she learned the truth. "Lissa, I'd been dealt a heart flush running from eight through jack. You don't back off a hand like that. Once I got the queen, the sky was the limit. He tossed in the ownership certificate and I threw in everything I had to stay in the hand." He held back from telling her that 'everything' included his grandfather's pocket watch, his one and only family heirloom.

Conflicting emotions had been running across her face. The gamut from curiosity to understanding to acceptance. The last one was what he'd been waiting for.

He reached out and placed his hand over hers on the railing. The urge to touch her was always at the edge of his awareness. "I want to continue what we started a few minutes ago. Or we can play a private game of poker. If one of those choices interests you, meet me in my cabin in ten minutes."

Her head snapped around, her blue eyes narrowed. "Why your cabin?"

"Have you forgotten? As captain, I have to be where the crew can find me—at all times." He looked around the deck, and then leaned close. "Last night was the longest stretch of peace and quiet I've had in the past two weeks. And, as I recall, it wasn't all that peaceful." He winked and, powerless to resist her rosy lips, pressed a lingering kiss on her mouth. "Ten minutes."

When he moved away, he saw that she watched him with dazed eyes and pouting lips. Oh yeah, she'd be there.

Whistling, he sauntered through the main gallery; his gaze scanned the tables he passed and met the gazes of his employees assigned to check the status of games in progress. A few minutes to confer with his floor personnel and a couple minutes for arranging the service of refreshments in the privacy of his cabin.

His thoughts lingered on the woman these refreshments were for and his groin tightened. He huffed out a breath of sheer anticipation.

Mike Templeton raised a hand to grab his attention and approached. "Captain?"

Roark stopped, filing away the intention of quizzing this

man on his past relationship with Lissa. "Yes, Templeton." His gaze wandered the room, watching for a glimpse of Lissa reentering the cabin.

Mike stepped to one side and turned to survey the room. "I thought you needed to hear this. A couple poker players came to me with complaints about the singer."

"Complaints?" The instinct to protect Lissa's reputation ran through him, and he turned a hard stare on Templeton. "Go on."

Mike cleared his throat and rubbed at the back of his neck. "Yessir, they were grousing about a riverboat employee playing against passengers at the public tables. Mentioned a couple other riverboats with policies preventing this."

Damn, Roark's suspicion of the players' growing discontent had been right. Now if she'd lost a similar amount of money, he'd bet no one would object to her participation at their table. "Appreciate the information. Having any problems in your assigned area?"

Mike glanced over his shoulder. "The older gentleman down at table four has been drinking heavy, but still seems in control."

"Good work, Templeton. Inform Louie and then keep a close eye on that situation." Roark glanced toward the back door to the gallery. Had Lissa already gone upstairs? "We don't need a drunken brawl or broken furniture."

"Will do, Captain." The thin man strolled away, circulating among his assigned tables.

Roark walked to the roulette table and waited as Louie, the croupier, executed the current spin. When the bets were paid, he stepped closer. "Things running smoothly?"

Keeping his gaze on the action on the roulette table, Louie straightened. "I saw you with Templeton, so you know what's being said about our chanteuse with the lucky streak."

"Heard about that." He dreaded restricting her gaming, but he couldn't risk alienating other passengers. "What else?"

Louie shook his head and raised a finger. "Place your bets, folks." He spun the wheel with one hand and rolled the ball with the other. "Oh, a passenger asked why we weren't using the calliope like the previous owner. Said he almost missed the boat's departure."

"Noted." The echo of Lissa's similar question asked earlier ran through his head. He might have to reconsider that decision. "I'm headed to my cabin—for privacy."

"No more bets." Louie looked up and nodded. "I'll run interference down here, boss."

That's all Roark needed to hear. He spun on his boot heel and strode for the stairs leading to his cabin, anticipating the arrival of the intriguing Lissa Tayte.

Standing in front of the oval wall mirror, Lissa fluffed the curls around her face and pinched her cheeks. Roark's offer was too tempting to ignore. Granted, he probably hadn't taken her statement about winning back the boat seriously, but the lure of being alone with this man was irresistible. She stepped back and inspected her appearance one last time.

Because of the informal ambiance of Roark's cabin, she'd removed one layer of petticoats and changed from her buttoned-up boots into satin slippers. Comfort could be the key to gaining the upper hand tonight.

After checking the hallway for other passengers, she hurried across the Texas deck and tapped on his cabin door.

The door immediately swung open and he gestured her into the room. "Welcome. I'm glad you came." He grasped her hand and tugged her inside.

The act of stepping inside his cabin set her stomach dancing with nervous tingles. Last night, she hadn't felt this way, probably because she'd been in control. Her room, her invitation. Tonight, he'd set the stage.

He'd removed his jacket, revealing a shirt tailored to accent the breadth of his chest and the leanness of his waist.

Images of the body underneath his fine linen shirt raced through her thoughts. She sucked in her lower lip and nibbled.

His gaze focused on her mouth and flashed a heated green. "Keep making movements like that, and we may never shuffle the cards. You're here, so have you decided?"

"Decided?"

His hand ran up her arm and cupped her shoulder. "About what will happen here tonight?" Leaning close, he whispered close to her cheek, "Tell me, Lissa, poker or pleasure?"

Her knees wobbled and she forced them straight. When his voice lowered to that whiskeyed timbre, she wished for something solid to lean on. "I don't ever get enough poker playing."

"Could say the same about the other choice."

At his words, she closed her eyes and sucked in a breath. Such temptation. Was he deliberately torturing her? She cleared her throat. "Can we start with poker?"

"As you wish." He stepped to the side with a seductive grin. "The cards await. I realize my setup here is not as intimate as yours at the hotel was."

The table was set with a silver tray holding decanters, glasses, cups and a cloth-covered plate. Beside the tray sat a deck of playing cards.

His preparations for making their time together special was touching. "Oh, you arranged for refreshments. How thoughtful."

"Players often have to keep up their strength. The endurance factor."

Her sideways glance only caught his profile as he turned away, and she couldn't tell by his tone if he was teasing.

"What would you like? I have coffee, whiskey, and sherry. I also requested a selection of tarts and cakes."

"Coffee with a splash of whiskey, please. I'll save dessert for later." She set her reticule on the table and loosened the strings, ready to set up her coin stacks.

He set two cups and saucers on the table between them and lowered himself to the bench. "Should we decide up front what's at stake?"

"I thought we were playing for money? Out on the deck, you mentioned a private poker game." The aroma of the southern coffee with a hint of chicory wafted to her nose and she inhaled its richness.

"I needed to make my offer irresistible." His eyes lit with mischief over the rim of the coffee cup. "While I waited for you to arrive, I contemplated that offer. We've already played poker for money this evening." He trailed a fingertip along her hand holding the coffee cup. "What about another type of winnings?"

Everywhere he touched, tingles ran along her skin. Her heartbeat raced. "Another type?" she murmured.

"The stakes I want are more personal. You want the challenge of a poker game." His gaze heated and his fingers ran up the back side of her arm. "I want a repeat of last night's fun between the sheets."

His words conjured up the memory of their bodies moving in rhythm—touching, tasting, exciting each other past the point of reason. Need spiraled deep in her belly. She shifted against the bench to ease her ache, moisture seeping along her pussy lips. Rather than appear like a bitch in heat, she sipped her coffee and fluttered her eyelashes. "That's the prize when you win. What's my prize?"

His eyes narrowed and his lips tightened. "What do you want?"

Her thoughts went to the ultimate game she had planned but

knew the timing wasn't right. That game to retrieve her family's boat would have to wait until her winnings had grown. "I'd want you to listen to my suggestions for how to spread publicity and increase attendance."

"Easy enough." He leaned his elbows on the table.

His agreement was too quick. What had she missed? "Maybe 'listen' wasn't strong enough. How about enact my ideas?"

"Lissa, I've agreed to your terms. Get the cards and shuffle."

Impatience tinged his words, and her breath hitched in her throat. After the surprising, and so exciting, spanking she'd received last night, she wondered if his tension might reveal yet another new experience of the carnal act. She scooted her cup to the side and grabbed the deck, expertly shuffling. "A chance at . . ."

"Not a chance," his voice was raw, "another night like last night will occur. Or one that's better."

Her nipples ached and she felt a flush of excitement running up her neck. Before her traitorous body gave away the true state of her emotions, she focused on the guidelines for their wager. "How many hands will we play?"

"You like high stakes." He leaned back and crossed his arms over his chest. "One game, winner claims the stated prize."

One? She studied his face, but his eyes were hooded, the eyes of a predator intent on prey. If she lost, another night of frolic with this fantastic man could hardly be considered bad. But a part of her resisted letting on how much his proposal excited her.

For tonight, she could put aside thoughts of the relationship between Roark Sheridan and her family.

She returned his perusal with a blatant appraisal of her own. "If the wager is decided in just one game, then we're playing stud."

A laugh burst from his lips.

She dealt the first card facedown on the table in front of him. "Stud poker, of course." She glanced at her hole card, a ten, and slid it in front of her and then paused before dealing the second cards face up. "We didn't discuss the ante."

"Since we know how this will end—"

The arrogance. Her hands stilled. "We do?"

"I certainly do. Let's add to the excitement." He rested an arm on the table and leaned close, his eyes smoldering with green fire. "I propose low card holder of each deal removes a piece of clothing."

By some force of sheer willpower, she managed to keep her eyelids from closing in anticipation of the end of the hand. In most circumstances, she'd be offended that another player assumed such a domineering attitude. But he was swaying her with his words, making her want to toss in the cards right now.

Five cards in a hand. The potential to be sitting within a few feet of Roark wearing five fewer items of clothing. With each card dealt, she could be seeing more of his tanned, muscled skin. Hell, he was a man—his outfit probably only consisted of five or six articles.

With a hand that trembled only slightly, she flipped over the first card and met his gaze with a sultry look. "At least one piece." The card she laid on his stack was a seven of diamonds. Lots of higher cards to beat him.

Without breaking eye contact, she slid the next card off the deck and turned it over onto her side of the table. "Who will be undressing?" She glanced down and saw a nine of clubs. "Does the winner get to choose the article of clothing?"

Roark stood and put his hands on his hips. His legs were braced in a wide stance, the evidence of his arousal filling the front of his trousers. "Why not?"

For an instant, the image of Roark as a ravaging pirate flashed through her mind. She shook away that fanciful thought and concentrated on the real choices before her. He'd made this decision easier by removing his jacket before her arrival. His pants? No sense in exposing bare skin she couldn't see once he sat again to play. "Your shirt."

To have something to occupy her hands, she sipped at her now-cold coffee while watching him unbutton his creamy linen shirt.

He started at the top, each loosened button revealing another few inches of tight muscles covered with a furring of dark hair.

Her fingers itched to feel the coarse texture of his chest hair against his muscled skin.

A quick yank, and his shirttails pulled loose from his trousers, exposing the narrow line of dark hair below his navel.

Her throat dried and a heated flush ran over her skin. She never realized anticipation could be so arousing. A glance at his face told her he knew her thoughts—and that he shared her feelings.

Once his cufflinks were unfastened and dropped at the far end of the table, he let the shirt slide off his arms to the floor. His eyes were crinkled with laughter when he sat again at the table, muscles rippling sinuously with each movement. "Ready for the next card?"

The cup clattered on the saucer as she set it down and fumbled for the top card. "All right." That single word sounded like it was scraped from her mouth. She couldn't drag her gaze away from all that masculine skin within her sight.

King of diamonds. A grin spread across his lips. "I like the possibilities of that card."

Not much chance she'd win this one. With her heart beating against her chest, she flipped over the next card and looked down.

Nine of hearts. She'd lost, but she'd be damned if she would do it with anything but style. Pressing her hands on the table, she rose off the bench and leaned forward, displaying the plumpness of her breasts. "What piece of clothing do you choose?"

His gaze brushed across her face, lingered on her décolletage and focused on her skirts just above the level of the table. "Your pantalets."

7

Had she heard him correctly? "You want me to remove a piece of my underwear?"

"Yeah, I want to imagine your pussy exposed." He covered her hand with his and stroked a thumb along the inside of her wrist. "While we're playing the rest of this game, I want to think of how your petals will blush then redden with anticipation of the final prize."

As she listened to his cajoling voice, her womb clenched and her cream seeped onto the crotch of her pantalets. Oo, this man's words could seduce.

She straightened and stepped away from the bench. Two could play at this seduction. Uncertain how he would respond, she hitched up her skirts and reached underneath for the ribbon ties. Yards of stiff petticoats impeded her search. Women's outfits were supposed to be removed in a certain order, and this was not the preferred one.

Roark leaned an arm on the table and gazed at what she'd exposed. "Your legs have a nice shape. Curves that taper to a slim ankle."

The tone of his words urged her to flaunt her assets. She untied the knot and eased the fine-woven fabric along her curves, shimmying her hips to shake the garment down her legs to pool at her feet.

His gaze followed the path of the garment and heated at her movements.

Watching him made her legs wobbly and she steadied herself on the table. Two steps removed her slippers from the pantalets and she lowered herself to the bench. The stiffness of the petticoats pressed against her pussy, reminding her of her nakedness under the dress. Inside her corset, her nipples beaded in response and ached with tension.

She gasped in surprise. One simple change in her clothing, and she was suddenly aware of each and every part of her body that ached with wanting.

And the man sitting across from her knew. His steamy gaze told her he'd achieved exactly what he wanted.

"Deal the next card?"

For a moment, she'd forgotten they were in the middle of a card game. This felt more like a battle of wills. She grabbed two cards off the top and flipped his first and hers second, secretly wishing for the low card. Disrobing for an interested audience was more erotic than she'd ever imagined. Watching him enjoy her body gave her a thrill.

His card was the seven of spades.

Hers the ten of diamonds. A card that bettered her hand *and* gave her momentary control. "My choice."

"Yours." His voice purred out the single word.

Why not surprise him like he'd surprised her? "A sock."

His brows scrunched into a frown. "Really?"

With a broad smile, she leaned an elbow on the table and rested her chin on her palm. "Yep, a sock." He probably didn't realize what she'd gain. In anticipation of her next move, she surreptitiously toed off her slippers.

From under the table came the scuffling sounds of boots pushed against one another, and he kicked it out from under the table. Then he reached down, pulled off a white knitted sock and tossed it over his shoulder. With eyebrows raised and a wide grin, he declared, "Done."

Not quite. She dragged her gaze from the sensuous movements of his arms to the boot, his right boot, lying two feet away then eased her feet along the plank floor until they surrounded his right foot. With kneading movements of her toes, she massaged his foot and ran a toe under his trouser cuff and along his shin.

His grin widened. "The lady's true motives are revealed. Nicely played."

Each movement of her legs rubbed her bare pussy against her petticoats, keeping her aroused. Squeezing her thighs together only increased the friction. She squirmed sideways, and then bit her lower lip to keep in the moan threatening to escape.

The hand that reached to deal the last upturned cards faltered.

"Let me help."

Expecting him to reach for the cards, she was shocked to feel the nudge of his foot against hers, easing it to the side. One moment his toe teased her ankle, the next it tickled her knee.

Her hands grabbed the edge of the table and she closed her eyes to concentrate on the sensations his foot aroused. Her nipples pulsed and ached to be fondled. Her breath hitched in her throat.

His warm hands covered hers at the same moment his foot skimmed her inner thigh, heading straight for her hot, wet pussy. With slow moves, his toe stroked her sensitive folds, pausing to circle and press against her clit.

She jerked and instinctively moved her legs closer.

"Lissa, keep your legs apart." His voice was rough and thick with desire.

His words caressed her ears, compelling her body to respond, and she complied, pressing her hips forward. Her breathing labored.

"That's right. Let me feel your heat." His foot stroked her outer lips, and then his toe returned to her engorged nub, alternating quick flicks with circling caresses.

Her body flushed with arousal, the swirling deep in her belly spiraling down to her core. The breaths allowed by her corset weren't deep enough, and she felt lightheaded. A whimper escaped her lips.

"Good." His toe circled with firmer strokes. "Let me hear you." Strong hands wrapped around her wrists, as if keeping her captive.

With her hands anchored, she could flex her hips to change the angle of his invading toe. A rhythm was established and she pressed against his foot, feeling her cream ease the gliding of their bodies.

"Lissa, listen to what your body tells you."

The spiraling in her womb intensified and her eyes flew open. She wanted to be watching him as he brought her to climax.

His hot gaze sent her over the edge.

Her breath rasped through a dry throat and her pussy clenched around his foot in waves. Her moans started on the low end of the scale and rose as her release climbed in intensity. His toe caressed her until the last spasm spent itself; then his hands released her wrists.

She flopped forward on the table, her head dropping onto her forearms. "Oh god, that's never happened." She shivered at the tingles of the aftermath and looked up at him with what she knew was a glazed expression. "That was amazing."

"I've never before heard a climax sung."

A giggle escaped over her dry lips, and she licked them.

"Is that an invitation?" His gaze focused on her lips; then he reached out a hand and traced her lower lip with his thumb. "Because my cock is about to burst through my trousers. And I'd like to be buried deep inside you when I go over the edge."

The image was erotic and she gasped. Nobody had ever talked to her like this. "What about the game?"

He kicked off his other boot. "Screw the game. You knew what I wanted when you arrived at my door." His gaze pinned her as he leaned sideways and reached under the table.

Her options of winning this hand were diminishing by the second. "Don't you want to look at your cards?"

A white sock flew over his shoulder. "Only if you're lying naked on top of them."

Oh my! His commanding manner was intoxicating and she felt excited blood pump throughout her body. "But those weren't our rules."

"Situations change and the rules get adjusted." He rose from the bench and his hands went to the buckle of his belt, pulling the leather from the clasp and edging the prong from the punched hole. A reversal of a similar action he intended to do after disrobing.

She couldn't drag her gaze away from the determined movements of his hands. Would he really demand the winning prize before they'd played out the complete hand?

With quick twists of his hands, he unbuttoned his trousers, then leaned over and dragged the trousers and his long johns down his lean legs. When he stepped from the pile of clothes, he stood naked before her—reddened cock jutting proudly from the nest of dark curls at his groin.

All that glorious male skin and muscle on display. Her mouth watered at the thought of tasting him all over, and the tip of her tongue traced her upper lip.

"The invitation has arrived." A groan rasped from his throat, and his emerald gaze pinned her. "I want you sitting on the end of the table with your skirts around your waist."

She doubted her legs would support her weight. The compelling look in his eye gave her strength. She paused only a second to reach to move her cup and saucer to the floor.

"Leave them." Strong hands grabbed her waist and lifted her to the table. Her toes barely touched the floor and she grabbed the edge of the plank table for balance.

He stepped close and shoved back her skirts. "Your legs go around me."

She raised quivering legs to his hips and immediately felt his cock run the length of her pussy.

She moaned.

His lips nuzzled her neck while one hand pulled at the closures on the back of her dress.

"Too many damn buttons." His fingers twisted and pulled until he loosened several.

She buried her nose against his chest, inhaling the scent of sultry night air, a touch of bay rum, and tobacco. Her lips feathered kisses along whatever muscled skin she could reach.

The shoulders of her dress slipped down her arms and he reached a hand inside her bodice, stroking her nipple.

Answering pulses in her pussy wet her curls for his gliding cock.

He tugged a breast from her bodice and leaned down to lick and taste her nipple, circling his tongue around the bud and pulling the breast deep into his mouth.

Her hips flexed, seeking the head of his cock. She tightened her legs and he pressed inside with one strong thrust.

The girth of his cock filled and stretched her channel. Her cry rang throughout the room.

His mouth moved to hers and their tongues tangled to the rhythm of his invading body.

With her hands on his shoulders, she used that leverage to push against his long, slow thrusts. Her need rising in tempo with each stroke.

Her hand drifted down his chest and rubbed the flat disk of his nipple into a hardened pebble.

A guttural rasp sounded from deep in his chest. His grip on her hips tightened and his pumping increased, causing the wooden table to groan under the onslaught.

The tinkle of breaking porcelain sounded.

She flexed her hips so each stroke rubbed her clit, the friction setting her aflame. She vowed to hold on and match him stroke for stroke, but his cock filled her so fully that each deep stroke sent her more out of control. Then waves of climax overtook her and all she could do was cling to his shoulders for the ride.

Strong arms scooped under her butt and lifted her off the table. He braced his feet wide and held her hips in place while he pumped with hard, fast strokes. At the point of his own release, he threw back his head and groaned.

Harsh breathing sounded and the scents of their lovemaking filled her nostrils. Sensations that were forever imprinted on her memory.

Roark's legs trembled with the effort of unclenching from his climax without buckling and forcing him to drop the treasure in his arms. He'd pushed her, bending her to his terms because a part of him hoped the sex they'd shared hadn't been as spectacular as he'd remembered.

He'd been wrong.

Damn. What the hell was he going to do with this realization? He didn't create ties. Life had taught him to keep on moving.

Panting breaths tickled his neck and he turned to lean his butt against the table, shifting her closer. The plank bit into his flesh, but he couldn't resist her warmth against his chest.

"If your intention was to impress me, gambling man, you succeeded."

He chuckled. "No intention to impress, ma'am, only to pleasure."

"You're such a smooth talker . . ." She pulled back and looked into his face, her gaze serious and searching. "I don't know whether you're telling the truth or painting a pretty picture."

"Keep them guessing, that's my motto." He swung her legs away from his hips and cradled them before crossing the room to the interior door.

"Eek." She grabbed tightly to his neck. "We're going to . . ."

He stopped at the threshold and kicked at the door he'd earlier left ajar, planning ahead for this possibility. "We're moving to a different playground."

With a frown creasing her forehead, she gazed inside the room. Slowly her eyes widened and a smile crept across her lips. "This wood was underneath all of Pa—, um, the handbills and steamboat pictures? Wow, it's beautiful."

He scanned the room, appreciating again the grain of the polished wood reflected in the glow of two oil lanterns nestled in wall sconces. In only three steps, he reached the built-in wooden bed and laid her on the velvet coverlet. "You're looking at several days' work of scraping and sanding, but the result is worth the effort. In a short time, the boat's become home."

Resting a knee on the edge of the mattress, he leaned over the bed and captured her lips in a kiss, one he meant to be short.

But her hands grabbed his jaws and she slanted her mouth to one side for better access, then tunneled inside with her tongue.

At her heated response, he inhaled and ran his hand along her hip and her stomach, coming to rest on her breast. Her corseted and clothed breast. His cock stirred and pressed against the fabric of her skirts, the friction teasing him. He broke away and rested his cheek on her temple. "That was meant to tide me over while I retrieve the drink tray from the other room."

She nibbled at his neck. "Sorry, just a reaction."

With a push of his hand on the mattress, he lifted himself off the bed. "Be wearing fewer clothes when I return."

Her gaze ran the length of his body and he paused by the bed, enjoying the blue fire in her eyes when she watched his cock lengthen.

He turned and sauntered out the door. At the shuffling of clothing and the creaking of bed slats, he smiled. She was preparing for his return.

The card game was still arranged on the table, just shoved a bit askew. He scooped up each hand, placed them on the tray, and deposited the remaining cards in the middle. Carrying the tray, he returned to the room and glanced at her before setting it on a table.

Big mistake. The sight of Lissa naked and waiting in his bed, reclining on one side, stabbed a pain through his chest. His hands shook and the glassware rattled until he slid it safely onto the table.

"I did as you commanded. Are you pleased?"

He eased down onto the edge of the mattress and glanced at her. Her blond waves covered one shoulder and breast, her waist dipped low and her hip rounded high. He couldn't resist reaching out a finger to tickle through the curls covering her mons.

Lissa moaned and shifted her legs, ran her hand down his arm to his fingers, and then twined her fingers with his and eased them away from her body. "I owe you some special attention, Captain. So lie back against this pillow and relax." She pressed against his shoulder until he flopped back and ran her hand down his torso.

He settled the pillow higher behind his head, wanting to get comfortable. The feisty widow lady had returned, and he couldn't wait to see what she'd do next.

She sat at the edge of the mattress, her hip touching his, and reached for the decanter. "I'm having a drink. Would you like something?"

"What I want to drink doesn't fit well in a cup."

Her eyes rounded. "Your choices are whiskey, sherry, or coffee—but I'm sure that's cold by now."

"Whiskey."

She poured a couple inches into a glass. Bracing one hand on the mattress and stretching her arm out to extend the glass caused her breasts to plump together.

He watched them jiggle and started to reach out for a caress, but saw the warning in her eyes. She wanted to take charge and he needed to let her.

Holding the glass over his middle, she tipped it until enough whiskey dribbled out to fill his navel. "Oops, so sorry. Let me clean that up." She extended the glass within his reach and waited for him to accept it. With a grin and a flash of mischief in her eyes, she braced her hands at the sides of his hips, leaned over until her mouth closed on top of his navel and sucked hard.

The sensation rocked him. His left hand fisted in the sheets and his hips flexed, pressing his cock along the edge of her breast.

Her pointy tongue lapped at the few drops of warm liquor, swirling deep inside and around the rim. "Mmm, tasty."

When he caught his breath, he sipped at the whiskey, watching for what Lissa might do next.

She eased away from his body and turned back to the tray. Peeling back the cloth, she displayed the assortment of tarts and cakes. "Oh, Floyd's pecan tarts. I've always loved these." She lifted one to her mouth and bit into it, closing her eyes as she chewed.

That simple act was so sensual, Roark felt awareness tightening the length of his entire body.

She held out the remaining piece. "Do you want a bite?"

"I'm enjoying it from right here."

Her gaze focused on his rigid cock and she grinned. "I see you are." The last bit disappeared into her mouth and she sipped at her sherry, gazing into his eyes over the rim. "You should probably finish your whiskey now." Without breaking eye contact, she reached to the side and returned her glass to the tray. "Or set it aside."

He continued sipping, narrowing his gaze at her warning.

With a gleam in her eye, she rose on her hands and knees and crawled to his side. One hand caressed the inner skin of his thigh while she swung her hair across his abdomen and flicked it on his cock.

At the tickling sensation, he tossed back the rest of his drink and set the glass at the corner of the mattress. The fire traveling down his throat mirrored the fire building in his loins.

Her tongue swirled around the head of his cock. Then her mouth closed over the tip, alternately licking and sucking.

His body clenched and he tunneled a hand through her thick hair, needing to touch her. To let his caressing fingers convey his feelings for her ministrations on his body. Wary of hurting her, he refrained from flexing his hips, but every inch of his being wanted to plunge deeper into her hot, moist mouth.

As her mouth moved, she moaned and the vibrations only increased his pleasure. She shifted positions and grazed the tips of her breasts along his upper thighs, then circled her hand around the base of his cock and pumped.

His restraint weakened and he pressed upward with one tentative stroke, butting the head of his cock against the roof of her mouth.

She pulled back her lips enough to graze her teeth along its length, using light, but steady, pressure.

The sensation intensified as she lifted away from his body, coming closer to the tip.

"Whoa, slow down. I need to taste you." He grabbed her shoulders and pulled her against his chest, his mouth planting kisses on her forehead, her cheeks, her nose, and finally settling on her moist lips.

Her soft hands moved over his chest and shoulders, caressing his skin, then plunging up his neck into his hair. She responded to his kisses with nibbles along his lower lip and thrusts of her tongue into the corners of his mouth.

The heat between them raged and Roark positioned her hips over his groin, rubbing his cock along her slick pussy.

She wiggled her hips and eased her honeyed folds over his cock, rocking with gentle movements.

He was too far gone for gentle. He flexed his hips upward and stroked until he was inside as deep as he could go. Her tight channel surrounding him, she clenched him with her inner walls, and embraced him with her heat.

Pressing against his shoulders, she arched her back and drew up one leg until her foot rested near his hip. She pushed against his thrusts, moaning with each move.

The friction intensified. He slid his hand along her leg, circling caresses along her inner thigh until his thumb reached her swollen nub.

At his touch, her head dropped back and she cried out, a high keening sound.

Her satisfaction was what he'd been waiting for. With the next thrust, he pumped his cum deep inside, letting the rhythmic pulls of her inner walls milk him. When their releases were complete, he eased Lissa's relaxed body down on top of his and enfolded her in his arms.

She settled her cheek against his slick chest, right above his thundering heart.

The heart now inscribed with her name.

8

"Untie the rope and shove off."

The deckhand's yell pulled Lissa from a lingering dream and she stretched. Muscles in various parts of her body ached with delicious soreness. She reached out a hand to touch the man who'd participated in last night's rollicking game. No man, just cold sheets. Again. Disappearing before morning seemed to be one of Roark Sheridan's more irritating habits.

Why had he let her sleep? She sat up and brushed her hair away from her face. How was she supposed to get back to her cabin now that the crew and passengers were up and about? And wearing her gown from last night. Resting her cheek on her upraised knees, she gazed at the room, her fingers running over the smoothness of the velvet coverlet. This cabin held none of the cluttered hodgepodge that had decorated Papa's old one.

Swathing her body in the sheet, she wandered the perimeter, touching leather-bound books on the shelves and a ragged gold nugget glued to a rough board, gazing at the shiny brass sconces on the walls and on the bureau drawers. Someone, namely Roark, took pride in the way this room looked. On top of the small dressing table, she found a neat pile of her belongings—underclothes and a clean calico dress for daytime wear.

He'd taken the time to retrieve them from her room and, she glanced around again, remove her gown. His thoughtfulness touched her. Gone was the tray of drinks and desserts. In its place was a bowl with a pair of towels, a soap bar, and a porcelain pitcher. She touched the side of the pitcher, surprised it still radiated warmth. The sheet dropped to the floor as she prepared for a quick sponge bath.

When she looked closer at the soap, she realized the bar was pressed with the shape of a Queen of Hearts playing card. Lathering a washcloth released the scent of magnolias to fill the cabin. A classy touch.

After her refreshing bath, she dressed quickly and stepped into his outer cabin, hoping he waited there. But the cabin was empty. For a moment, her shoulders sagged with disappointment, and then she spied the tray from the previous night and moved closer. The cards from their unfinished game lay spread across the silver surface.

Did he intend for them to finish it? That would fit well in her plans.

After consulting with the pilot about the day's run, Roark headed toward the lower deck. Abreast of his cabin, he paused with his hand wrapped around the doorknob, debating about waking Lissa. He suspected—no, he knew—if he entered the cabin, he wouldn't leave for a long time. Their night together had convinced him his appetite for the seductive lady would not soon be satisfied.

The next item on his list of business concerns could be answered by his steward. Roark moved away from the temptation of his rooms and set off through the Queen, finally spotting the man leaving the galley. "Hold up, Driscoll."

Driscoll turned, a stack of paper in his hands. "Yes, Captain?"

Roark eyed the paper with mild curiosity. He had questions; he didn't want to know all the duties of his employees. "You've served on how many boats?"

"The Queen is my fifth, sir."

"Did the others have regulations preventing the boat's employees at gaming tables?"

"Two did, but the owner banked either a faro or roulette table for the crew below decks. As you know, poker games spring up anywhere." He shifted the paper to the crook of his arm. "One finer boat included select employees in private games only."

"Any opinion on passenger response to such regulations?"

Driscoll frowned. "I'm not sure I understand what you're asking, sir."

As he worked out his question in his mind, Roark pinched the bridge of his nose. "I'm wondering whether or not the boats with the stricter regulations saw more repeat passengers. Could this be better for business?"

The sun shone red through the treetops lining the riverbank. High in the sky, the first stars twinkled. Inhaling the last puff of his cheroot, Roark leaned against the railing of the guard deck opposite the back stage area. He'd propped open the door to be sure to see Lissa when she arrived for her performance.

How they hadn't crossed paths all day on a 175-foot boat, he had no explanation. Sometime during the afternoon, he'd suspected she was ignoring him but could think of no reason. That would not be the case after the conversation he intended to have tonight.

The tapping of quick footsteps sounded along the hallway and a blonde wearing a green gown flashed by.

"Lissa? Um, Miss Alyssum?" He stepped to the doorway and waited for her to reappear. "May I have a few words before your performance?"

When their eyes met, she smiled. "Captain Sheridan? Good evening." She walked to the doorway and looked around the immediate area. "Well, I've had a busy day. Have you seen the—" Her gaze narrowed and her brows pinched together. "Roark, what's wrong?"

"Lissa, we need to discuss a few passenger complaints."

A low laugh escaped. "That conversation was a bit embarrassing last night at the poker table. Don't worry, though, I rearranged my song selections—dropped the opera and added a couple sea ballads. Need to keep the audience happy." Her words were light and confident. "You knew that's why I questioned the men last night, didn't you?"

He dragged a hand over his jaw and felt the prickles of his beard stubble. At times like this, he wished for more experience as a business owner. For hints on how to make this conversation easier. "I'm not talking about the songs."

Eyes wide, she stepped closer and rested a hand on his arm. "Oh, no, someone heard us last night?"

Her words, combined with her scent of roses mixed with magnolias, conjured images of their lovemaking, and he willed his body not to respond. "No one has mentioned someone overhearing any noise we might have made."

"Then what are you talking about?" Her mouth drew into a straight line. She started to raise her hand to his cheek but looked around at their location and dropped it. "Your expression is much too serious. How can I help?"

"There is a way for you to help. Because the complaint is about you joining the gambling at the public tables." He leaned against the railing and crossed his arms over his chest.

"About me? I don't understand."

"Other passengers are grumbling because you're a boat employee and you're winning too much of their money." He ran a hand through his hair, uneasy at her shocked expression. Listening to an outburst here on deck was not his preference.

"Well, that's easy to solve." She smiled and patted his hand. "Explain that I'm not an employee."

"Maybe not an employee in the true sense of the word." He pointed a finger between their bodies. "You and I know a separate contract exists, but think about how the situation looks to the public, Lissa. A woman performs on the boat's stage during the scheduled passage between their chosen cities. The performances are included in the passenger fare. As far as they're concerned, you are employed by the boat owner, namely me. Then they go to the gaming salon to relax and end up losing money to you."

She stiffened and narrowed her gaze. "So what does this mean?"

"If I had thought through the whole situation last night, I could have prevented this. For that I apologize." He girded himself for the outburst he knew was coming. "I hate like hell to say this. Lissa, you are banned from the gaming salon here on the Queen."

"Banned?" Her body jerked as if she'd been slapped. "That hardly seems fair."

His gaze scanned the side deck, hesitating on several figures on the foredeck. "Not so loud."

She paced a few feet away and returned. "Just last month during my engagement on the Clarkson Steamer, I sat every night at the poker tables." Wild thoughts ran through her mind. How could she win back the boat for Papa? Her stake wasn't big enough yet to challenge Roark.

"Boats operate with different rules. I checked with an employee who has experience on several riverboats." He huffed out a breath. "Lissa, I'm not the only captain imposing this regulation."

Footsteps sounded behind them, and Rolly strolled along the guard, sax case swinging in his hand. "Evening, folks."

"Evening." Roark clasped Lissa's elbow and drew her back

against the railing until the man passed. Although her arm was stiff as a poker, he held on, needing the fleeting connection. "Another solution exists. Stop performing. If you're not the headline singer, the passengers will have no reason to complain."

"Then what will I do?

He shrugged. "Be a paying passenger and enjoy the sights."

Her hands jammed onto her hips and she leaned close with narrowed eyes. "I've never walked out of a contract, and I won't do it now."

Bending his head until he looked her directly in the eye, he enunciated each word, "Then you'll refrain from gambling on this boat." He spun on his boot heel and strode along the planking, his steps sounding like shots in the otherwise calm evening.

With each of Roark's loud footfalls, Lissa's anger notched higher. Sure, she'd won a fair amount of the bank's money at roulette. But the man operated a riverboat, her win would surely be offset by someone else's loss. How dare he restrict her free time! Playing cards relaxed her. He was being plain ornery to take that away!

More important thoughts tumbled in her mind. How could she possibly earn enough money to challenge him for the boat? She thought of the handbills she'd worked on for hours that morning and then had paid Floyd's nephew to distribute upstream that afternoon.

If the promotion worked like in past years, the audience should be half again bigger tonight. The number expecting to see and hear Miss Alyssum perform had been increased by her efforts. She couldn't quit. Her reputation was on the line.

She'd have to find another way to increase her stake. Papa had run a different route along the river, and she wasn't familiar with the town at this particular landing. Someone on the crew must know which saloon in Boggstown ran the best poker games.

Three hours later, Lissa wondered whether her temper and stubbornness hadn't steered her wrong. The steward warned her that the Boggstown saloons were rougher than she was probably used to, but she'd forged a path anyway. If she'd put that information together with the coarser appearance of the majority of the audience, she might have remained on the Queen.

Now she sat at a table where the splinters kept snagging the sleeve of her dress. The playing surface was marred with gouges and stained with rings from beer mugs. Instead of crystal chandeliers, kerosene lanterns flickered and smoked, giving the air an acrid smell that stung the back of Lissa's throat.

But the cards had been favorable for the past hour, and she was ahead almost a hundred dollars.

"Show 'em, lady." The dealer, a dark-haired man with bushy eyebrows, ordered.

Inside, she cringed at the man's surly tone. Early on, she realized her usual flirty banter might be misinterpreted here. Thank God, she'd had the sense to change into one of her day gowns with a high neckline. "I've got a full house, tens over sixes."

A fist slammed onto the table. "Damnation, that makes four hands in a row."

"What can I say, gents?" She reached for the pile of coins and pulled them toward her, careful to avoid scraping her fingers on the table. "The cards are coming my way tonight."

Near her left elbow, a man with a stained vest leered. "I say the big winner ought to buy a round of drinks."

The stench of stale clothes and an unclean body wafted her way. Drinks would not be offered by this player. She had a purpose for each and every coin she won. "Now, sir, I remember asking whether this table had any special rules." She plastered on a pensive expression that she hoped looked like she was searching her memory. "Deuces as wild cards and jokers as bugs for filling straights or flushes were mentioned, but nothing was said about buying drinks."

"A man can get mighty thirsty when he's losing."

"Ought to get something out of watching a stranger take our money." The dark-haired man grumbled. "Where you from again?"

She rattled off her prepared line that didn't give away too much information. "I grew up on the river, on my family's riverboat."

"Then you must be rich. Why are you here, taking our hard-earned money?" He jammed his thick hands close to her face. "See the scars and cuts on my hands? Those're from picking cotton."

Take—not win. Her stomach churned and her palms grew moist. Only once before had she sensed animosity this strong around a gaming table. That time, her brother Forrest had been with her and stepped in.

If they weren't prepared to lose, they shouldn't have anted into the game. The thought, so like Roark's statement about the high-stakes game, echoed in her thoughts.

Time to consider a safe route back to the boat. The winnings in her reticule weighed heavy in her lap. As she fanned the cards into her hand, she scanned the room for familiar faces. Maybe she'd better start losing.

9

Roark stood near the roulette table and surveyed the gaming salon, pleased to hear the hum of conversation and the clinking of money being wagered. By his estimate, tonight's crowd was larger by at least twenty players.

As he moved his gaze over the room, he told himself he wasn't really looking for her blond head among the gamblers. His message couldn't have been any clearer, but she'd surprised him before. The fact she'd disappeared immediately after her performance nipped at his conscience. Probably off in some nook on the boat. He'd give her until midnight to lick her wounds, and then he'd start his search.

He stepped behind Louie and spoke in low tones. "The crowd's bigger tonight."

The croupier nodded, his hands moving to rake in the bank's latest winnings. "Must be because of Lissa's handbills."

How had Lissa distributed handbills? Rather than appear ignorant about happenings on the boat, he pressed his lips tight. From behind him, he heard the latch on the aft door from the galley squeak open. Maybe that was her. Roark turned and spotted a disheveled deckhand in the doorway. What in hell? "Didn't the crew get my message?"

Louie glanced over his shoulder. "Driscoll made the announcement below decks before my shift started."

Templeton approached, his gaze shifting between the man in the doorway and the roulette table. "Captain, Malloy is here to report a problem."

Where was the steward when he was needed? Irritation ran through Roark, and he pinned the man with a glare. "Send him to Driscoll."

Templeton winced at the harsh tone. "Says the matter is urgent and you need to hear it."

Roark strode the ten feet to the doorway and out into the narrow hallway. "Let me hear it."

The man stood at the far end, his cap crumpled in his hands. "Sorry for the interruption, sir. I left my buddy Linden at the Balers Saloon but I think the situation needs your authority."

The thought of bailing out one of his crewmembers who'd bet too heavily rankled. "Are you serious, Malloy? Linden's in over his head in a poker game?"

"Linden's not the one in trouble, the lady singer is."

At the word 'lady,' Roark's breath caught in his chest and a muscle in his jaw twitched. "Tell me everything."

"Well, sir. The players at her table ain't too happy with her luck and they're getting mean."

"So she's winning?" Roark shoved open the door leading to the deck and headed toward the loading ramp.

"Yes sir, like at The Cotton Palace."

"Different crowd at Balers." Here he'd thought she was in her room licking her wounds or maybe below decks scaring up a friendly game.

"Right." Malloy trotted to keep up. "A couple of those players are real big. Linden won't be much help against them, but we figured not to desert her."

"Backing up another crew member is good." This section along the river was not safe for a woman alone at night, especially not one with a satchel of coins. Was poker so important that she'd pull this crazy stunt? Didn't the woman care about her safety?

"Malloy, ready a lantern and wait for me here." Roark dashed up the exterior steps to the Texas deck. He was not headed into an explosive situation unarmed. In less than two minutes, he strode toward Malloy, who waited on the ramp.

From the top of the embankment came the rattle and squeak of a wagon harness. "Whoa, Blackie."

Roark grabbed the lantern from Malloy and climbed the short hill. He spotted Lissa being helped down from a farm wagon.

She was safe! The tightness in his chest loosened and he took the first full breath since hearing of her dilemma.

"Thank you for the ride, Mr. Jenkins." She waved at the departing wagon, then turned and her eyes rounded. "Roark? Um, Captain Sheridan? Why are you here?"

She acted like she'd only been out for a Sunday drive. Through the buzzing in his head, Roark was dimly aware that Malloy had followed him. He didn't need a witness to what he planned to say to her. He passed the lantern to the deck hand. "Better go back and get your friend. And thanks, Malloy."

"Sure enough, Captain." The man took the lantern, raised his cap as he approached Lissa, and sauntered down the trail, whistling.

She approached, her blue eyes filled with curiosity. "Miss me? Were you starting a search party?"

He grabbed her arms and hauled her to his chest. For one moment, he needed to make sure she was all right. Her hair smelled of tobacco and the fresh night air. Lissa was unhurt. He savored the feel of her curves against him for a second longer, then set her at arm's length. "What the hell were you doing going into the Balers Saloon alone?"

She struggled away from his grasp. "I know how to take care of myself."

"Really? Against a table of disgruntled laborers?"

"Did you send someone to spy on me?" She flung a hand in the direction of town. "Is that what he was doing?"

"He happened to be there and came back to report seeing you, a fellow crew member, in trouble."

"And you were coming to rescue me?"

"Sounded like you might need help." Damn it, she was not going to turn this situation around. Although guilt over banning her from the Queen's tables kept coloring his thoughts. "Do you crave winning so much?"

She folded her arms over her chest and tapped her foot in the dirt. "I have a good reason."

"Cotton pickers in this region are dirt poor. When I think of what could have happened—" He swallowed against the tightness in his throat and paced a few feet up the path. Hands on hips, he gazed at the star-filled sky, trying to rein in his temper. "Dammit, Lissa, what was so important you'd risk your own safety?"

"I needed to win, to build up my stake. I told you on the day I arrived, I expect a chance to win back the Queen of Hearts." Her voice rose. "Don't you understand I owe this to my family?"

He looked over his shoulder, long and hard, at this headstrong woman. Family loyalty was an unknown feeling. What he did know was his chest still burned with the realization of how much this woman meant to him. The footloose gambler who never made commitments had finally fallen for a woman. Too bad she was hell bent on taking away the only home he remembered.

"One chance, one game. In my cabin." He pulled out his pocket watch and glanced at the time. "In thirty minutes, at midnight." Without waiting for an answer, he stomped down the path and across the Queen's deck.

Lissa stood within the smoky glow of the oil lamps lighting the path down to the boat ramp. She fought to control the tears of indignation stinging the backs of her eyes. How dare he treat her like a disobedient child! She'd been gambling long enough to know never to enter a saloon without a derringer in her reticule or a knife strapped to her leg.

She wandered down the path and onto the ramp. Roark had been spitting mad, his face almost purple with anger. Nobody had yelled at her like that since Papa learned all the Springer kids had canoed over the Cuyahoga Falls in Ohio. He'd yelled long and loud about how stupid they'd been to put themselves in danger.

Walking to the exterior stairs, her thoughts went to her father's apology afterwards, and how he'd explained the anger came from worry over their safety. In Papa's book, worry equaled love.

Her hand gripped the railing and her breathing quickened. Was Roark's reason the same?

Impatient to see Roark after her new insight, Lissa arrived at his cabin a few minutes before midnight. She'd dressed in her favorite blue satin gown, the one that highlighted her eyes, and had brushed her hair into long flowing waves. Balancing a small wooden box and her bulging reticule on a hip, she knocked twice.

Roark opened the door and extended his arm into the room, a wide smile on his mouth. "Don't you look beautiful? Please come in."

With a hesitant step, she entered his cabin. Where was his anger? She'd figured on meeting the same scowling, terse man who'd left her on the riverbank and had prepared arguments to get around that man.

The charming gambler she hadn't counted on.

The door closed behind her with a snap. "How shall I address you? Are you Miss Alyssum or Mrs. Tayte tonight?"

"Roark, in the privacy of this room, why can't you call me Liss " He looked every inch like the boat's captain—wearing a black jacket with silk lapels, white shirt with black silk tie, and matching black trousers. Tonight, he obviously intended his manner to be as formal as his attire.

"Demands of the game, you taught me that. Can't get too personal." His gaze dropped to the wooden box with her bulging reticule on top and he reached out his hands. "I'll put this on the table for you. Please make yourself comfortable."

"I'll carry it, Captain Sheridan. Please do call me Mrs. Tayte. After all, that is how we first met." As she stepped toward the table, she purposefully rubbed a shoulder against his chest, pleased when he straightened and hissed in a breath.

At least, his attraction to her hadn't changed.

She scanned the table, looking for the silver tray to see whether he'd left their previous game intact. With a glimmer of disappointment, she spotted the deck of cards sitting in the middle of the table. "I see you have the cards ready."

"No need for delay." He swept his hand toward the table and benches. "Choose your place." He moved to a built-in desk and poured amber liquid into two glasses.

She walked to the far end of the table and set down her box. "To be absolutely clear, what are the stakes tonight?"

"Ah yes, Mrs. Tayte and her rules."

Where had his cynicism come from? "This is an attempt at fairness."

He stood opposite her with feet braced apart. "We both know what I'm wagering. What have you brought to this challenge?"

Was he deliberately baiting her? "Cash totaling $814.23 and

my mother's pearl necklace that has been in the family for three generations."

"That's all you're pitting against an entire boat?" His mouth spread into a cajoling smile but he shook his head. "Not enough. I want more."

"But it's all I have." She thought of her trunk of costumes, but didn't think he'd consider those of much value.

"I want your word you'll never again claim I stole this boat from your family." He chuckled, a dry rasping sound. "Of course, that's only if you lose. If you win, you can say what you like because I won't be around to hear it."

Her stomach churned at his words. Not here? Since coming aboard, she hadn't pictured him in any other setting. She dropped to the bench, suddenly aware of the hurt her accusations had caused. "I promise."

He reached into his jacket, pulled out a folded paper and tossed it on her box. "Here's the owner certificate." He moved to the opposite bench and sat. "If you don't mind, I'll deal." With expert motions, he shuffled the deck and set it in front of her.

She cut it, lifting off about a third of the cards and setting them to the side. The green eyes staring at her could have belonged to a stranger. His gaze gave away none of what he was feeling. How was she going to reach him?

"Since we won't be raising the ante, I call the game is stud poker. Five cards to decide the Queen's future ownership."

Too fast. That meant within a few minutes, their relationship would be forever changed. "Stud, it is. But let's add a bit of interest . . . Captain."

His eyes flashed and he straightened.

For a moment, she remembered their game on the previous night as she assumed Roark did, too. Even with his brows drawn into a frown, he was the handsomest man she knew. His lips were pressed into a tight line, but she remembered the blazing trail his kisses had left on her body. And on her heart.

"What do you mean?"

"For each card dealt, low card has to answer any question asked."

He hesitated for only a moment, then grinned. "Then I'll be learning a lot about you." Lifting his glass, he downed half of the liquid and raised an eyebrow. "Ready for the first card?"

She mirrored his action with her drink and, with the heat in the back of her throat, could only nod her agreement.

He placed an eight of clubs in front of her and a seven of diamonds next to his glass.

She was high card! Her mind reeled with all the things she wanted to know about him. One question could not encompass it all. "Where is your family?"

With a wide grin lighting his face, he threw out his arms in an expansive gesture. "My family is right here on board this boat. Driscoll and Jimmy, Louie and Tug."

"Not fair, you know I meant your real family."

His gaze narrowed. "Ma was buried before I was old enough to remember her. I left Pa in a Colorado mining camp when I was fifteen."

So young! Her heart hurt for the tough times he must have had, but made sure none of what she felt reached her eyes. "Sounds rough."

Roark kept his gaze on her face while he dealt the next cards. Nine of clubs for her and seven of spades for him.

Her question again. She met his gaze and saw the hard challenge there, as if daring her to comment on his admission. "Do you enjoy the traveling life of a gambler?"

"What's not to enjoy? I travel to whatever part of the country I want, stay in fine hotels, and while away my evenings enjoying my favorite pastime."

Two cards snapped against the table planks. Six of clubs for her, ace of hearts for him.

"Finally, my turn." With a gleam in his eyes, he leaned back. "Was there ever a Mr. Tayte?"

Interesting that's the information he wanted. She grabbed a lock of hair and twirled it between her fingers. "Nope. When I struck out on my own, I adopted my grandfather's name. Mama died when I was ten. Papa approved, telling me I was strengthening my connection with her..." She swallowed against the sudden dryness in her mouth. "Besides, the name's more sophisticated than Springer." She grabbed her glass and took a small sip. "Next card."

His hands moved quickly and set out the next pair. Eight of clubs for her and ace of clubs for him.

His expression tightened and he tossed back the rest of his whiskey before speaking. "Tell me why this boat is so important you risked your life."

Unexpected tears burned at the back of her eyes, and she dropped her gaze to the cards. "This boat is the last home I shared with my family. I come back here every summer and winter."

On the table lay their hands.

Hers—five, six, eight, and nine of clubs. A potential flush, with a possibility of a straight flush.

His—a pair of sevens and a pair of aces. Definite two pair, and a potential full house.

Either hand could win with the seven of clubs. The reality was they both couldn't.

She raised her gaze to his and searched his face. A face that had become so special. A face she loved and one she didn't want to disappear from her life. She covered his hand to keep him from dealing the next cards. "Don't."

Still holding his hand, she skirted the end of the table and wiggled herself into his lap. "I don't want to know what the cards decide." She kissed his stiff jaw and wrapped her arms around his neck.

He reared back his head, his brows drawn low. "Is this a trick? We need to finish this game."

She stretched to kiss his mouth after every few words. "No, Roark. I want us to decide our future."

He wrapped an arm around her back and pulled her close. "Tell me what you mean."

"First, put down the cards." Her gaze challenged him. "Better yet, swipe your arm across the layout." When he didn't move, she cupped his cheeks with her hands and attacked his mouth with a ferocious kiss, using the love for him she'd discovered in the midst of his tirade on the riverbank. She didn't stop her assault until she felt both of his hands roaming her back and grabbing fistfuls of her hair.

She broke away and leaned her forehead against his. "I love you, Roark Sheridan. And I've figured out a way for both of us to have what we want."

His lips nuzzled the tender spot along her neck. "All the accusations are gone?"

"They disappeared at the table in Balers Saloon, when those men accused me of the same thing I'd said to you. They weren't prepared to lose but played the game anyway." As she spoke the words, a knot of tension released in her chest. That had needed to be said.

His lips found hers and his tongue invaded in long, sweeping strokes. She grabbed his shoulders and let herself float in the warmth of his affection.

With a surge, he stood, the bench clattered behind him, and he moved toward the bedroom, holding her high in his arms.

"But you haven't even heard my plan."

"I can hear it all while we're getting naked." With a kick, the door crashed open and he crossed to the bed. "Anything longer will have to wait. Until after." He kissed her hard, then dropped her the final foot to the mattress. "Besides, I've already heard the best part—you love me." He stepped back and pulled off his jacket, then started on the buttons of his shirt.

She stared at his hands and the skin revealed as his hands moved.

A chuckle escaped his lips. "Better start talking, Lissa. And definitely start shedding those clothes."

Scrambling to sit, she reached for her slippers and yanked them off. "I figure we hire my family to run the boat." She pulled at the buttons down the back of her dress, trying to watch him as his shirt sailed across the room and he reached for his belt buckle. "Papa's great with promotion and Forrest is a certified pilot."

"Stand and turn around. I'll undo those buttons."

He stood before her, his trousers half open, the fly bulging.

She sucked in a breath at the delights she knew were coming, then spun around. While he worked on the buttons, she leaned over to reach under her skirts and untie her petticoats. When her dress slid down her arms, she felt his hands at her waist, tossing her to the mattress. She landed on her hands and knees.

He pulled her dress free from her body and threw it over his shoulder. "Okay, so I couldn't wait for you to be naked."

She looked over her shoulder and started to turn over to lie on her back, ready for him.

"Stay like that." His hands clamped on her hips and he climbed onto the mattress behind her. Heat from his body flowed against her skin. When he leaned forward, running his hand from her hip to her breast, his stiff cock tickled the back of her leg.

With each pinch, tweak, and pull of his fingers, Lissa's breathing increased and cream flowed in her pussy. She'd never made love in this position but his commanding attitude aroused her senses.

"Spread your legs."

She braced her hands and moved her knees apart. His fingers traced from her hip to her mons, delving into her juicy folds and rubbing over her swollen nub.

"Glad you're wet because I can't wait." With the final word, he entered her and stroked his cock deep inside. One arm circled her waist and the other held her hip in place as he pumped with long, slow strokes.

"Oh!" Lissa arched her back and circled her hips, moving herself against his girth. Deep in her belly, the spiraling started. She pushed her hips back against his groin, wanting to feel every inch of his masculine shaft.

His strokes increased and his hands were everywhere, caressing her hips, her stomach, her breasts. Her skin tingled with wild sensations, her channel throbbed from his invasion, and she cried out her satisfaction, elbows wobbling from the exertion.

Roark held both of her hips and pounded with several more strokes until a groan rasped from his throat and his seed emptied deep inside her. He leaned over her back, then eased them both sideways onto the bed, maintaining their connection.

Still gasping for air, she cuddled against him and crossed her arms over where his hugged her stomach. This was blissful and she wanted to stay in this bed forever. Or at least with the man who made her feel this wanted. "I didn't hear an answer about my plan. Do you like the idea?"

His lips moved along her shoulder with lingering kisses. "You make me crazy at times, but, Lissa, I can't imagine living on this boat without you. I don't have much experience with family, so I can't judge about them being here."

This conversation was too important to be having without seeing his beloved face. As much as she hated changing positions, she scooted away from the cocoon of his hard thighs and turned to face him.

She ran a finger over the wrinkles in his forehead and trailed her fingers through his hair. "Don't you see? That's the great part. With my family on board and managing the boat operations, we can leave anytime we want. We'll visit any city that interests us, and we'll find the best places for playing poker. You won't be giving up the time you used to have for your favorite pastime."

His hand brushed her hair away from her moist cheek. "Or I can stay right here and concentrate on my new favorite game."

"Something that's better than poker?"

"I think so." His green gaze turned emerald and his words were husky. "I'll be spending time with my new Queen of Hearts."

TOUCH OF MAGIC

MYLA JACKSON

1

1872, Abilene, Kansas

Catarina Novak settled the heavy purple cloak around her bare shoulders, pulling the tie-string away from choking her throat. Lightning danced in a circle, held tightly by her assistant Nora Jane Sims. The cloak spooked the solid white Arabian stallion she'd inherited from her mentor, The Amazing Mancini.

"Are you sure you want to do this?" Nora Jane fought to hold the stallion steady.

Leaving their bags at the hotel in Abilene, they'd ridden out early that morning before sunrise to prepare for her introduction to potential theater patrons. Now, half a mile east of the city, they prepared for the grand entrance to the Golden Garter Theater and Saloon. This would be Catarina's first magic show without Marco Mancini. The old magician had insisted she was ready, telling her she was as good, or better, than he had ever been.

That had been a few minutes before he'd passed on due to a nasty bout of pneumonia.

Cat wrinkled her nose at the smell of the stockyards, reminding herself that horrendous stench was the smell of money. The town was teeming with cowboys, merchants, and cattle. There should be a good crowd at the theater tonight. Especially if she made a spectacular display and enticed more people to come to the show.

"I have to do this. We need the money to pay our hotel bill and get us to Chicago." Catarina settled the cape over the hindquarters of the stallion and reached out. "Let me have the reins."

"I don't know about this. I can get a job washing clothes or something. You don't have to do this, you know. Lightning only likes to be ridden by men," Nora Jane said.

"Nonsense, as a laundress, you'd never save enough money to get to Chicago and your sister. We have to do this. Besides, Lightning won't know the difference between me and Mr. Mancini, other than the side saddle."

Nora Jane shook her bright copper curls. "You don't weigh no more than a tumbleweed, Ms. Catarina, and that horse knows it. Why he could throw you so fast you wouldn't know what hit you until you woke up dead."

"I'm an excellent rider. Don't worry about me, nothing bad will happen." She hoped her streak of bad luck and little accidents didn't jinx this show. She and Nora Jane needed the money to stay alive and move farther east. "Now, I have to get or I'll miss the afternoon crowd in town."

"I don't know." She handed Cat the reins but held the strap by the horse's mouth. "Lightning ain't likin' that cape, none."

"He'll have to get used to it." She glanced down at her black satin dress sprinkled with painted silver stars and smiled at the gift Signor Mancini had bestowed on her before their last show together. Her vision blurred. If not for Mancini, she didn't know what might have become of her. He'd taken her in as a young widow when her husband died of pneumonia on their way out West.

She didn't have time to ruminate on the past. Her future awaited. "Let go, Nora Jane. I have a job to do."

The redhead stepped back. "Break a leg, Ms. Catarina."

"Thanks." She took a deep breath, turned her mount in the direction of the Golden Garter, and sank her heels into the horse's flanks.

Trace Adams trudged across the busy Main Street of Abilene, Kansas, bone-weary and covered in dust and grime from months on a cattle drive from Amarillo, Texas.

"Can't wait for that drink you promised me a hundred miles ago." Jay Tyler clapped his hat against his thigh, sending up a puff of dust.

"And you'll get that drink. You and the boys worked hard."

The excitement of reaching Kansas was more over the prospect of a bath and a new set of boots and clothing than from actually delivering the animals. Sure, he was glad to get his herd to the stockyards and he'd be even happier to get paid for the six-hundred head of longhorns he'd driven over hundreds of miles with minimal losses. But what he wanted most was a clean body, a soft bed, and twenty-four hours of uninterrupted sleep.

"Well, since we're finally in Abilene, have you made up your mind?" Jay asked.

Trace took a deep breath and let it out slowly. "Nope."

"You can't keep Martha hanging." Jay pounded him hard on the back. "You need to shit or get out of the outhouse."

"I know. It's just that we've known each other all our lives. I've never thought of marrying anyone else, but still."

"What you need is to sow a few wild oats. Ride a few other fillies before you settle on the mare of your dreams."

"I'm not buying a horse." No, Martha wasn't a horse, but

Trace felt like a horse trader being stuck with one horse to choose from and he was chafing at the prospect. Not that Martha wasn't a good horse—woman. She was one of the best, a fine solid woman with everything a man wanted and needed for a ranch wife. When he'd left, she'd insisted on a parting kiss—their first. A chaste kiss for a proper woman.

For the two months he'd been on the trail, he'd thought about that kiss and how he'd felt nothing—no spark, no connection, no stirring in his loins.

Nothing.

Perhaps Jay was right. He needed a comparison, a chance to experience other women before he settled with Martha. The catch being, he was more or less promised to Martha. Trying out other women would be like cheating on his future wife. He respected Martha too much to cheat on her. No, he had to make this decision without perusing the corral of other fillies.

When he and Jay were only halfway across the thoroughfare, a loud whooping sound caught Trace's attention. Men gathered on the broad boardwalks, every one of them facing to the east. A shout went up as a cloud of dust blew their way.

"What the hell?" Jay turned to face Main Street.

Too tired to really care, Trace made it across to the front entrance of the Golden Garter Saloon, bent on ordering a whiskey before tackling the job of cleaning up.

As he set his foot on the boardwalk, he turned to Jay.

"Whoa, will ya look at her." Jay's mouth hung open, his eyes wide.

Emerging from the cloud of dust was a solid white horse racing through the street at breakneck speed. Perched in a sidesaddle on its back was a beautiful woman with a long, flowing black mane of hair, as beautiful and wild as the horse she rode. She wore a star-sprinkled black dress and a purple cape that appeared to be choking the living daylights out of her. By the way she leaned back on the reins, she was nowhere near in control of the rampaging horse and if she didn't slow the horse soon, someone was likely to get hurt.

"Damn, that horse is a runaway," Jay said.

Without thinking, Trace leaped off the boardwalk onto the hard-packed dirt of Main Street and directly into the path of the charging horse. When he didn't move out of the horse's way, the horse planted its hooves in the dirt, skidding to a halt. Then he reared, his rider hanging on to the saddle horn, her eyes wide, her long black hair swirling around her face.

Trace reached out, captured the reins and brought the horse back to the ground.

When all four of the horse's hooves were firmly planted on the ground, the woman grasped the string around her throat and pulled it away from her skin, a thin red line marring her pearly-white throat. She gulped air for several seconds and then turned a brilliant smile toward the men lining the boardwalk. With a wide and graceful sweep of her arm, she shouted, "Gentlemen, let me introduce myself." In a voice only Trace could hear, she said, "Step away from the horse."

"Are you crazy?" He held the horse's nose down. The animal's ears still lay back against its head and the whites of its eyes shown. If he let go, the woman would be flat on her butt in the dirt. But then maybe she needed that lesson.

"I need the room for my entrance," she hissed for his ears only. For the crowd, she stood in the single stirrup and waved her hand again. "I am The Amazing Catarina, magician and mesmerist extraordinaire!" After she said the words, she gathered her skirts and jumped from the horse's back. When she hit the ground, she flung her heavy purple cape in a sweeping arc.

The cape flapped in Trace's face. The Arabian stallion reared again, lifting Trace from the ground. Holding on with all his might, he fought to calm the horse.

The woman continued. "Join me at the Golden Garter tonight at eight for daring feats of magical wonder and delight."

When she waved her cape again, the horse leaped forward, taking Trace with him, dragging him down the length of Main Street. All he could hear over the thundering hooves, so dangerously close to his own feet, was the woman saying, "See? I can make a cowboy disappear with just the wave of my cape."

Laughter followed him to the end of the street and out onto the prairie.

2

"It's a full crowd, Ms. Catarina." Nora Jane peered through a gap in the heavy black curtain covering the theater stage. She wore the royal-blue corset and short skirt Catarina had worn for the years she'd played magician's assistant to The Amazing Mancini. Nora Jane made the corset appear almost obscene. Much of her heavy bosoms spilled over the top into the thin white muslin of her chemise.

The matching royal blue of the tulle dancer's skirt reached down to mid calf. Her pretty little ankles ended in a shiny pair of button-up black boots. Nora Jane drew a crowd all her own, with her bright copper curls piled up on her head and cascading down her back in loose ringlets.

Nora Jane was another one of Marco Mancini's strays he'd accrued on his travels around the countryside with his magic act. He'd insisted he needed beautiful assistants to help him with his routines. Nora Jane fit that description, until she opened her mouth and demonstrated her lack of education and couth. But Mancini had found her beaten and abused in the alley of a whorehouse and had insisted she work for him.

"Let's hope they like us well enough to come back for the next three nights we're here." Catarina tucked a loose curl behind her ear and leaned over Nora Jane's shoulder. "Let me see."

Just as the assistant attested, the room was full to standing room only. Mostly men with a few of the saloon girls draped over their laps; raucous laughter echoed off the high-beamed ceiling. Most of the men were cowboys, in from riding herd over cattle to bring them to market. Having been on the trail for weeks, they were ready for a little fun.

Catarina hoped the fun didn't include destroying the theater or anyone in it. She also hoped all six-shooters were checked at the door. She and Mancini had performed in a saloon where one particularly liquored-up young cowboy started shooting. One man ended up with a finger missing.

A hole remained to this day in Mancini's magic top hat. The thought of which had Catarina hurrying to the table draped in black fabric to inventory the items she'd use that night in her magic show.

"I suppose your grand entrance impressed the men so much they spread the word." Nora Jane joined her and bent to test the latch on the doves' cage.

Of all the men who came to see her show, Catarina hoped one in particular showed. The man who'd more or less saved her life during the disaster of an entrance earlier that day.

She hadn't seen the gruff-looking man with the shaggy beard in the audience, although there'd been plenty of shaggy men out there. Given a chance, she'd like to apologize for her behavior and that of her horse. The saloon owner had ushered her inside before the crowd converged on her, otherwise she would have stood out front until the man returned with her horse.

Maybe it was better to wait. Her cavalier behavior might have angered him. She'd asked the saloon owner, Martin Sheridan, to be sure to allow him and a guest to attend the show free for rescuing her from the runaway horse.

Martin poked his gray head through the curtain. "You ready?"

Catarina's nerves jumped and she shot a glance at Nora Jane.

When the older woman moved across the stage to the curtain, Catarina nodded at Mr. Sheridan. "Yes, if you'd be so good as to announce us as I instructed and then open the curtain, I'd be forever grateful."

"Of course." The man ducked out of the curtain. "Ladieeezzz and Gentlemen. Tonight for your viewing pleasure, I present to you . . . The one . . . the only . . . The Amaaazzzing Catarina!"

Catarina nodded to Nora Jane, who grabbed one side of the curtain while Martin grabbed the other and they walked the curtain to the sides.

As the curtain opened, Catarina's smile spread across her lips and she stared out at the audience, willing the butterflies to give up the attack in her belly. As a calming routine, Mancini had taught her to make it a point to think of each member of the crowd sitting there in their undergarments in order to take the edge off her nerves.

As she panned the room of mostly men, she fought back a chuckle. The thought of the rotund gentleman with his trousers hanging low on his hips wearing nothing but his underwear had her resisting the giggles in no time. She was beginning to feel good about her impending performance when her glance caught the blue-eyed glare of a gorgeous sun-kissed blond Adonis sitting dead center in the front row with his arms crossed over his chest. And a very broad chest he had, straining beneath his blue cotton shirt.

Catarina's gut tightened, but not from nerves. She'd gone a long time since taking a lover—one of the advantages of being a widow. Her trick of imagining him in his underwear had her body flushing all over.

How could someone that blessed have such a sour expression? Wouldn't she enjoying kissing it away, if she had the time or the opportunity?

Catarina launched into her routine. One after the other, she revealed amazing acts of illusion. But Adonis sat with his arms crossed and his brows furrowed over his tanned forehead. Pulling Oscar the Rabbit out of the top hat didn't move him. Card tricks, producing silk flowers from thin air and doves from beneath a handkerchief . . . nothing softened his acerbic stare.

By the time she was halfway through the show, she could feel perspiration popping out on her lower lip. Why couldn't this man show some sign of enjoyment or surprise?

The rest of the crowd laughed and clapped, cheering her on. But not Adonis, who sat as bold as he pleased in the front row.

It became an obsession for Catarina to make him smile or look at her in wonder. An obsession nearing mania.

When pulling a long string of silk scarves from between her bosoms only got a quirk of his eyebrow, Catarina had decided enough was enough.

"And for my next demonstration," Catarina called out to the men in the room. "I'll need a volunteer." This was a trick that never failed to awe the masses.

Half of the men in the theater shouted at once, "Me!"

If her next ploy didn't get so much as a smile from the man, Catarina would give up and find a job as a seamstress or something equally mundane.

She chose a thin, impressionable young man standing near the stage. He took the steps two at a time, skidding to a halt amidst laughter and raunchy jibes from the men not chosen. He stood with a goofy grin and red face in front of Catarina.

She gave him a gentle smile. "What is your name?"

"Luke."

"Luke, have you ever been in front of a crowd before?"

"No, ma'am."

"Do I make you nervous, Luke?"

"Yes, ma'am." The poor man was shaking and looked ready to run.

A grizzly old man close to the stage called out, "Hey, Luke, you ever been with a woman?"

When Luke flushed beet red, the crowd roared with laughter.

Catarina assumed her best schoolmarm look and stared out at the audience, avoiding looking at Mr. I-am-too-good-for-this-Tomfoolery Adonis. "I'll need complete silence for this next act."

The laughter died down with an occasional snort or chuckle trailing off into the silence.

Lifting a gold watch on a chain, Catarina schooled her voice into a lulling cadence. "Luke, keep your eyes on the watch and relax. I'm not going to hurt you. Just watch the shiny gold watch tip back and forth . . . back and forth." While she talked, the room grew hushed.

As instructed, Luke concentrated on the watch.

"The only thing in your world is the watch. Nothing besides the watch. Back and forth. You'll feel yourself getting sleepy as it tips back and forth. Back and forth."

Luke's eyelids dipped once . . . twice . . . and closed as he stood straight as an arrow in the middle of the stage.

Cat turned to the audience and smiled, the strain making her cheek muscles ache. She'd be damned if she let this man off the stage without a little more than he came onto it with.

For the benefit of the audience and Luke she spoke louder. "Luke, when you hear the word 'woman,' you will crow like a rooster. When you hear me clap three times, you will no longer crow like a rooster. Do you understand?"

With his eyes still closed, Luke swayed. "Yes, ma'am."

She leaned close to him and whispered, "Luke, you're a handsome man. You will be confident, but gentle, with women from now on. When I clap once, you will no longer crow when you hear the word 'woman.'" She raised her voice for the audience. "Wake up, Luke."

Luke's eyes opened and he stared around at the theater, blinking several times. "Did you do the trick? Did I miss it?"

"I did the trick and no, you didn't miss it."

Luke frowned. "What was it?"

"First, we'll need a woman." Catarina held her breath. She'd performed hypnosis on many occasions and Signor Mancini had said she was a master. But there was always someone immune to her skills and she was afraid the one immune would turn up in front of a large audience.

When Luke opened his mouth and crowed like a strutting cock, Catarina could have squealed her delight. The entire room roared with laughter. When the laughter quieted, Cat clapped three times and Luke stopped crowing.

Her gaze darted to the Greek god sitting in the front row. His scowl was still firmly in place but he was standing, his head and shoulders rising above the stage. "This is all a bunch of bull. You planted young Luke in the audience. He's just playing along with your trickery."

The room grew still.

"What trick?" Luke's confusion appeared genuine to Catarina. Why would he fake it?

"Only a gifted mesmerist can perform this feat." Catarina stared into Adonis's eyes, daring him to disagree.

The Adonis snorted. "You're not a mesmerist, you're just a woman."

On cue, Luke crowed again and continued crowing until Cat clapped three times.

The gentleman standing in the front row planted his hands on his hips. "He's faking it. Luke, you crowed because she told you to, didn't you?"

"Crowed?" Luke stared at Catarina. "Did I crow?"

Men laughed out loud, shaking the walls with the volume.

"I'm not swallowing this. It's all a hoax."

She'd seen hecklers in every crowd, but this man went too far. "Sir, would you care to put your money where your mouth is?"

A nasty twist marred his sensuous lips. "I'll only expose you for the fake you are."

Catarina forced her smile wider when all she wanted to do was throw something at the man's handsome, smirking face. "Try me."

His gaze traveled from the hem of her black dress up to the rounded curves of her breasts rising above the low-cut gown. "Now, that's something I'd go for."

"Then please join me on the stage." Catarina clapped once to release Luke from the suggestion of crowing. "Luke, thank you for your cooperation."

"But I didn't crow, did I?" Luke's face scrunched in a worried frown.

"Yes, Luke, you did. And quite well, I might add." Catarina nodded at Nora Jane, who hooked her elbow through Luke's and led him to the steps.

Adonis still stood with his hands on his hips, his eyes narrowed to slits.

Catarina planted her fists on her own hips, pushing the cape back with her elbows. "Well, sir? Are you afraid I'll make a fool of you?"

"Ha!" The man smiled for the first time since she'd seen him, the gesture knocking her back a step. "You'd have to go a long way to make a fool of Trace Adams."

So his name was Trace Adams. Catarina liked that she had a name to the pretty face. "Well? What will it be?"

The crowd rumbled and someone called out. "Do it, Adams! Show us you ain't afraid of no girl."

Trace turned and glared at the offender. "I'll do it, but not because of your big mouth. I'll do it to prove . . ." He turned to face her. "That she's a fake."

Catarina's chest tightened. If she failed in this one event, the rest of the week would be a shambles. No one would come to see her magic show, she and Nora Jane would be tossed out as laughingstocks, and they'd never get Nora Jane back to St. Louis.

On the other hand, she couldn't back down from this challenge and she'd be damned if she let him walk away without paying for making the crowd doubt her abilities. "Step right up, sir." *Let the humiliation begin.*

When the sun-kissed cowboy stepped onto the stage, Catarina's breath caught in her throat. He was even more overwhelming up close than as a face in the crowd. The closer he moved, the more breathless she grew. Physically magnificent in size and breadth, he was a man worthy of bedding. A long silence stretched as she struggled to slow the volcanic rush of lust through her system.

As he stared down at her, a smile played on his lips.

Catarina had the unsettling feeling this man could read her sinful thoughts.

"Cat got your tongue?" He circled her like a lion teasing his prey. The rippling muscles stretched his shirt taut over his chest, emphasizing every bulge.

The effect had Catarina panting and unable to form a single intelligible comment for five seconds.

Trace leaned close to her ear. "Are you afraid, little witch?"

Nora Jane, a frantic look on her face, stepped to center stage. "And now, The Amazing Catarina will mesmerize this doubting cowboy and make him perform her bidding."

"Like she made him disappear this afternoon?" The man who'd been sitting next to Trace shouted above the rising cacophony of male voices.

As the crowd erupted in loud guffaws of laughter, the cowboy's ruddy complexion reddened.

Could this be the man who'd saved her from her runaway horse today? The man she'd promised to thank? "You?"

His mouth twisted into a smirk. "That's right, me."

Her face heated and she looked at him anew. "But the man who stopped my horse was much . . . hairier."

The handsome cowboy rubbed a hand across his cheek. "The magic of a barber's razor." His hand dropped to his side and his eyes narrowed.

Because their words were spoken in soft murmurs, the crowd couldn't hear them.

"What are you waiting for?" shouted the rotund gentleman by the bar. Answering shouts erupted, filling the theater to the rafters.

"Yes, what are you waiting for?" Trace turned to the crowd. "I think The Amazing Catarina is afraid."

"I am not." Anger quickly outweighed shame for her poor behavior earlier. This man could ruin her chances of getting Nora Jane to Chicago and Cat's dream of settling down to a respectable position. "If you'll step this way, I'll amaze even you." *Just give me half a chance and I'll show you.* She could think of a lot of ways to show him how good she was. Her nipples tightened and her belly ached at some of her more interesting ideas. And the best part was, he'd never know he'd done it and she'd get all the satisfaction. All it took was a whispered suggestion while the man was mesmerized and she'd have him at her beck and call.

Cat could almost feel the devil's horns sprouting from the top of her head.

Trace opened his eyes to the roar of laughter filling the theater. "What? Why are they laughing?" Anger and frustration shot like a firecracker through his head. He couldn't remember falling asleep while on stage with the witch, Catarina. He glared at her. "What did you do to me?"

A secret smile curled her lips, the same one he remembered seeing on the fat tomcat who lurked around the barn. The look he'd gotten when he'd swallowed a fat mouse he'd played with first. The smile twinkled in Catarina's eyes and she laughed out loud.

"You howled like a coyote, Trace," Jay shouted from his seat on the front row, slapping his thigh with his hat, tears streaming from his eyes. "Funniest thing I ever saw."

"I did not," Trace bristled.

As one, the entire crowd yelled, "Yes, you did!"

Catarina turned to him, her lips twitching as if she were fighting her own mirth. "Thank you, sir, for being such a good sport about everything." Then in a soft whisper he could barely make out, she said, "I'll be seeing you later."

Trace shook his head. That must be wrong. Why would she say that when he had no intentions of seeing her later, or any other time? "What did you say?"

A smile lit her face and she turned to the crowd. "Please thank our volunteer for his participation in our little experiment."

Applause filled the room, the noise so loud Trace's ears rang. Still angry and confused, he decided leaving was his best option at this point. He should never have come to torment the witch who'd made a laughingstock out of him. Twice, now. He knew when he'd been bested, and he'd be damned if he let it get to him. A room with a nice soft bed awaited his tired body. He had better things to do and sleep was number one on his list.

After one more parting glare at the smiling Catarina, Trace stomped down the steps and past Jay, who didn't bother to get up and follow him.

To hell with him and to hell with The Amazing Catarina. He forced himself not to look back at the wild-haired beauty in the black dress. She was like a gypsy weaving spells and Trace didn't believe in magic.

As he moved through the tables, men pounded him on the back. "Never seen a man who could howl like that, unless he was bedding a wild woman."

Yeah, he'd like to bed Catarina. That would show her whose magic was strongest. If he didn't have Martha to think of, he might just do that.

3

Catarina paced across the floor in her night clothes, her dressing gown cinched tightly beneath her breasts. Would he come? Did the suggestion work? Based on the circles that had been beneath Trace's eyes, he'd been tired and he'd succumbed to the trance much sooner than she'd expected. Had he faked it?

Nora Jane had helped her out of her star-sprinkled gown and into her night clothes before she'd left to talk to a gentleman she'd met after the performance. She'd said she'd be gone most of the night and Catarina shouldn't wait up for her.

Which meant she had the room all to herself. Well, at least until midnight, when the Greek god of a cowboy showed up at her door as she'd 'suggested,' ready to please her in any way she wanted.

Her body ached for the stroke of midnight at the same time her guilty conscience nudged at her gut. She shouldn't have used her gifts to take advantage of an unsuspecting cowboy, even though the cowboy tried to ruin her show.

Her fingers twisted together as she thought about what

Mancini would say if he knew she'd abused her position. He'd probably fire her on the spot. But Mancini wasn't there to pass judgment. She had only her sense of fairness as her guide, and Trace Adams hadn't been too fair with her when he'd publicly mocked her during her performance.

Her shoulders pushed back and she stood to her full height of five-feet three inches. Besides, Nora Jane was probably flat on her back with her beau by now. Why shouldn't Cat be allowed a bit of relief from months of abstinence? She was a widow, after all. And how long had it been since she'd taken a man to her bed? Her shoulders sagged. Not since Rupert's shy attempts in the hotels they'd stayed in at the train stops on their way west to California.

Dear, sweet Rupert. He'd offered to take her to California and give her a home, maybe children, God willing. But Rupert hadn't made it to California. He'd taken ill along the way and died. If not for The Amazing Mancini, she didn't know what would have happened to her. She'd probably have ended up like Nora Jane, working in a whorehouse the rest of her life.

History tended to repeat itself. She'd gone from one man's protection to another, only for both men to die. Catarina wondered whether she was cursed.

A soft tapping on the door made her jump. All her thoughts of the past had made her forget she'd tricked a man into coming to her room. Should she open the door and let him in to play out her wicked fantasy? Or should she ignore him and he'd go away, none the worse for her little prank?

Another knock on the door made her jump again. Cat reached for the door, fully intending to end the hypnosis and send him on his way back to his room.

When she opened the door and stood face to face with the handsome cowboy whose countenance no longer bore the frown of earlier that evening, all her resolve melted away.

"C-come in." She held the door wide and he stepped through. The walls pulled in around her as his broad shoulders filled the small space.

"I'm here to please you," Trace said, a smile curling the edges of his lips—full, sensuous lips.

The sight of his lips up close and the sound of his voice warmed her insides to a toasty inferno. Cat said the first thing that came to mind. "Kiss me."

He didn't plant a chaste kiss on her quivering lips. No. He gathered her in his arms and smoothed his hands through her hair until he cupped the back of her head. With the grace of a panther, he leaned in and claimed her lips. The firm pressure eroded her last shreds of resistance.

Catarina clung to him, certain her knees would not withstand the assault on her senses. Weak with desire, she returned his kiss, opening her mouth to his tongue.

Not until Trace lifted his head did Catarina realize the kiss had ended. With her body ablaze to the very tips of her extremities, she couldn't let go. Her fingers dug into his arms and she leaned her forehead against his chest, forcing air into her lungs.

This was wrong. To trick a man into pleasuring her was wrong. But how could something that felt so right be wrong? She stared up into Trace's mesmerized gaze. What would it be like to have him look down at her with the same amount of craving she had for him?

As if she'd willed him so, his face softened and he gathered her closer. "Are you pleased? Do you want more?"

"Yes." Where was her reserve as a lady, her resolve to undo this wrong? Shattered and forgotten as she dissolved against him, her heart hammering against her chest, her fingers aching to ease across naked skin.

She reached between them and released the buttons of his blue cotton shirt, revealing a magnificent tanned chest, sprinkled with tight blond curls.

Shoving aside the fabric, she leaned forward to kiss a small brown nipple. He tasted fresh, of soap, leather, and the prairie. Catarina inhaled and laid her head against his chest, the sound of his heart beating against her ear.

"Do you always wear so many clothes to bed?" He eased the robe from her shoulders.

"Yes." She didn't have a man to share her bed; otherwise, she'd sleep in the nude. In the heat of the summer, she preferred as few clothes as possible, even leaving off the required undergarments of a lady. She straightened her arms and the robe drifted to the floor in a pool around her feet.

Standing in her thin cotton nightgown, she felt about as desirable as a little girl in her daddy's home. Until she stared up into Trace's eyes.

The dazed expression was gone as he stared at her throat. His hands slid around her neck, his thumb rubbing the sensitive area beneath her ears. Then his fingers reached to untie the string holding her nightgown together. Gently, he tugged the bow until the ribbon loosened and fell away, leaving the neckline of her gown gaping open, her shoulders and the tops of her breasts exposed to the night air and his roving gaze.

Fire leaped in his blue gray eyes. Rough hands skimmed the fabric across her shoulders, pushing the nightgown down her arms. All that kept the gown from falling was the swell of her breasts. A gentle tug sent it to the floor and she stood naked in front of the handsome stranger.

Modesty decreed she should cover herself, but her body reveled in her naked glory, with a man's gaze skimming over her peaked nipples and lower. She felt beautiful, desirable and wanton.

"You're a beautiful woman, Catarina." His voice stroked her skin with warmth.

Catarina practically purred, her core creaming in response to his praise. Then she was shoving the straps of his suspenders over his shoulders and pushing his shirt from his back, anxious to see more of this glorious man.

His hands stopped her fevered fingers and a low rumbling chuckle echoed from his chest.

For a moment, Catarina thought he might not be under her hypnosis. She stared up into his face. Had he been awake during the performance and only played along to get what he wanted of her?

The tender lines around his mouth were so foreign to the anger of earlier that he couldn't be faking it. He'd been completely livid on stage before and after the performance. Dark circles beneath his eyes indicated a tired man—a man susceptible to the power of hypnotic suggestion.

A twinge of guilt nudged at Cat. She'd taken advantage of him when he wasn't at full strength. A glimpse of sinfully sinuous shoulders made her want to weep with the struggle over her conscience. Her hand smoothed across his chest, feeling the steel beneath the skin, and she couldn't resist pressing her taut breasts to his chest.

A fire lit within, and she couldn't douse the flames with any less than a full round of lovemaking with this man. Perhaps then she'd slake her rising lust and get him out of her system. She unbuttoned the fly of his pants and peeled away the stiff fabric, revealing the blatant lack of long underwear and a cock straining for release.

Walking Trace backward, she sat him in the only chair available in the room and bent to remove his boots. Leaning over his feet, she tugged at the stiff leather of new boots.

He chuckled. "In a hurry?" With one toe on the back of his heel, he helped her remove the boot and reached out to fondle her breast in the process.

Cat's breath caught in her throat and she struggled to pull the boot from his other foot. If she didn't get him completely naked soon, she'd come apart. With the removal of the second boot, she straightened, a glimmer of perspiration rising from her skin even the cool night air couldn't contain.

Trace sat in the chair, still clad in his trousers, his cock peeking out from the open fly, a smile curving his lips. "What's next?"

Starting to weary of telling him what to do, Cat planted her hands on her naked hips. "If you do not know what to do, maybe you should go back to your own room."

He stood. "Whatever pleases you." Then he turned to the door.

All the air flew from her lungs and Cat threw herself in front of the door. "I didn't mean for you to leave."

His brow wrinkled. "No?"

"No." She grabbed his hand and led him to the bed. "Don't you know what to do with a woman without me telling you?"

"Of course."

She threw her hands in the air. "Then do it."

Trace grinned and scooped her into his arms.

Cat laughed out loud, relief washing over her fevered body. She'd thought for a moment she'd lost him. That he'd walk right out of her room, leaving her in a dither of aching need.

Instead, he buried his face in her breasts, laving attention one at a time on the hardened beads of her nipples. "Is this what you want?"

"Oh, yes!" She wound her arms around his neck, pulling him closer, loving the feel of being held aloft by a powerful man. "More, please."

"Whatever the lady wants." He laid her on the counterpane and stood back, slipping out of the last bit of his clothing. When he stood naked in the light from the oil lamp, Catarina counted her blessings—especially the hard, thick, incredibly sexy one in the middle.

Then he climbed into the bed with her, lying next to her, skin-to-skin. One hand trailed a line over her collarbone and down to follow the full curve of her breast. "Do you like that?"

"Ummm, yes."

At the tip of her nipple, he paused to tweak the beaded round nub, leaning forward to take it into his mouth, sucking hard on it.

Catarina arched her back, her fingers lacing behind Trace's neck to pull him closer. Her core burned, throbbing to be filled and stroked in the most primal way a man can touch a woman. Her knees fell to the side and she pushed his head downward.

His fingers moved lower, followed by his lips and teeth as he licked and nibbled a path downward. When his tongue dipped into her bellybutton, his fingers found her mound of curly hair. He parted her folds, deftly sliding his hand over the sweet little nubbin of her desire.

An igniting sensation had her planting her heels in the feather mattress and lifting her bottom off the bed—anything to get closer to his magic touch.

Catarina had never had a man touch her in this intimate fashion. Even her husband had made love to her in the only way she knew—a few kisses, hands on her breasts, and then his cock sliding inside her. A few short minutes later, it was over.

This was simply marvelous, the best feeling she'd ever had. How could it possibly get better than this?

Then Trace slid lower off the bed, dragging her arse to the edge. Down on his knees, he draped her legs over his shoulders, his lips hovering above that spot he'd strummed with the tips of his fingers.

"What are you doing?" Cat's eyes widened and she looked down at the top of his sandy blond head. Surely he wasn't going to kiss her there. What manner of lovemaking was this? Shouldn't she be disgusted or repulsed by such an attempt? Cat opened her mouth to tell him to stop.

Before her words left her mouth, Trace's tongue flicked her clitoris and all thoughts exploded in a kaleidoscope of powerful awareness.

The only sound out of Cat's mouth was her shout of pleasure. "Oh, my!"

He lapped at her pussy, allowing her to return to earth, but without extinguishing any fires. Then he moved back up to the center of her clit, teasing it with his warm, moist tongue.

As he flicked the tip, the tension built until her body peaked, her insides pitching into that bright orgasmic chasm, where pain was pleasure and pleasure was so powerful it hurt.

When Cat finally drifted back to Earth, she lay spent and boneless against the bedding, drawing in ragged breaths to refill her starved lungs. "Trace," she breathed. "That was incredible." Her body was spent, completely devoid of any ability to move.

"I know." The smile he gave her almost had her believing he wasn't hypnotized.

Wasn't he? Cat stared down into dancing blue eyes. "What do you mean, you 'know'?"

He climbed up her body until his erection lay between her legs, nudging the opening to her channel. The velvety head of his cock pressed into her core. "I know how to please a woman."

"You do, don't you?" Her gaze raked across his chest, devouring his handsome physique. "Show me more."

"Anything to please you, witch."

"Call me Cat."

"As you wish, Pussy Cat." His lips descended, claiming hers in a soul-defining kiss that stole Cat's breath away. The taste of her on his lips only added to the experience. No one had ever done to her what Trace had. She'd be absolutely ruined for any other man.

While she'd thought her muscles wouldn't work again, her legs lifted automatically, opening her wider to accept him fully inside.

Glazed with the juices of her womb, Trace slid all the way in until his balls bumped into her arse.

Cat's back arched off the bed and she wrapped her legs around his waist. "Do you always please your women in such a manner?" She could never recall lovemaking with Rupert being this intense or satisfying.

"Of all the women I've pleasured, you are the first to make it all feel like magic."

Her breath caught in her throat, even as he moved slowly in and out of her. "What do you mean, 'magic'?"

"You're incredible, Pussy Cat." He leaned over her and kissed the sensitive skin beneath her ear. "Your skin is like cream, your hair like silk."

She could get used to the way he made her feel with the touch of his hands, the stroke of his words, and the thrust of his cock. "How many women have you pleasured?"

"Not so many. And none could hold a candle to you." Then he kissed her hard on the mouth and his thrusts became more urgent, until he slammed against her so hard the iron bed shook.

The frenzy of motion and the fact that others might hear titillated Catarina's senses and she climbed that jagged peak once again. When she reached the top, she screamed and fell over the edge.

Trace's body stiffened at the same time. He threw back his head, thrust one last time, and held still, the expression on his face one of exquisite pain and pleasure. When the tremors in his cock lessened, he collapsed on the bed beside her, turning her so that their connection would not be broken.

Catarina lay in his arms, the afterglow of ecstasy warring with the guilt she felt for tricking this man into her bed. How could she make him come back to her, short of hypnotizing him all over again?

4

_____

"No one could hold a candle to you, Pussy Cat." Trace *smoothed her beautiful black hair back from her forehead and pressed a kiss to her ruby-red lips.*

"Will you come back to see me again?" she asked, her breath tickling his chin.

"Wild horses couldn't keep me away, sweetheart."

She smiled up at him and a slim leg slid up over his, her sex pressing into his thigh, warm and wet.

The sound of pounding jerked Trace away from the alluring witch. No! He wanted to stay with her, drive his cock into her creamy depths, and hold her unbelievable body until she cried out his name.

But the pounding continued and began to mirror the pounding in his head. Who the hell was knocking on his door in the middle of the night? As he surfaced from the wooly darkness of sleep, he realized he'd been dreaming and whoever it was at the door would wake the entire hotel if he didn't stop soon. A dust cloud of disappointment filled him. He wanted to

212 / Myla Jackson

sink back into slumber and continue where he'd left off with the woman he'd conjured.

When the pounding continued, Trace forced his eyelids opened and sat up. "I'm coming, damn it."

It wasn't until his feet hit the warm wooden floor that he realized sun streamed through the windows at a high angle. Did the sun rise sooner in Kansas than Texas? How could it be daylight already? He couldn't have slept more than an hour by the feel of the grit in his eyes. Despite his exhaustion, his body somehow felt replete and satisfied, as if his dream had provided the relief he'd needed. He scratched his head.

Must have been a hell of a dream.

Marching to the door, he flung it open, ready to do battle with whomever had the gumption to wake him so early and from such a wonderful dream.

Jay stood with his hand poised to pound the door, an anxious frown denting his normally smooth, tanned forehead. "I almost thought you'd left without me, or died, or something. Why the hell didn't you answer the door?"

"I was asleep." Trace pushed a hand through his hair. "What time is it anyway?"

"Almost noon and we have to be at the stockyards in less than fifteen minutes, in case you forgot."

"What? Almost noon?" He hurried back to the table beside the bed and lifted his pocket watch. Jay was right. "How the hell did I sleep so long?"

"I don't know, but you better hurry. I hear ol' George Tanneby won't wait for no one. If you want to sell your herd, you better be on time."

"Damn." Trace grabbed his new shirt and his cowboy hat and headed for the door, not stopping to question why he still wore his boots and pants, even though he specifically remembered removing them sometime last night before he went to bed.

The two men ran down Main Street to the stable, tossed saddles on their horses, and raced for the stockyard on the edge of town. They arrived in time to make their appointment with Mr. Tanneby. Despite his extreme fatigue, Trace sold his six-hundred head of cattle for the price he'd hoped and all he had left to do was gather his men and head back to Texas.

After he left his horse at the stable, Trace trudged along the hard-packed dirt of Main Street with Jay beside him. The late summer heat must be affecting him. He couldn't remember a time he'd woken up this tired. An image of the night of the big storm came to mind, when they'd rode hard to make sure the lightning and thunder didn't spook the cattle into a stampede. The next day he'd been exhausted, but not with the same kind of exhaustion he felt now. He walked around in a somewhat happy daze, as if nothing could go wrong. He shook his head to clear his strange thoughts. "Think the boys will be ready to leave tomorrow?"

"Are you crazy?" Jay smiled at the pretty woman in the bright red dress standing outside the Golden Garter Saloon. "The boys will expect at least a week in Abilene to rest up and spend their money. Why are you in such a hurry to get back?"

"I've been away from the ranch long enough." Truth was he didn't like this feeling of being out of kilter, and he had a suspicion that something about Abilene had him off balance.

"I'm sure your brother can handle running things while you're gone." Jay pounded Trace's back. "Have you made your decision? Is that it? Are you finally gonna marry Miss Martha and you can't wait to get back to tell her yourself?"

Trace grunted to avoid a response. Martha wanted to name a date for their wedding. He scratched his head. Funny, but he couldn't recall having ever really asked her to marry him. Both their families had assumed they would marry for as long as they could both remember. When he'd left the ranch in the Texas panhandle, he'd promised himself he'd make a decision to either set a date or call it off by the time he reached Kansas.

214 / Myla Jackson

The only conclusion he'd come to was that if he was having this much trouble making up his mind, he had no business marrying Martha. She was a good woman who deserved a man completely committed to her.

"I take it you haven't decided?"

"No. I have."

"I'm glad you decided to take my advice and sow a few wild oats before you saddle-er settle." He cleared his throat. "Before we head back, at least let me and the boys have *our* fun for a few days."

Sow oats? What was Jay talking about? Then, recognizing the signs in his friend, Trace stated, "You found a woman, didn't you?"

Jay pulled his hat from his head and stared at it. "Well, as a matter of fact, yes."

Trace shook his head. "I should have guessed."

"Remember the pretty lady from the show last night?"

A frown pulled Trace's brows downward. The black-haired beauty with the clear blue eyes came to mind, as did the laughter of the crowd. "You met up with her?" He ignored the fact he felt like he'd been elbowed in the gut. Jay had every right to pursue the pretty witch and Trace had no interest in her. None whatsoever.

His friend blushed, his tanned skin turning a ruddy red. "She's the purdiest thing this side of the Mississippi and she has the sweetest disposition."

Trace couldn't deny The Amazing Catarina was the prettiest woman he'd ever had the displeasure of meeting; in fact, his dream woman looked surprisingly like her. But sweet disposition? "She is pretty, if you like black hair and pale skin."

"What do you mean black hair? I was talking about Nora Jane, the redhead." Jay shot a curious look at Trace. "You still mad at The Amazing Catarina for making you howl? I thought you'd gotten over it when I saw you go into her room last night."

The last part of Jay's sentence came to Trace in a fog as a wash of relief loosened the knot in his gut. Jay hadn't been talking about the magician. He'd been talking about her assistant. Then Jay's words sank in. "What do you mean, when I went to her room?"

"As if I didn't know. I met Nora Jane outside the room she shares with Miss Catarina. You were headed our way as we left. Don't tell me you're gonna deny you spent the night with her. I won't believe you for a moment."

Trace stood on the boardwalk, his head spinning in a haze of satisfied exhaustion. Had his dreams really only been dreams? Or had the witch put a spell on him and lured him to her room last night? He shook his head. No, he didn't believe in magic. There had to be another explanation.

"There she is now." Jay hurried forward to grasp the hands of the red-haired woman from the show last night.

Trace hung back as the couple said their hellos with silly smiles and disgusting displays of affection.

Glad for Jay's distraction, Trace pondered his friend's revelation. What had happened last night when he'd thought he'd been peacefully sleeping in his own bed? He managed not to reach down and test his man parts. What would that prove? His dream had felt so real and he could have gotten hard in his sleep.

At that moment, a woman wearing a sapphire-blue dress with long black hair piled high on her head stepped out the door of the shop behind Nora Jane. She was laughing and talking to someone inside as she pulled the door shut behind her. Then she turned toward him, her smile still affixed to her beautiful face—a smile that rivaled the sunshine. It almost blinded Trace's tired brain. If he wanted answers about last night, she might be the one to provide them. "I think you're right, Jay. The boys worked hard. They deserve a rest before we make the journey back."

Jay grinned at Trace, his hand on Nora Jane's elbow. "Now you're making sense. If you'll pardon me, I promised I'd take Nora Jane to lunch." He escorted his prize past Trace and disappeared into the hotel restaurant.

Which left Trace standing in front of The Amazing Catarina, wondering whether she was more amazing than he'd originally given her credit for. With a couple days on his hands, he decided he'd find out just how amazing she was.

Just the man she wanted to see. Catarina advanced on Trace Adams, determined to apologize for her behavior the previous day. She'd been a complete clod and deserved his anger at the show last night.

After his performance in her bedroom, she knew mending fences was in order if she wanted him back in her bed under his own cognitive abilities.

When she stopped in front of him, all her feminine instincts ripped into motion and her entire body flushed with red-hot lust. The fire ignited low in her belly and rushed upward, burning into her cheeks. Thank goodness she carried a fan and the day was rather warm. With a flick of her wrist, she popped open the black lace fan and waved it beneath her chin. Let him think her coy, not sweating like a horse.

"Mr. Adams, you're just the man I wanted to see." *And touch and make love to.* At the rate her heart beat, the heat wouldn't subside in the near future.

His brows rose and a smile spread across his face. "And I wanted to see you."

Her eyes widened. "You did? After last night?"

Was that a slight narrowing of his eyes? "What do you mean, 'after last night'?"

Images of his naked body flashed through her mind. Catarina forced those thoughts back, even as her core creamed. "Th-the show, of course. I was talking about the show. What else would I mean?" Her words rushed out and her cheeks burned hot like the embers of a blacksmith's fire. Did the man know what she'd done? Catarina stared into his face, trying to read into those impassive gray eyes, while guilt made her mind race with the possibilities. Should she confess and apologize?

Confess? Egad. How could she confess to a perfect stranger that she'd tricked him into coming to her room and making mad, passionate love to her? No man liked being made a fool of. If she read this one right, he'd be more than displeased. She would be better off apologizing for her behavior before and during her show and leaving out the rest. "I wanted to offer my apologies for my appalling behavior yesterday when I rode into town. You saved my life and I repaid you by making a mockery of you."

"Oh, that. I'd forgotten it already."

"You did?" Did she sound as inane as she felt? "Well, then let me also apologize for making you howl on stage last night."

"No need to apologize for something I don't even remember. If you'd join me for lunch, I'd like to learn more about mesmerism."

"Oh, I couldn't possibly." But if she didn't, how could he get to know her on a personal level? How could she manage a repeat performance of last night's incredible lovemaking? She wanted that more than she wanted to breathe—which reminded her to inhale and exhale. She wished she hadn't had Nora Jane tighten her corsets so much. Had she had this much difficulty breathing when she left her room? Cat gulped and nodded. "All right, I accept your kind invitation to lunch. However, I must warn you I don't give away my magic secrets."

"What a shame. I'd hoped to learn more about what you did to me."

Cat stumbled on the boardwalk. If not for Trace's warm hand cupping her elbow, she might have landed on her face.

"Are you all right?" he asked, his words stirring the tendrils around her ear.

Tingles of awareness shivered through her, raising goose-flesh on her exposed skin. She straightened so quickly her head hit his chin and she saw stars twirling around the edges of her vision. Again, if not for the pressure of his hand on her arm, she'd have fallen.

Once she could see without annoying little bright lights flickering in front of her eyes, she shot a glance at Trace.

He flexed his jaw, and rubbed his chin, where a dark red circle marked his face.

"Oh, did I do that?" Cat reached up and touched his face, wishing she could fall through the rotting boards of the walkway. "No matter what I do, I always seem to be hurting you in one manner or another. Here, let me have a look." She brushed his hand away and ran her fingers across fresh stubble.

Trace had been clean-shaven the night before. He'd apparently chosen not to shave this morning, a fact that caused her insides to turn flips. How would it feel to have that stubble rubbing against the tender skin of her inner thigh, tonight?

During her mesmerizing act, she'd only planted the suggestion for him to come to her room last night. Too bad she hadn't requested him every night for the entire week she'd be there. That stubble intrigued her more than she cared to admit. Fighting the overwhelming urge to drag him up to her room and test it against her skin, she smiled up at him. "Once again, I find I'm in the position of apologizing."

"No need. I probably deserved being hit, and a lot more, for being such an oaf in the audience."

"You were a rather odious heckler."

"Odious, huh? Odious enough to punish?"

"Are you feeling particularly punished, Mr. Adams? I assure you, your performance last night was exemplary." She hid her smile behind her fan. If only he knew how exemplary he'd been.

"So, I'm told." He guided her into a small café farther down the street from the restaurant Jay and Nora Jane had entered. "Howling, huh? How is it I 'performed,' as you say, yet I don't remember a thing? Or can't you tell me?"

"I can tell you that I planted the suggestions while you were in a trance, and you performed them based on a key phrase or sound." Like a clock striking midnight sending him to her room last night. As he held a chair for her, she sank into the ladder-back chair, where she perched on the edge of the seat, on her guard for his next barrage of questions.

As he scooted her chair beneath her, his hands brushed her shoulders, the tingles of awareness spreading from the point of contact throughout her body. Once again, she wondered how she could renew her suggestion for him to come to her room at midnight.

He leaned close as he slipped the chair closer to the table, his breath warm on her neck. "Does your magic work on everyone?"

"It works best on those in a more susceptible frame of mind."

"Such as young Luke or, say, a tired cowboy, fresh off the trail?"

Catarina concentrated on spreading the cloth napkin across her best blue dress before she answered noncommittally, "I suppose."

While the owner took their order, Catarina studied Trace. Last night she'd concentrated on his body; today, she promised herself she'd study only his face. Without the hairy beard from yesterday, he was incredibly handsome.

After the owner left with their orders, Trace turned his attention back to her.

"Are you a cowboy, Mr. Adams?" Catarina asked, thinking how formal 'Mr. Adams' sounded when she'd made passionate love to this man.

"I like to think of myself as a rancher taking my livestock to market. Cowboy sounds like I'm not quite a grown man."

"I would never accuse you of being a boy, Mr. Adams." As soon as her words left her mouth, Catarina wished them back.

The smile lifting the corners of Trace's mouth held a fair amount of mischief. "Why would you say that, Miss . . ." He frowned. "It is Miss, isn't it?"

"Actually, it's Mrs. Novak. I don't think we've been properly introduced."

"I would think we're well past proper introductions." A frown creased his forehead. "Mrs. Novak? Is there a husband lurking in the shadows I should beware of?"

"No, there's no husband hiding in the shadows, God rest his soul. Rupert died a year ago of pneumonia on our way out West. That's why I work as a magician now."

"I'm sorry to hear that. What a tragedy for such a young and lovely woman."

"Yes, indeed. Rupert was a good man." Although her husband had never stirred her lusty side quite like the man across the table from her. Something about Trace's earlier comment niggled. "Why would you say that we're well past the point of proper introductions, Mr. Adams?"

A wicked grin crossed his face at lightning speed and was gone. If she hadn't been watching him so carefully, she'd have missed it altogether. "Only that since I've known you, I've been slapped in the face with a cape, dragged down Main Street by your horse, humiliated in front of my peers, and forced to do things I wouldn't normally do. All because of you, Mrs. Novak."

She touched her fingers to her lips. "Oh dear, when you put it that way, I do sound the bumbling oaf. If I were you, I'd steer well away from me. I must be jinxed." She tipped her head to the side. "Which begs the question that, if I am such a liability, why are we sitting together sharing a meal? Aren't you afraid I'll set you on fire or something equally disastrous?"

His chuckle warmed the air around her. "I figure I'm better off knowing where you are than not."

"Like being less afraid of the snake in the grass you can see than one you can't?"

"Something like that. I also think you're pretty, smart and, when you're not making me howl or being annoying, you can be . . . passable."

Passable? Catarina's back stiffened. As much of a wildcat as she'd been in bed last night, she wouldn't call herself passable. Passionate, fervent, phenomenal maybe, but not passable. Her mouth opened to say just that.

Before she declared her opinion on his unfortunate adjective, Catarina recalled that Trace had no memory of their little tryst in her room. He was completely in the dark about how she'd screamed his name aloud in the throes of passion. Thank goodness. How embarrassing would it be to have to wake next to a strange man after behaving like a common tramp?

The ache in her thighs and the tenderness in her private area only emphasized how foolhardy she'd been. To get away with it once was a miracle. She'd be a fool to wish for more.

Yet, the remembered sensation of Trace's tongue licking a path across her belly, down to her—

A hand waved in front of her face, interrupting her perfectly lovely image—Trace's hand.

"I thought I'd lost you for a moment there. Is that bump on your head still affecting you?" He rubbed his jaw. "I know I'll never be the same."

"I seriously doubt I'll ever be the same, as well," she mut-tered and thanked her lucky stars the food arrived at that mo-ment to save her from having to explain her comment to Trace. Taking a very unladylike chunk of buffalo steak, she stuffed her mouth full and hoped it deterred the curious cowboy—er . . . man—from asking her further questions.

Trace took his time cutting his steak and almost had Catarina believing he'd dropped his line of questioning for the enjoy-ment of his food. "Have you ever suggested anything more . . . challenging to your volunteers other than howling like a coyote or crowing like a rooster?"

Catarina swallowed the half-chewed chunk of buffalo, which proceeded to lodge firmly in her throat. Gratitude for the op-portunity to avoid answering Trace's question quickly shifted into panic as Catarina struggled to breathe past the hideously large piece of flesh. When air refused to pass to her lungs, she clutched her throat, her eyes widening. Death appeared immi-nent.

"Is there a problem, Mrs. Novak?" Trace leaned close. "Catarina? Your face, it's turning blue."

She clawed her throat as the air around her eluded her lungs and fuzzy gray edged her sight. She wanted to yell, *I can't breathe, you idiot!* But she couldn't get air into her lungs, much less out past her vocal chords.

Trace leaped from his chair and pounded his palm between her shoulder blades. A sharp smack launched the meat from her throat across the table.

Cat placed her hands on the tablecloth and sucked in a deep breath of the most beautiful air she'd ever breathed. She gulped in more until she could see everything as clearly as a freshly washed sky. It was then she realized Trace had his arm around her shoulder, and worse, she was leaning into him as if her life depended on it. "I'm quite all right, thank you, sir." She sat up straight and folded her napkin in her lap.

When Trace returned to his seat, laughter danced in his gray eyes.

Disturbed by her own rude behavior, Catarina didn't need this dusty cowboy laughing at her in public. "What?" she asked, her voice a little sharper than the man who'd saved her for the second time in as many days deserved.

He stared at the chunk of half-chewed buffalo lying atop his own uneaten steak. "You have good aim for a woman. Like to see what you could do with a bullet instead of buffalo steak."

Indignation rose to the surface and quickly fizzled. The mirth in his eyes stirred the humor in her soul and giggles bubbled up in her throat. Catarina pressed her hand to her mouth to hold them back, but a few managed to leak out. "I'm sorry. I've completely ruined your meal." Another giggle erupted. "Really, I am sorry."

When she looked up at Trace, all hints of humor had disappeared from his mouth and eyes.

The force of his stare pinned her to her seat and she squirmed. What had she done now?

Trace reached across the table and laid his work-callused hand over hers. "You are very amazing, Catarina."

Warmth seeped through his skin into hers, sending heat to the center of her being. How did he do it with a simple touch? The better question was how could he stare at her with such intensity after she'd spit a hunk of meat onto his plate? Her stomach did flips and she willed her heart to slow to a normal rate.

Was that desire she saw in the stormy gray depths of his eyes, or was she projecting her own longing onto this hardworking man? How could she have tricked him? He deserved better. "No, I'm not so amazing." She pushed her chair back and stood. "If you'll excuse me, I just recalled an appointment I have with the haberdashery. I'd better hurry." She pulled coins from the hidden pocket in her skirt and laid them on the table.

"Please, stay and order a fresh lunch. I'm sorry I spoiled yours."

A scowl appeared between Trace's brows. "Keep your money. I invited you to lunch."

"But I ruined it for you. I insist."

He captured her hand and turned it palm upward, placing the coins in them. "Will I see you again?"

How could she, knowing she'd tricked him into making love to her? She was a pathetic wretch of a woman to do such a thing. "No, I don't think so." She ducked her head and moved past him, when all she wanted was to fall into his arms and beg his forgiveness. Walking away from him, knowing she could never see him again, was the hardest thing she'd ever done.

Trace gave her a moment or two to leave and then he followed. Whatever he'd said had her running like a scared rabbit. Or was it guilt for having tricked him?

When Catarina walked right past the haberdashery without even looking up, Trace knew he'd touched her in some way. Good. When he'd heard her laughter, she'd more than touched him. He'd felt like he'd been pole-axed in the gut. He slowed his pace and stood still until she turned into the hotel where they both had rooms.

Why was he pursuing her when he had a good woman waiting to marry him at home in Texas? Because Martha's kiss didn't stir inside him the same amount of fire The Amazing Catarina did with her smile and laughter. What was it about the witch that had his gut tied in knots and his groin aching for more? Had she really hexed him with her magic and lured him to her room last night?

His dreams had been of the lusty woman with the pale skin and raven-black hair. Could his dreams have been reality? If so, why the hell couldn't he remember them more clearly? The throbbing in his cock remembered something and wanted more.

Trace had to know the truth one way or another.

Although she had the right to decline his invitation to dinner or lunch, she couldn't have him thrown out of the theater if he paid his way in.

5

―――――――

"Calm down, Catarina. This crowd isn't nearly as rowdy as last night." Nora Jane peered through the gap in the curtain.

Catarina refused to look. She didn't want to know whether or not a certain cowboy sat in the front row as he had the night before. She could wait for that disappointment until the curtain opened.

"Oh, there's my fella, Jay." Nora Jane practically hopped up and down, her bulbous breasts all but falling out of her costume.

Making a note to have a seamstress add a bit of lace to her assistant's bodice, Catarina checked her supplies and tapped the bird cage for good luck. Only four more nights in the theater and they'd be on their way to Chicago. The first night's earnings had been good, but not good enough for train tickets and seed money to get the two women started in the bustling Illinois town. They didn't know how long it would take to find work or how much it would cost to live. They'd need every cent they could earn.

"Ready?" Martin poked his head through the center curtain.

"Yes, sir." As ready as she'd ever be.

Martin made his introduction and, with Nora Jane's help, he opened the heavy black velvet drapes.

Despite her warnings to herself not to be disappointed, Catarina couldn't help the stab of misery when her gaze scanned the front row of men and none of them were her golden Adonis with the storm-cloud-gray eyes. She pinned a smile to her face and began the show.

The saloon's theater was even more crowded than the night before. The saloon owner had told her that young Luke and others from last night's audience had spread the word around town about The Amazing Catarina and her magic show. The response was overwhelming and she should have been happy.

What did she expect? She'd told him she didn't want to see him anymore. He was only honoring her wishes. Why would he be there, anyway? She'd been a nuisance to him from the moment they'd met.

Throughout the magic portion of her routine, she smiled, her cheeks aching with the effort. When it came time for the hypnosis, she breathed a sigh. The show was almost over and she could go back to her lonely room and get a full night's uninterrupted sleep.

Nora Jane leaned close to her as she cleared away the props and magician's table. "I won't be in the room again tonight. Jay's taking me out for a late dinner." She winked. "A really late dinner, if you get my meaning."

Oh, Catarina got her meaning, but she couldn't even summon a smile for her friend. At that moment, she was unbecomingly green with envy for the woman's newfound love interest. Catarina had secretly hoped Nora Jane would be in their room that night so that she didn't have to face it alone. Now, even that option was taken from her. Where was Trace? She peered over the stage lights into the audience. With so many faces in the crowd, she couldn't see the one she longed to see the most.

* * *

Trace stood near the rear of the theater, drinking in every word and movement of The Amazing Catarina's performance on stage.

Since he'd left her earlier that day, all he'd thought about was Catarina—the way the lights danced in her pale blue eyes when she laughed and the musical sound of her voice. So, she'd made a fool of him and tricked him into howling in front of an audience of ruffians. He couldn't get his mind off the wicked dreams from the previous night and the intriguing possibility they weren't dreams at all.

If she truly could make him howl without his knowledge, perhaps Jay was right and Catarina had summoned him to her room the previous night. It would explain why he'd been exhausted when he'd gotten up this morning, and why his cock ached as though he'd had his share of romping in the sheets. He couldn't have conjured dreams as vivid as those he'd had, could he?

When he'd tried to question her, she had been evasive and he could have sworn he'd seen guilt written across her pretty face. But he couldn't be absolutely certain and to flat-out ask her would be forward and rude, deserving of a slap in the face. Now watching her with the audience, he paid close attention to her words and movements.

"Now for the next portion of The Amazing Catarina Show, I'll need a volunteer from the audience." Catarina's brows winged upward as she stared out at the crowd.

A hundred voices shouted "Me!" echoing off the ceiling beams like thunder.

Catarina smiled and gestured to a painfully thin man leaning against the wall, his hands tucked into his pockets and his gaze nervous. "How about you?"

The man's eyes widened and he shook his head.

The hulking man next to the thin man shoved him to the side. "He don't want to, how about me?"

Catarina planted her hands on her hips. "Let the man speak for himself."

"You don't want him, that's stuttering Stephen. He can't talk."

She turned her gaze on the smaller man. "Is that true? You can't talk?"

Stephen shook his head. "N-n-n-no m-m-m-ma'am. I c-c-c-can t-t-t-talk." He shrugged and smiled sheepishly.

"Please, Stephen, come up and help me with the next trick." Her smile could have lured a lion from his den.

Trace wanted to leap onto the stage for that smile. A glance around the room confirmed that so did every other cock and dandy. He crossed his arms over his chest and maintained his position against the back wall.

Stephen shot a glance at the big man next to him and ducked around him to climb the steps of the stage.

Once there, his ears turned a bright shade of red to match his cheeks.

Catarina lifted her gold watch and commenced her witchery of placing the man in a trance. Within minutes, Stephen's eyes were closed and the magician was speaking softly to him. Then louder for the crowd, she said, "When I say Shakespeare, you will recite the words from *Romeo and Juliet* I just told you."

"He'll never do it," the big guy who'd shoved Stephen earlier shouted. "He can't say his name without s-s-s-stuttering."

The crowd laughed.

Catarina hated when men made fun of others who were different. "Please, sir. I need silence for this to work."

The man snorted. "Fat lot of good that'll do you. The man's a stuttering fool."

Her gaze narrowed at the man, then she turned her attention back to Stephen. "Wake up, Stephen."

Stephen blinked and looked at her and then the audience. "Did you do the trick?" He clapped his hand over his mouth, his eyes widening. His hand fell away and he stared at Catarina. "Was that me? Did I just say that? Did you hear that? I'm not stuttering!"

"Stephen," Catarina said softly. "Have you ever heard of Shakespeare?"

Stephen straightened, his eyes glazing over. "But soft. What light through yonder window breaks? It is the east, and Juliet is the sun."

The crowd went wild, cheering so loudly the curtains shook.

When the noise died down, Stephen blinked and stared at Catarina. "What did you do to me?"

Her brows rose. "You just recited a passage from a play called *Romeo and Juliet*."

"I did?" He shook his head. "I don't even know this man named Romeo." Stephen grabbed her shoulders. "Never mind that, what did you do? I'm not stuttering!" Then he wrapped his arms around her waist and lifted her off the ground, his grin stretching across his face, lighting a previously sad countenance.

Anger coursed through Trace and he took a step forward, ready to pry the man's hands off Catarina.

Stephen set her back on her feet and dropped his hands. "Thank you, Miss Catarina. You really are amazing. You've given me a gift."

Catarina's eyes glistened and she smiled softly at the man. "I didn't give you anything you didn't have inside you to begin with." Then she turned to the audience. "Please thank our volunteer."

A huge round of applause followed and more shouts of, "Me next!"

Trace had seen enough. He left the room and wandered outside onto the boardwalk. What he'd seen The Amazing Catarina do on the stage fed his suspicions. She'd had to have tricked him into her room last night and, if his dreams were anything to go by, he'd made love to her until the small hours of the morning.

Staring up at the stars in the Kansas sky, he wondered what he should do with this knowledge. He should be angry with her for fooling him. He was a practically engaged man with a woman at home waiting for him to set the date. Guilt knotted his gut when he thought of sweet Martha, waiting patiently back in Texas. Guilt burned in his gut, but not love. He stood straighter. Who was he kidding? If he had loved Martha, he'd have married her long ago. Tomorrow he'd send a telegram apologizing for leading her to believe he'd marry her when his heart wasn't in it.

No. A woman needed to hear that kind of news in person, not delivered in a telegram anyone could see.

Damn. Women were nothing but trouble. The Amazing Catarina was a perfect example. What bothered him most was that no matter how hard he tried, he couldn't clearly remember last night. Strangely, regret outweighed anger. The woman was beautiful. The vague images of her naked body in his dreams were not nearly enough to go on. He had to know more, see more, touch more of The Amazing Catarina. This time while he was awake, not asleep or in a trance.

As an idea formed, he smiled up at the stars. He'd have the beautiful witch tonight. On his terms, not on hers.

Catarina climbed into her empty bed, smoothing the sheets she'd shared with Trace with an unsteady hand and wishing she'd had the forthrightness to ask for what she wanted to his face. What was it she wanted? She wanted Trace Adams in her bed. If she hadn't tricked him into her bed the first night, she wouldn't have known what a magnificent lover he was and she wouldn't be lying there in a lather of sweat, wishing he was beside her.

She pounded her fist into her feather pillow and threw aside the covers. The sound of a clock striking midnight drifted through her open window and she tensed. That had been the trigger for Trace to come to her room last night. Catarina padded to the window and stared out at the night. Laughter and piano music could still be heard from the saloon next door. She leaned her forehead against the window pane and sighed.

A knock at her door jerked her upright. Who would be at her door at this hour? Her chest tightened. Surely it couldn't be . . . No, she'd only asked for last night . . . Could it be? With wings on her feet, she flew to the door and flung it open.

Filling the doorway with his broad chest was the man of her day-and-night dreams. The once cranky, now sexy cowboy Trace Adams.

Breathe, Catarina, breathe! The previous night, she'd expected him at her doorway and didn't have any expectations of his sexual prowess. Tonight, she hadn't expected him and had a very good idea about how well he performed. . . . "Why are you here?"

Was that a twitch at the edges of his lips? "To pleasure you." His face was as blank as the best poker player.

Hmmm. Her suggestion must have been more powerful than she'd originally thought. Then why the hell was she hesitating?

Still, she blocked the doorway with her dressing-gown-clad body. Was he really there based on her hypnosis, or had he figured out her trick? Why should she care? He was here and she wanted him with a passion that made her tremble. Cat moved to the side. "Please, come in."

Once Trace stepped through the doorway and Cat closed the door behind him, she clasped her hands together, suddenly nervous, as if she were a bride on her wedding night. She almost laughed out loud. Like she'd ever be Trace Adam's bride. He'd marry a sweet young woman who'd make his family proud, not a widow with a questionable occupation. "This is foolish."

"What's foolish?" The man who'd filled her heart and thoughts all evening moved about the room. He shed his leather vest and dropped the suspenders from his shoulders. When Trace unbuttoned the top button of his white shirt, Catarina's heart rate increased.

With each button Trace released, Catarina's breathing became more ragged until she was panting in shallow breaths. "How will you pleasure me?" Was he in a trance? How could she test him?

"However you want me to." He stopped at the last button and glanced up, his gaze meeting hers.

Cat's breath caught in her throat and she gulped it down. "What if I don't want you to pleasure me?" Was she crazy? Where had that statement come from? She wanted him more than she could recall ever wanting a man, even her dead husband.

Trace's brows drew together. "Isn't that why I'm here?"

"I don't know, you tell me."

"Do you want me to go?" His hand moved the opposite direction, buttoning the loose buttons.

"Wait!" Catarina reached out and stopped his hands. "I want you to stay." If he was in a trance or not, she didn't care. What she did care about was getting the rest of his clothes off and then getting naked herself. "Please, stay."

Trace's hands moved from his buttons to her arms. "Are you sure? If you don't want me here, I'll go." He hesitated, then added, "I'll stay if that pleases you."

Oh, yes, it pleased her. Catarina fought not to dissolve at the way his fingers heated the skin beneath her gown. "I'm sure," she said, breathless and throbbing in places still aching from the previous night's activities. Her fingers touched his chest through the opening in his shirt and she could feel his heart beating almost as fast as hers.

She stared up into his eyes and in little more than a whisper asked, "Do you even know you're here?"

6

Ah-ha! Up until the point The Amazing Catarina had asked her quiet question, Trace held out hope that her duplicity was a figment of his imagination. He had wanted to believe the beautiful woman was not capable of extending such a carnal suggestion to a stranger. Anger surged through him at how easily she'd tricked him—as easily as she'd tricked young Luke. Damn it, he wasn't a boy still green about the ears. He was a man who knew his own mind.

While he knew he should confront her with her lie, he couldn't deny what his body craved and obviously knew. Two could play her game. She'd had her way with him last night, leaving him with nothing more than vague dreams of fulfillment. This time he'd be awake and aware. He'd satisfy his own desires and leave Catarina begging for more. Then he'd force her to confess her deception.

In order to play her ruse, he had to convince her that he was here because of her mesmerism. "If this is a dream, don't wake me," he said and pulled her into his arms, crushing his lips to hers. This part he didn't have to fake.

She fit against him as though she belonged, her soft curves melting against the hard planes of his torso. Her hands moved inside his shirt and around his back, bringing him closer until the ridge of his cock nestled against her soft belly. He'd never known a woman as greedy with lust as she and fires ignited deep in his soul.

"Too many clothes," she gasped as she struggled against him, her hands working to free the tie holding her dressing gown together. In her hurry, she only managed to knot the string.

Trace hid his grin by kissing her earlobe.

"If you want to please me," she cried, "You'll help me out of this confounded thing."

He brushed her hands aside and eased the knot from the silken ribbon beneath her breasts. As he pushed her thin cotton garment from her shoulders, he kissed the base of her throat. "What do you wish me to do next, witch?"

Her soft body stiffened when he said the word 'witch' and she pushed him back, enough to look him in the eye. "Did you call me 'witch'? You called me that on stage." Her look was wary, guarded, as though she doubted his trance was real.

Damn. He hadn't meant to slip and call her something his wakeful self would say. "You have bewitched my dreams. Does that not please you?" Lifting one of the hands braced to his chest, he turned it over and pressed a kiss to her palm. "I'm here only to please you, my lovely Catarina." His mouth moved to her wrist, sliding back the lacy sleeve of her nightgown. With the sensitive flesh at the inside curve of her elbow exposed, he pressed kisses in a sensuous procession up the length of her arm. She smelled of springtime and tasted of honeysuckle and she bewitched him beyond recognition.

What kind of a man could fall so deeply under a woman's spell? And here he was, a man promised to another until he could break it off. The thought niggled in Trace's lust-filled brain. A kiss turned into a nibble, a nibble into a nip, as the anger resurfaced.

"Ouch!" Catarina jerked her arm away, her pretty dark brows drawn together in a frown. She stared down at the red mark marring her pale skin, a smile quirking at the corners of her mouth. "Is this a naughty dream?"

The animal inside Trace responded to Catarina's teasing question with a low, guttural growl. He grasped her around the middle and backed her against the wood panels of the door. "My dreams of you are anything but placid. I want you."

Catarina laughed a sensuous, throaty laugh and reached up, stretching in his embrace, the movement pulling the thin cotton gown taut over her breasts. Rosy-brown aureoles showed through the material, tempting Trace. "Ummm, I like it when you play rough."

His groin tightened, his cock surging, lengthening against the thick fabric of his trousers. When he thought he was being cruel, she enjoyed it. What manner of woman was this? One who appealed to his baser instincts.

With his hands beneath her breasts, his thumbs circled the pebbled peaks and he leaned forward to capture one in his mouth. Through the fabric he could taste her.

Her back arched away from the door and she pulled him to her, a slender leg circling behind his thigh. "Oh, Trace, that feels so good."

Her softly spoken words spurred him on and he stooped to skim up her gown and cup her bottom, lifting her higher.

Slim white legs circled his waist, her hips rising and falling, rubbing her pussy across the hard ridge of his cock through his trousers.

"Patience, sweet Cat."

"No, I want you hard and fast. Fuck me like you mean it. Like I'm the last woman on earth and our time is coming to an end."

He'd never heard a woman use such vulgar language. Trace let it wash over him, working past the shock to the way it made his body flood with desire. He wanted to fuck her, fast and furious.

His slight hesitation seemed to frustrate her and she clamped her hands on either side of his face, staring into his eyes. "Are you a man, or only a cow*boy*?" she asked, emphasizing the word 'boy.'

Her comment hit a chord in him. With her legs wrapped around his waist, Trace spun toward the bed and tossed her onto the feather mattress. He kicked off his boots and shucked his trousers, freeing his engorged cock with all intentions of mounting this filly and riding her into a full lather.

She lay on the mattress, a smile sliding across her face. Then her smile turned to giggles and finally full-out belly laughs. "I wish you could see how determined you look. I almost felt like a steer being thrown to the ground for branding. Do you attack your ranching with as much vigor as you attack your women?"

He couldn't even dream about throwing Martha onto a bed and fucking the daylights out of her. She'd be appalled, mortified and frightened. "In most circumstances, I don't attack my women."

"No?" Her beautiful dark head tipped to one side. "Did they ever ask you to?"

"No." Of all the women he'd ever made love to, none had been quite as brazen as the widow before him, and Trace liked that. He could never be bored with a woman like The Amazing Catarina.

Even after a lifetime? He stared into her pale blue eyes and tried to imagine her as a gray-haired old woman sitting beside him in her rocking chair. He could imagine the teasing gleam in her eyes even then.

But with her nightgown hiked up around her hips, he struggled to imagine past what he was going to do next.

"No one ever asked you to play rough?" She sighed. "I have to admit, even with Rupert, lovemaking was rather staid."

"Let me show you how good it can be."

She sank back against the pillows, her hand straying to the triangle of curls at the apex of her thighs. "What are you waiting for?"

Trace advanced on her, dropping to the bed beside her. What crazy scheme would she think of next? His cock twitched in anticipation. "Tell me what naughty fantasies you dream about."

She stared at him as if trying to see inside his head. "You mean your dreams weren't naughty enough?"

He trailed a finger from her hip up to where the nightgown still draped over her upper body. "They weren't enough. Having you will be much more satisfying." The fact she was still toying with him about being in her room the night before made his hands a little rough when he grabbed the hem of the gown and jerked it up over her head. With the gown around her wrists, he twisted the fabric until her hands were bound together. Then he bent to nip her lower lip. "Tell me your wildest fantasy."

Her bare breasts rose and fell to the erratic rhythm of her breathing. "I've always wondered how it would feel to be bound and taken by force, by a very virile man." Her cheeks flamed with her admission.

With one hand holding her arms over her head, Trace moved the other from the slender column of her throat to the swell of her breasts. "I've captured you. You're mine to do with as I please."

"You won't hurt me, will you?" Her voice sounded less frightened than hopeful.

At the excitement in Catarina's tone, every nerve in Trace's body ignited. "I'll do whatever I want, Pussy Cat, and you will do as I command."

A shiver ran the length of her delicious body. She struggled against the hold he had on her hands. "Let me go so I can touch all that lovely skin."

He pinched the tip of her pebbled nipple hard enough to hurt.

"Ouch! That hurt." A tiny frown turned into a sensuous smile and she struggled again. This time she threw her hips into the fight, tossing to the side until her nest of curly hairs rubbed against his straining cock.

He jumped back as if she'd burned him simply by touching him. As excited as he was, even the slightest contact to his penis was excruciatingly sensuous. He reached out and tweaked the other nipple in retaliation.

"Ouch! Let me go." She rolled from side to side.

Trace had his hands too full to hold her down and pleasure her at the same time, so he used her gown to tie her wrists to the white iron bed.

"Ooh, that's not playing fair. How am I to touch you, if I'm tethered to the bed?"

"Exactly the point. You wanted to know what it was like to be held captive. Now you will." He stood next to the bed and waved his hand toward her bound hands, then planted his fists on his hips. "You're my captive. I'll do as I please."

Catarina's inky black brows rose. "You will? What if I don't like it?"

"That, my dear, will not be a possibility." He grabbed her knees and dragged her across the bed until her legs dangled over the edge and her wrists pulled tight, stretching her arms high over her head. Her naked body was fully exposed to his view and he liked what he saw: from the full, rosy-tipped breasts to her tiny waist to the dark curls covering her cunt.

"I could scream, you know." Not that she sounded like she had enough air to carry through on her threat.

He nudged a path between her legs and his cock touched the entrance to her pussy. "Oh, you'll scream all right." He pulled back without penetrating her glistening entrance.

"Where are you going? You can't stop there." She tried to wrap her legs around him to keep him close. "This is my fantasy, you're supposed to perform the way I want."

"Are you forgetting whose dream this is?" Trace crossed his arms over his chest and stared hard at her.

Catarina chewed her lip. She should tell him he wasn't dreaming and wake him from his trance. It was the right thing to do, the honorable thing.

Still, her pussy ached with the need for him to come into her, fill her to full, and rock the iron bed into the wee hours of the morning.

This new promise of playing out her fantasy had her in a frenzy of longing. It also had her in a compromising position. If Trace walked away and left her tied to her bed, surely she'd perish from unfulfilled lust. And Nora Jane wouldn't drift through the doorway until some time in the late morning hours to free her. Pleasuring herself to relieve this manic need would not be an option. Frustrated and fearful he'd leave, Catarina asked, "What are you going to do?"

She could swear a little frown dipped his brows, if only for a second, as if her words disappointed him. Then a feral smile filled with danger and sheer orneriness shifted across his lips and made her body hum in anticipation of what was to come.

"I'm going to torture you until you beg me to stop." He paced the floor in front of her, his hand to his chin as if contemplating the types of torture he would inflict. His magnificent cock jutted hard and thick, ahead of each step.

Catarina groaned. "You're killing me. Decide my fate and do what you will, but don't make me wait any longer."

He stopped, his brows rising. "Anxious, are we? I was just trying to think of a suitable punishment. Any suggestions?"

"I could think of a few," she said, her mouth going dry as he pointed his most lethal weapon at her.

He dropped to the bed beside her and traced a line from her breasts down to the apex of her thighs. "How's this for a start?"

She wiggled and squirmed but couldn't get him to take those fingers to the spot she wanted him to touch most. Frustration bubbled up inside and she flopped back against the mattress, blowing a strand of hair off her forehead. "Definitely punishing. Why am I being punished?" As soon as she opened her mouth with the question, she wished she hadn't asked. She could think of a great big reason she should be punished. Trace was there under a trance—a trance she didn't want him to wake from. Not yet. She liked playing this game and loved what he did to her insides. If only he were doing this on his own and not under the influence of hypnosis.

He leaned over her and followed his fingers with his lips, trailing kisses down the side of her breast, stopping to swirl his tongue around the taut nipple.

She wanted to touch him and run her hands through his hair. "Please let me go. I have to touch you, too."

"Do you want me?" He blew a warm stream of air across her damp aureole.

Her back arched off the bed, pushing her breast closer to his mouth.

Instead of taking it between his lips, he leaned back. "Uh-uh. This is supposed to be torture."

"It is, damn it!"

"Tsk, tsk." He pressed a kiss to each of her ribs on his path downward. "Such vulgar language for a pretty lady."

"If you don't get down to business, I'll show you vulgar."

His eyes widened. "Now *that* sounds interesting."

"Trace! I'm dying here." She jerked against her bonds. "Please let me play, too."

"Maybe. If you're very good." Although his look was stern, a wicked gleam glowed in his eyes from the oil lamp's reflection.

With her body on fire, Catarina cried, "Tell me what to do and I'll do it. Just please come inside me soon."

He nodded, his mouth curving into a satisfied grin. "Open your legs."

She almost laughed out loud with relief. At last he'd give her the fulfillment she longed for. Spreading her legs wide, she waited for him to mount her and plunge his cock deep.

He didn't. Instead, he trailed his fingers down over her clit, stroking just enough to titillate, then slipping lower to dip into her cunt for a hot coating of cream. Dropping to the floor on his knees, he spread her legs wide, draping one leg over each of his shoulders. With slow, deliberate moves, he dragged his tongue from her creamy entrance upward to that special spot that yanked every nerve to attention and made her blood sing for more.

Alternating between light flicks and nips, he had her moaning steadily, her thighs clamped around his ears. She rose to the point where every muscle, nerve, and cell in her body teetered on the precipice of igniting.

Just as she thought she'd burst, Trace laid her legs to the side, pressing a kiss to each inner thigh. He rose to his feet and plunged his cock into her slick channel, sliding all the way in, filling her, completing her. As he pumped in and out of her, he flicked her clit with his fingertips, bringing her with him.

Catarina shouted Trace's name and burst over the edge in an explosion unrivaled by any Fourth of July fireworks. A myriad of colors and sensations tumbled through her body, making her jerk and spasm uncontrollably.

Trace thrust harder until his entire body stiffened. He slammed into her one last time before holding her tight against him, his seed spilling into her womb.

When the tremors abated, he leaned over her and untied her nightgown. Then he climbed into the bed and pulled her up beside him.

With her lusty thirst momentarily slaked, Catarina curled up in Trace's arms and rested her cheek against his bare chest, allowing the hairs to tickle her nose. "That was wonderful."

"Yes, it was pretty phenomenal . . . for a dream."

"I wish we could stay like this forever."

"You do? Then you'd miss the little things, like this." He pulled her closer and nuzzled her neck until she giggled.

"No, I wish we could be close like this, always." She sighed and nestled even closer, draping her leg over his. "I wish it wasn't just a dream," she whispered.

7

Trace saw her before she saw him the next morning as she stepped out of the hotel onto the busy boardwalk. She stopped to check the contents of her reticule, giving him time to study her in the light of day. Her rich black hair rose in soft waves up into an elegant knot with ringlets spilling down from the back. Her cheeks were rosy and her lips were kiss-swollen from two nights of loving. Damn, she was beautiful.

With little sleep to go on, he leaned against the building and waited for her to come to him, not wanting to appear overly anxious to see her. He'd left her sleeping a little before dawn a mere three hours earlier. When he'd gone back to his room, he'd lain on top of the covers with the window wide open, hoping for a breeze to cool his heated hankering for the black-haired witch. The late summer air had hung warm and unmoving, adding to the fire simmering inside.

Sleep eluded him when all he could think about was returning to Catarina's room and climbing into bed beside her. He wanted to bury himself deep inside her and make her shout his name over and over.

The wish she'd whispered just before she'd drifted off to sleep haunted him. All this time, he'd been fooling himself into believing he was only after revenge for the trick she'd played on him that first night.

The joke was on him and he wasn't laughing. He hung on her every word and the sun didn't fully rise in the morning until he saw her. What the hell had happened in the short time he'd known her? Had she hypnotized him into falling in love with her? How could he love a woman he'd only known for two days? He and Martha had known each other all their lives. Now that was something you could build a lasting relationship on. Not two nights of tossing up a woman's skirts.

The more he pondered the problem of Martha versus Catarina, the more he knew he had to do something. He'd been at the telegraph office first thing that morning, sending a telegram to his brother asking him to break the news to Martha. He couldn't marry her and he was sorry he'd waited so long to tell her. For years he'd wondered what kept him from setting a date for their wedding. The cattle drive and having met Catarina made it all crystal clear to him. He loved Martha, but not like a man loves his wife, more like a man loves his sister. He couldn't set a date because he thought of Martha like a kid sister.

Not so the beautiful magician, The Amazing Catarina. He could never think of her as a sister, especially after what they'd shared in her bed the past two nights. He didn't know whether he and Catarina had a future, but he did know that he had to be with the magician as long as he could, at least until he left for Texas in two days' time.

If he showed up at her door that night, would she believe him again, or would he be pushing his luck?

At the exact moment Trace was thinking about the night ahead, Catarina turned his way, her clear blue gaze connecting with his.

Even without touching her, his body responded. The placket of buttons on the front of his trousers grew tight and uncomfortable and he resisted adjusting them.

Mrs. Catarina Novak strolled down the boardwalk dressed in a polonaise, its pale, blue-striped bodice with an overskirt draped modestly over a white cotton skirt. She looked as prim and proper as a schoolmarm on her way to teach the town hellions. When she passed within two feet of him, she nodded, a hint of a smile on her lips, her eyes reticently downcast. "Good morning, Mr. Adams."

"Mrs. Novak, nice to see you, ma'am. I trust you slept well?"

"Why, Mr. Adams, how kind of you to be concerned over my sleeping habits." She glanced up, the light in her eyes dancing with mischief. "I fear the heat kept me awake far later than I anticipated."

So, she still pretended what happened last night didn't. He must have played his part much better than he'd anticipated. Covering his mouth, he feigned a yawn. "It was hot last night. I don't think I slept more than fifteen minutes at a stretch. I'll be glad to be on the road home. The heat is much more tolerable out in the open."

A pout formed on her lower lip. "Are you leaving so soon? I thought you just got here."

"That's right. I came in with a herd of cattle," he said. "We have more that need tending where they came from."

"And where might that be?" she asked.

"On a ranch a short piece out of Independence, Texas." He nodded toward the restaurant where they'd shared lunch the day before. "Care to join me for breakfast?"

"I'd be delighted."

Over beef steak and eggs, Trace told Catarina all about the 3,200 acres of land where he and his brother raised cattle. Other than the women who'd ranched alongside him, he'd never met a city woman who didn't change the subject within half an hour or smother a yawn and excuse herself.

Catarina sat forward, her gaze intent on him, asking questions about everything. "Tell me how you go about branding a calf, Mr. Adams. Just how do you get one to be still long enough to complete the process?"

When the image of a naked widow woman tied to a white iron headboard sprang to mind, Trace almost snorted coffee through his nostrils. When he could get his tongue working properly, he replied, "Now, Mrs. Novak. It wouldn't be gentlemanly of me if I talked branding at the table, now would it?"

"Such a shame. I find the entire concept fascinating, don't you?" She batted long dark lashes like miniature fans, raising and lowering them over the gleam in her eyes. Twin red flags flew high in her cheeks, an indication her thoughts were not far from his own.

He'd be better off changing the subject or he wouldn't be able to walk out of the restaurant. "I've talked enough about me. Tell me more about you. Are you originally from Kansas?"

Her smile faded, the color in her cheeks fading with it. "No, my family hailed from Johnson City, Tennessee."

Now, what took the bloom out of her skin? "Do they still live there?"

"No." She sighed. "Sadly, my parents passed on two years ago."

"What about your husband?"

"Rupert?" Her face softened. "He was a kind man with a big heart. We married after my parents died. I don't know what I would have done without him."

Trace's gut tightened over the way her voice went soft when she spoke of her husband. He bit back a flash of envy for the dead man. "What did your husband do?"

"My mother and father died in a house fire. I was the only

one to escape alive. Everything they owned burned in the house." When her head shook, her black curls swayed from side to side. "You see, my father didn't believe in keeping his money in a bank."

"So you were left without a family and nothing to live on?"

A smile lifted the corners of her lips. "Don't go feeling sorry for me. Rupert came along and asked me to marry him. Of course, I said 'yes.'"

"Did you love him?" Trace leaned forward. Her answer meant more to him than he cared to admit.

"As much as I could."

Her words said what he wanted to hear. She hadn't loved her husband. "If he married you in Tennessee, how did you end up in Kansas?"

"Rupert heard there were jobs out in San Francisco, so we packed up and set off on the transcontinental railroad." Her gaze took on a glassy, faraway look. "It was such a grand adventure. Until, outside of Laramie in the Wyoming Territory, Rupert took ill of pneumonia. He died within a week."

"That explains how you became a widow. What I don't understand is how you ended up as a magician? Was your father or mother in the trade?"

She laughed, the sound like angels singing. "My father was a Baptist minister. He'd be appalled at my chosen profession. But then he's not around to know better, is he?" The laughter died from her eyes and she looked down at her hands clasped together in her lap. "There are lots of things he's better off not knowing."

Was she thinking about what she'd done to him? Perhaps feeling guilty? As mad as he'd been at her deception, he couldn't stop the feeling of wanting to release her from her burden of guilt by telling her he knew and that it was all right.

Trace opened his mouth to do just that and closed it again. If she knew he knew she'd tricked him, and she found out he'd tricked her, how would she react? He had two more nights left in Abilene. If he played his cards right, he had two nights he could spend with The Amazing Catarina. During the day, he could share her company at a safe distance.

Although, his natural reaction to her presence didn't seem safe sometimes. If he found a dark corner, he might be tempted to steal a kiss. Would she pretend to be offended and slap his face? It would be worth it to find out. Glancing around the room, he searched for just such a dark corner. Unfortunately, tables dotted every spare inch in the small eatery. The more he thought about being alone with her, the more he searched for alternatives. "Would you care to go for a ride this afternoon?"

"A ride?" Her face brightened and then creased in a frown. "Did you bring a buggy with you?"

He pretended to be serious. "Can't say that we have much use for a buggy on a cattle drive, but I think I saw one for hire in the stable. What do you say? Do you trust me to take you out unchaperoned, Mrs. Novak?"

"Oh, I don't know. I fear my virtue will be at stake." She fanned herself with a lace-gloved hand. "But if it means getting away from the stench of the stockyards for a couple hours, yes, please. I'd be delighted to accept your kind invitation."

"Then shall we say two o'clock outside your hotel?"

"I'll be there."

After Catarina left the restaurant and Trace, she frittered her time away shopping for a new hat for her buggy ride with him. She could ill afford the extravagance, except that the last two nights' proceeds from the magic show plus the coins tossed onto the stage were adding up nicely. By the end of the week, she and Nora Jane would have a tidy sum to get them to Chicago with a little nest egg to start them off while they searched for suitable work.

Wearing a pretty straw hat festooned with pale blue feathers and a wide brim to keep the sun from her skin, Catarina stepped out onto the boardwalk.

Chicago seemed so far away from Abilene, Kansas. What did she have waiting for her there? It was Nora Jane's sister, not hers. With no family left to her, Catarina had no ties to any one place. Her father and mother died in a house fire. Rupert Novak had promised to take her to California and give her children and a home. He'd died before he could realize his dream or hers. Marco Mancini had taken her in like the grandfather she'd never known and he'd died. Everyone she'd ever loved, all the family she'd ever known, had passed away. The emptiness of her life gnawed at her gut, reminding her she belonged with no one and no one belonged with her. Even her short relationship with Trace would be just that—short. He'd go back to his ranch in Texas, and Catarina? Well, she'd follow Nora Jane out to Chicago to build a life there.

Catarina wandered the streets, reflecting on where life had left her. She pondered the choices available to her and found herself wondering what it was like in Texas. Would the life of a rancher be any lonelier than a woman living alone in a city of people she didn't know?

By the time two o'clock rolled around, she'd sunk herself into a sad state of longing for a life she couldn't have. A life with a tall, blond Texan. He was only a day or two away from leaving, himself. His fascination with her would end with his stay in Abilene. A man like Trace married sweet, young virgins, not lonely, mature widows.

At the ripe old age of twenty-four, she was well past marriage material, not that Trace would ever marry a woman who'd lied to him and tricked him into her bed.

Her feet slowed as she approached the livery stable where she'd agreed to meet Trace for their buggy ride.

The man who'd been with Trace at the theater the first night hurried ahead of her, a sheet of paper in his hand. He ducked into the shadowy doorway, calling out as he went, "Trace?"

Since she was looking for the same man, Catarina followed.

As she stepped inside the barn, she removed her hat so that her eyes could adjust to the shadows more quickly. The earthy scent of manure, combined with the pungent odor of urine, stung her nostrils. Not even the smell of livestock could keep her away from the man. Catarina pressed her gloved hand to her nose and picked her way carefully past the rows of stalls to the far end of the stable.

On the opposite side of a faded black buggy, Trace knelt in the dust, adjusting the straps of a harness around a sturdy black horse. He glanced up and smiled at his friend, apparently unaware of Catarina's presence. "Jay, how was your night? Get any sleep?" The horse whinnied and danced in place. "Will you give me a hand with the traces?"

Jay grabbed one side of the leather harness and slipped it beneath the horse's neck. "No sleep for this cowboy. That Nora Jane is a wildcat, if you know what I mean."

Realizing she was eavesdropping on a private conversation, Catarina backed farther away. A man leading a horse blocked her only exit and she was forced to slide into a stall nearby.

"Yup, I do know what you mean," Trace replied. "But spare me the details, will ya?"

"What about you? Noticed you didn't come back to your room last night." Jay's brows waggled. "Spend another night with The Amazing Catarina?"

Realizing they were talking about her, Catarina held her breath, wondering whether Trace had any memory of what they'd shared.

Trace lifted the straps of the buggy harness up over the horse's shoulders. "Now, Jay, you know I don't kiss and tell."

What the hell kind of answer was that? Catarina stared through the slats of the stall, hoping to catch a glimpse of Trace's face to read into his vague comment. Had he been awake and aware the entire time last night? Was his performance just that—a performance to make her believe he was still in a trance? Her brows arrowed downward. If so, he was one sly little snake in the grass, and she was a desperately gullible widow.

Jay latched the tug strap to one side of the buggy and strode around to the other side. "Never met a woman quite like my Nora Jane. She's growing on me like a wildfire on the late summer prairie." He shook his head. "Might have to keep this one."

Trace's hands froze on the buckles of the breast strap and he shot a glance at Jay. "You thinkin' about marryin' her?"

Jay hooked the second tug strap to the buggy and stepped back, holding his hands high. "Now, just you listen before you say anything."

Trace stood straight and crossed his arms over his chest, a frown pulling his brows down over his eyes. "I'm list'nin."

"I know it's only been two days, but there's something about her that keeps me coming back and wanting more."

"Wouldn't any two-bit whore do the same?"

From her position in the stall, Catarina smothered a gasp and fought the urge to scratch Trace's eyes out. For all intents, he'd just called Nora Jane a two-bit whore. And for all she knew, he thought the same about her.

Jay's eyes narrowed and he raised his fists. "You shouldn't oughta said that, Trace. I've a good mind to knock the meanness out of you."

"But you won't, because I can best you any day."

"Say what you did again, and I will knock you down." He let out a deep breath. "Nora Jane's had a tough row to hoe, but she's got a good heart. She'd make me a damn fine wife."

Trace's arms fell to his side and the frown faded into a concerned crease between his brows. "I just wanted to make sure you were thinking this through. It's hard to get to know someone in only two days. Even tougher to decide you want to marry a woman on such short acquaintance."

"I know, I know." Jay turned away and stared at the stall in which Catarina hid.

Catarina held her breath, afraid he'd see her crouching in the darkness.

But then he sighed and faced Trace. "You aren't telling me anything I didn't think of already. Two days ain't much. But it's enough for me to know I don't want to go back to Texas without her."

Catarina's eyes welled with tears at the love she heard in Jay's voice for her dear friend Nora Jane. She wished someone felt the same about her. No, she wished Trace felt the same.

Trace laid an arm over his friend's shoulder. "Who am I to talk? I've known Martha all my life and I couldn't make up my mind until I got here."

Martha? Catarina's tears evaporated.

"So you've decided to marry her?" Jay closed the gap between himself and Trace and pounded his friend on the back. "Congratulations, old man. About time you married that girl. She's been waiting long enough."

Something lodged firmly in Catarina's throat, making it impossible to swallow. Trace had a girl back home, one he planned to marry, and her name was Martha.

Catarina had to get out of the barn, and fast, before she made a complete fool of herself in front of a man she'd grown to love in only two days. A man who'd promised to marry another woman.

A grizzled old cowboy led a draft horse toward the door about the time Catarina determined she'd have to leave even if Trace saw her. Slipping out of the stall, she walked with the horse between her and the buggy all the way out of the livery stable and on to Main Street.

Trace was going to marry another woman. She fought the urge to drop to the earth and clutch at the pain eating a hole through her belly. Instead, she pasted a smile on her face, lifted her chin, and hurried along the boardwalk to her hotel.

Once inside the safety of her room, she threw herself onto her bed and cried. The misery of her past two years of loss combined with the knowledge Trace was spoken for *and* he'd played her for a fool last night welled up and overflowed onto her feather pillow.

When someone knocked on her door fifteen minutes after two o'clock, she lay huddled against the pillow, holding her breath. It was probably that two-timing Trace on the other side. While part of her wanted to run to the door and throw herself into his arms, the other part wanted to throw something at his face.

Fighting both urges, she lay still and waited for him to give up and go away. After several knocks, she heard the click of boots on the wooden floorboards move away.

Catarina rose from the bed and brushed at the wrinkles from her dress. If only she could brush the man from her heart as easily. Even though she'd fooled him into coming to her room the first night, she hadn't had a fiancé waiting somewhere else. And to come to her room the second night, pretending to be in a trance while he had a fiancée back home, was just . . . well . . . low.

Catarina wasn't one for wallowing in self-pity for long. She was a woman of action and she wanted a plan to get back at Trace Adams for making a fool out of her and breaking her heart. She didn't know how, but she would. Then she'd take herself off to Chicago, as originally planned, and live happily ever after, despite the dratted man!

8

When Catarina didn't show up at the livery stable for the buggy ride, Trace hadn't thought much of it. Like many women, perhaps she was being fashionably late. After fifteen minutes, worry ate through his resolve to wait for her and he went in search of the black-haired beauty.

He knocked on the door to her hotel room and got no answer. With the buggy waiting at the stable, he worked his way down the street, ducking in and out of business establishments in search of Catarina or anyone who might know where she was.

At the end of the boardwalk he bumped into Jay and Nora Jane. Nora Jane had a smile as big as the Texas panhandle spread across her face and Jay had a similar grin.

Before Trace could ask them where he could find Catarina, Jay blurted, "She said 'yes'!" He picked up Nora Jane and spun her around once before setting her back on her feet.

The redhead giggled and slapped a playful hand at Jay. "Now, Jay, behave yourself." Though her voice was stern, her face glowed with happiness. She smiled up at Trace. "Guess you'll have more company on the ride back to Independence, Mr. Adams. Hope you don't mind."

"Not at all." He forced a smile despite his desperation to find Catarina. "I'm happy for you both."

"Then why do you look like you ate something bad?" Jay asked.

"I'm sorry, I was just thinking." About Catarina and how he'd like to take her back to Independence with him.

Jay's smile faded and he stepped forward. "Tweren't nothing bad in that telegram I brought you at the stable, was there?"

The telegram had been in response to his message breaking it off with Martha. The note was from his brother and held nothing but good news for Trace. While he'd been on the cattle trail, his brother Daniel had married Martha and the two couldn't be happier. "No, there's nothing wrong back home. I don't suppose you've seen Mrs. Novak, have you?"

Jay frowned. "I thought you two were goin' on a buggy ride half an hour ago."

"We were supposed to, but Cat—Mrs. Novak—seems to have been delayed." Although he'd passed the mark of being anxious, he didn't want to sound as though he was.

"I haven't seen her since this mornin' when you two were comin' out of the restaurant together," Nora Jane said. "But I'll check her room."

"No need." Trace shook his head. "I went up there and no one answered my knock."

"Something probably came up with the show." Nora Jane patted his arm as if he were an overwrought child. "If I see her, I'll let her know you're looking for her. I'm sure it's nothing to worry about."

Nothing to worry about? Trace didn't know what to think, and he spent the rest of the day searching the town for the missing magician. It was as if she'd magically disappeared.

❋   ❋   ❋

Dressed in her star-sprinkled black gown, Catarina waited behind the curtain to perform her last show in Abilene, Kansas. If all went well and the train was on time tomorrow morning, this would be the last time she'd perform as a magician. She hoped Trace wouldn't appear and demand to know why she hadn't shown up for the buggy ride that afternoon.

Nora Jane had come into their room bursting with excitement and the news that she would not be going to Chicago after all. Instead she was going to a ranch outside of Independence, Texas, with her fiancé and soon-to-be-husband, Jay Tyler.

It was all Catarina could do not to burst into tears. Hadn't she been dreaming such foolish dreams earlier that morning? That was before she'd discovered Trace had no plans to marry the widowed magician and that he had a girl back home. Didn't she know better than to hope for a happily-ever-after? That kind of life was for someone other than herself.

She'd hugged Nora Jane, honestly happy for the woman. She deserved a better life than what she'd led, and Jay seemed to be the man to give it to her.

Which left Catarina on her own, again.

"But you can still go to my sister," Nora Jane insisted. "I'll write her a letter. She'll let you stay as long as you need to."

Catarina had no plans to accept Nora Jane's kind offer. If she wanted to make it in the big city, she'd do it completely on her own. Tomorrow, at the early hour of eight o'clock in the morning, she'd board the train for Chicago and her new life. A life without Trace Adams in it. But first, she had to get through her last night in Abilene.

Throughout the magic show, she panned the audience, hoping Trace would not be among the men filling the chairs and lining the walls. Deep down, she was disappointed when he didn't show up. She should have been happy, but she ended up swallowing a dozen times to clear the lump in her throat every time she thought about the golden-haired cowboy who'd sat in the front row the first night of her show.

After the last curtain call, she secured her belongings in the heavy trunks and scooped coins off the stage. Then she ran for her room, where she slammed the door and locked it behind her. Exhausted, depressed, and lonely, she crawled into her dressing gown and lay across her bed.

At the stroke of midnight, a knock sounded at her door. Surely Trace didn't expect her to believe her hypnosis trick would work for three nights straight. She'd been gullible last night because she'd wanted him there.

Lust welled up inside her just like it had the night before and she cursed her libido. Knowing that he'd tricked her in much the same way she'd tricked him made her less than sympathetic; she was downright angry. The man had a lot of gall to show up expecting her to fall into his arms and make love to him all night long, even if it was what her body craved. He deserved to be slapped in the face. No, he deserved to be hog-tied and strung up from the nearest lynching tree. Not only for fooling her and taking advantage of her in her weakened state of desire, but also for withholding vital information from her about a fiancée waiting patiently for his return to Independence.

The louse deserved to be taught a lesson.

When the knock sounded again, she climbed down from the bed and gathered her dressing gown about her. If he wanted to play this game, she had a few tricks up her sleeve that should serve her well. But she vowed not to make love to Trace Adams ever again.

When she pulled the door open and saw the handsome cowboy on the other side, her vow of celibacy crumbled as her belly tightened. Perhaps she'd make love to him one last time before she climbed aboard the train headed for Chicago. He'd already cheated on his fiancée once because of her and once on his own. What was one more time?

* * *

As Trace stared down into Catarina's face, all he could think was that he wanted this woman in his arms forever. Before she opened her mouth and said anything, he gathered her in his arms and held her close.

The long day of searching for her and not knowing why she hadn't shown up for their buggy ride had eaten a hole in his gut. For most of the day, fear had welled inside him. For a man unafraid of gunslingers, snakes, and stampeding cattle, the fear of losing Catarina brought him to his knees.

When he'd seen her on stage earlier, he'd been confused. Where had she been all day? Had she avoided him on purpose? Then she'd opened her door to him just like she had the night before.

Was it because she thought he was still in a trance? He pushed her away, his confession that he'd tricked her poised on his lips.

"Are you here to please me or not?" Her question caught him off guard and the words he'd been prepared to say froze on his lips.

Catarina stepped from his arms and walked toward the bed, dropping her dressing gown as she went. Light from the oil lamp shown through her thin white nightgown, silhouetting the feminine curves beneath.

Trace's cock jerked to attention and swelled behind the buttons on his trousers. "Yes. Of course I'm here to please you." No, that had not been the original phrase he'd been prepared to say, but it would do for the moment.

She glanced over her shoulder, her brows raised. "What are you waiting for? Come please me." She bent to lift the hem of her nightgown, pulling the garment up and over her head, tossing it to the bed.

Trace swallowed hard at the lump in his throat.

Silken black tresses hung to the tops of her buttocks, her

smooth white skin a stark contrast to the blue-black luster. She walked toward the bed, her hips swaying from side to side.

Feeling like a boy on his first night with a woman, Trace followed, led by the promise of touching her and driving hard into her womb.

The long day of worrying about where she was had made him aware of how much he had grown to love this woman in only two short nights. The thought of being without her left him feeling empty and directionless. He'd never felt that way about Martha, only The Amazing Catarina.

Now she stood before him, naked. She crawled onto the bed and lay back against the pillows, a beckoning finger crooking at him. Her bottom lip pouted. "You're wearing entirely too many clothes to please me."

With his cock straining against the front of his pants, he had to agree. But first . . . "Catarina, we need to talk."

"Talk?" Her thin black brows winged upward. "Talk, when we could be making love?" Her laugh sounded a bit forced, but she patted the bed beside her. "Let's talk later. Right now, I can think of better things to do."

Although Trace wanted to clear the air between them and confess to tricking her last night, he wanted to hold her in his arms more. They could talk later, when they'd spent their passions. He shucked his clothes in record time and stood facing her in the soft lamplight.

Catarina smiled, the light never reaching her eyes, and her gaze dropped to his protruding cock. "You are magnificent, aren't you?" Her knees spread wide. "Come to me."

Dropping to the bed beside her, he gathered her into his arms and kissed her long and hard. Had it only been that morning when he'd held her like this? It felt more like an eternity. When she hadn't shown up for their ride, he'd been beside himself with worry. He broke off the kiss and stared down into her face. "Where were you this afternoon?"

"Shhh." She pressed a finger to his lips. "This is my fantasy. We'll play it my way." Then she rolled him onto his back and straddled his hips.

Taken aback at first, Trace didn't resist. Not with his cock pressed to the entrance of her warm, wet pussy. He liked the wildcat in Catarina and looked forward to more of it in the near future, if she'd consider going to Texas with him.

With his hands clasped in hers, she crawled up over him. "My turn to play with you." Using her discarded gown, she tied his wrists to the headboard. As she leaned over him, the heady scent of her skin and rosewater filled his senses. A breast dangled in his face and her furry mound brushed across his belly.

He leaned up and captured her nipple between his lips and sucked it into his mouth.

Her hands paused in the process of tying his wrists and she pressed into him, allowing him better access to her breast.

Trace tugged at his bonds, not liking that he couldn't touch her or feel her warm skin between his fingertips. "Untie me so that I can touch you."

Her smile had a devilish gleam as she sat back, her creamy cunt oozing warm liquid over his cock. "Oh, no, this will be my way tonight." Then she slid down him, her breasts rubbing against the hairs on his chest. She paused to nip at his hard brown nipple.

"Ouch! Not so hard."

"Oops, sorry, didn't mean to hurt you." She smoothed a hand over his chest and then leaned over and nipped his other nipple.

"Ouch!" Trace strained his neck upward and glared at her. "If I didn't know better, I'd think you were trying to hurt me."

"Why would I want to hurt you, cowboy?" Her lips smoothed down his chest, trailing kisses down to his belly button.

This was better, much better. The wildcat had claws, but she knew when to purr and please.

When she reached his jutting cock, she grasped him in her hands and squeezed gently, rubbing her cheek against the tip.

Heat seared through him like a branding iron burning its way through his body. He bucked beneath her grasp, pressing upward.

Then she did something amazing: she took him fully into her mouth, swallowing the tip of his cock all the way down the length until he bumped against the back of her throat.

His breath caught in his chest and he held it there, savoring the intense surge of lust rushing over him.

Her mouth rose off him. "Like that?"

"Oh yes." He tried to reach for her, only to be restrained by her nightgown holding him fast to the headboard. "I'd like it much better if I could hold you and give you as much pleasure."

"Uh uh. This is my fantasy. And this is what I want to do." Her brows rose as if to challenge him.

He frowned. Something about the hard glint in Catarina's eyes made Trace wonder. Did she doubt that he was in a trance? Had she figured it out? He really needed to level with her and get everything out in the open.

When she climbed up over him, all thoughts raced south to where her pussy hovered over the tip of his cock. Now what was it he wanted to say?

She slid down over him, sheathing him in her hot, moist center.

"Good God, Cat, you're incredible."

"I am, am I?" She rose on her haunches until the tip of his cock almost slid free of her channel.

He wanted to grab her hips and slam her home, but his hands were firmly tied to the bed. "Untie me, Catarina. Please. I need to hold you."

"Do you?" She rose up again and sank down.

Trace thrust upward to meet her.

As she rose and fell onto him, her breasts bounced free, teasing him with their fullness.

His arms ached with the strain of pulling against the head board. If she didn't untie him soon, he feared he'd rip the rails out. He'd gladly pay for a new headboard for the chance to get his hands on her.

She settled into a rhythm, moving up and down over him.

He thrust upward each time she fell back on her haunches.

When she leaned back, letting her hair dangle between his thighs, the feathery-soft tips teased him to a frenzy. His body tensed and he shouted, "Come with me, Catarina. Now!"

Catarina let him come inside her, her heart breaking even as she felt his body's release. He'd yelled for her to come with him. How she'd wished he'd said it because he wanted her to go to Texas with him.

But Trace Adams had a girl waiting back home. He just wanted her for a few nights of lovemaking. Why would he want a woman who made a living on the stage when he could have Martha back in Texas?

While Trace lay spent against the sheets, Catarina wanted her own satisfaction. Hot and creamy from her ride on the cowboy, she was ready for a little more action.

Trace's cock lay against his belly, still stiff and wet with their shared juices.

Spreading her folds, Catarina rubbed her clit against his staff, her breathing ragged and jumpy in her throat. If she untied him, he'd take on this task and bring her to her pleasure much faster. He might even take her in his mouth like he had last night.

The thought of his tongue and teeth on her sensitive nub had her pitching over the edge and shattering into a thousand little pieces.

"You should have let me get you there." The disappointment in Trace's voice almost made her untie him and do it again.

Catarina resisted his entreaty and collapsed across his chest, drinking in the musky scent of man, leather, and the great outdoors.

"We really should talk, Cat."

"Later. We'll talk later." She promised, with no intention of talking to him. For a long time, she lay on top of him, soaking in everything about him.

Even though he'd lied to her and used her, she couldn't resist him. When his breathing evened out, she rolled off him and watched him in his sleep. Then she quietly moved about the room, packing her valise with the last of her personal belongings. She'd sent her trunks to the train earlier that night.

When she was dressed and ready to go, she hesitated.

Trace lay in the middle of the bed, sound asleep, with his wrists still tied to the headboard. His soft snoring made Catarina smile. She could have gotten used to sleeping beside this man.

She leaned over him one last time and kissed him. "Goodbye, cowboy."

The blast of a train's whistle woke Trace from his sleep. When he tried to turn over, his arms wouldn't move. His eyes flew open when he realized he was still tied to the bed. Worse, Catarina was nowhere in sight.

The train whistle blasted again as a last call for passengers boarding.

"Catarina?" Trace called out.

When he got no answer, Trace glanced around the room. It

was strangely empty, as if Catarina had never been there. Where was her valise and the dress that had hung on a peg on the wall the night before?

"Catarina!" Trace's heart thudded against his chest as a horrible thought took root in his gut. She was gone. Catarina had left and she wasn't coming back.

Then he yelled loud enough to wake all of Abilene.

Catarina sat in her seat on the train, her valise in her lap, her heart back in the room with Trace. If she went back to him, he'd just use her for another night and be on his way back to Texas the following day.

The last train whistle blew and the train jerked to a start, rolling slowly along beside the depot. It was going slow enough she could jump from the train and not hurt herself.

Why would she jump? Trace wasn't hers, she didn't own his heart. He had Martha waiting for him back home.

The devil on her shoulder whispered, *he isn't married yet.*

What chance did she have of getting a man like Trace to marry her instead? She didn't know anything about ranching; she was an older woman and a showgirl. Showgirls were tainted according to polite society. No, she was better off staying on the train to Chicago.

As the train picked up a little speed, Catarina balanced on the edge of her seat. She at least should have untied Trace before she'd left. He'd have to yell until someone showed up to loosen her nightgown from his wrists.

It was her only nightgown.

She stood and, holding on to the back of the seat, worked her way past the passengers to the steps leading down off the car. When she was on the last step, only inches from jumping to the ground, she heard a shout.

Looking back toward the train station, she saw Trace on the

white stallion she'd ridden into town—the one she'd sold the day before after Trace had returned the horse and buggy to the stable.

Her chest filled with hope. Was he coming to bring her back? Did he love her? The hope died before it could take firm root. No, she'd left him tied to the headboard. He was probably madder than hell and out for revenge.

At that moment, he spied her perching on the step. "Catarina! Don't go." His horse easily caught up to the slow-moving train.

She clutched the handrail with one hand and her valise with the other. He looked like he really didn't want her to go. Was it because he wanted to shout at her? "Aren't you mad about being left tied up?"

"Yes—no. Ah, hell, Cat. Don't go. We never got to talk and I have so much to tell you."

She gave an unladylike snort. "Like the fact you have a fiancée back home?"

"I did, but I don't anymore. Please, Catarina, get off the train."

That little ray of hope sprang up again in her belly. "What do you mean not anymore?"

He grinned like a fool. "She married my brother."

So he was free after all. For a moment, Catarina thought she could believe in a future with Trace, but then she realized she'd be a consolation prize after being jilted by his fiancée. "I'm going to Chicago."

"You can't." Trace nudged the horse a little faster to keep up with the train's increasing speed.

"Why?"

"Because I love you, Catarina."

"Only because your fiancée dumped you." She refused to be second choice.

"No, I couldn't marry Martha even before I met you because I didn't love her. I didn't realize it until I met and fell in love with you."

The train's speed was getting faster as they approached the edge of town.

"Stay with me, Catarina." Trace yelled, kicking the horse into a gallop.

Catarina's heart burst from her chest and she stared down at the ground speeding by. "I can't go with you."

"Why?"

"The train's moving too fast. I can't jump."

Trace moved closer to the train and held out his hand. "Grab my hand and jump!"

Catarina only hesitated a moment. She threw her valise off the train, grabbed Trace's hand and took a leap of faith straight into Trace's arms. Well, more like across the front of his saddle, landing hard enough to knock the air from her lungs.

As the train sped away, Trace hauled on the reins until the stallion came to a wheezing halt.

Catarina straightened herself in front of Trace. Now that they were still and her heart rate was returning to normal, she didn't know what to say to this man she'd fallen for in just three short days. "I didn't think you loved me."

"I didn't know until I couldn't find you yesterday." He kissed her and pushed a strand of hair from her face. "I thought my world was falling apart. All I wanted was to be with you."

"I thought you wouldn't want a washed-up old widow woman." She placed her hands on each side of his cheeks and kissed his lips.

"You're not old and I love everything about you." He kissed her lips and kissed each palm. "You make me laugh and you're amazing in bed."

"I don't know anything about ranching," she argued, though why, she didn't know.

"I'll teach you." He kissed her lightly on the lips and laughed out loud. "I love you, Catarina."

She snuggled into his arms. "I'll need a different horse. Lightning doesn't like women."

"I have just the horse for you back home in Texas."

"Home." She sighed. "I like the sound of that."

"You'll love it there. If you don't, we'll go wherever you want."

"I love you, Trace Adams."

"I love you, and you're amazing, Catarina." He smiled down into her eyes. "Will you marry this cowboy, showgirl?"

Cat's eyes brimmed with moisture. She'd only just dreamed he'd ask her this very question. "Yes, I will."

His brows rose. "I have one condition."

"Condition?" Her breath caught in her throat. How could anything dull the sun shining over her head?

"You promise to never again leave me trussed up in a hotel wearing nothing but my toenails."

"Can't promise you that, cowboy." She let the breath out and kissed his chin. "What if you make me mad?"

"I can see I've got a wildcat by the tail."

She smiled up at him with a twinkle in her eyes. "That, I can promise."

Don't miss this hot sneak peek at
MIDNIGHT CONFESSIONS II,
by Bonnie Edwards.

Available now from Aphrodisia . . .

1

Faye Grantham placed her cheek next to the smooth pine planking of the wall and peered through a peephole set at eye level. The angle of the hole gave her a perfect view of the bed in the next room. Odd how she already knew it would look like this. The walls were in shadow, with the bed spotlighted.

All she could see was the bed and a couple standing beside it. Their faces were obscured. The woman wore her long blond hair in a fall of cascading white and cream. Faye couldn't make out her face behind the curtain of lustrous hair.

She fingered her own shoulder-length waves. Hers were shorter, but the color was similar.

The man's upper face was in shadow. His jaw, strong and lightly bristled, glowed from the odd lighting. His mouth, mobile and hard, dipped in and out of the light so Faye couldn't see it clearly. A mystery couple about to do unmysterious things.

The man untied the laces at the bodice of the woman's nightgown to let it drift and skim down her body to her feet. White, cotton, chaste, the nightgown gave no clue to what era they were in.

The man wore trousers, but his chest was bare. Suspenders dangled at his hips. His erection strained for freedom until the woman guided it to peek out the top of his waistband.

Yum. Great chest, slim hips, hard belly, and a wide head on his cock. Faye responded as if she were the one cupping his balls and feeling his hot thumbs swirl across her nipples.

Odd, but pleasurable, the sensation of his callused hands aroused her.

Hot! She was suddenly aroused beyond tolerance by the seductively slow foreplay she witnessed through the peephole. She slid her hand to her crotch and pressed a fingertip to her clit through her thin silk nightie. She was wet and needy and the finger pressure made it better, but she still couldn't ease her need. She pressed harder, rubbed.

The narrow passageway she stood in closed in around her as she caught her breath. The man, naked now and gloriously hard, pressed the woman's shoulders down. She sank to her knees and took him into her mouth. Drew him in deep.

Faye's mouth worked in conjunction as she watched the woman suck him deep into her throat. Faye tasted hot man-flesh and swirled her tongue around her mouth, feeling him.

Slowly, carefully, the man pumped into her mouth while the woman continued to lick. He was big and she had to adjust, but eventually, she took most of his full length.

The man's face was still in shadow and he hadn't spoken. Silent but for the sound of mouth-work, lit from a spotlight, the two performed while Faye watched through the bullet-sized hole. The man pumped harder; the woman's head bobbed more quickly. Tension rose around the silent couple, while Faye's arousal deepened.

Faye closed her eyes in passion while she worked to bring herself closer to climax. Next time she could focus, the couple had climbed onto the bed and were writhing together, with deep kisses and rough and ready hands. Still, no sounds came to Faye. No bedsprings, no sighs or moans torn from the amorous pair.

The woman's pale calves flashed in the dim light from the bedside lamps, as she raised them to offer herself to her lover.

Was this *her* room? Was she watching herself with Liam?

The long, slick invasion stretched her wide and she felt the man enter her, knew what the woman knew. The man's heated scent, the feel of his weight on her chest, the incredible stretch of his cock as he pressed her deep into the mattress.

Faye rolled her hips in acceptance and began the dance of need.

Vaguely, she understood she was dreaming. In Perdition House, anything could happen, and often did. She lived with ghosts who saw nothing wrong with siphoning off her orgasms, inciting her to sex with strangers, and causing wild, insatiable desires to bubble under her skin.

Pleasure rose under her hand as she played voyeur and rubbed at her pussy. Suddenly, her nightie slid off her shoulders and drifted away on a breeze that caressed her heated flesh as she watched the lovers, moaned along with them, and felt every sensation they did.

She fought the rising tide, trying to see whose room they were in. As she focused her eyes away from the couple, the details of the room came clearer. Past the bed, light shone on a wallpaper design decades old.

With no French doors, no staircase to a widow's walk on the roof, it wasn't her room. Hers was larger, airier, prettier.

Comforted, she settled in to watch, unable to tear her eyes away even though the couple deserved their privacy. After all, the man had paid for it.

The light in the room dimmed, but still the wall danced with the lovers' shadow, grotesquely erotic. A woman prone, her legs raised, the man's head at her crotch. Finally, she heard sucking and licking sounds as the man pleasured the woman.

The lover's lips and tongue slid harder against her tender flesh, wilder and wilder until the woman crested and moaned, eyes closed, in a low, deep, delicious orgasm that pulsed out in waves from her lowest reaches. Faye rode out the come, closed her eyes and melted and shook along with the lovers.

A sudden scream rent the air, ripping into Faye. The piercing wail came through the wall, clear as a chime and full of terror.

Faye opened her eyes and tried to see what had happened, who had screamed, but the light in the room was suddenly bright as a cloudless day and hurt her eyes. She could see nothing, and all sound faded.

She rolled over and woke, fading pulses the only proof that she'd dreamed again.

A nap—it had all happened during a nap. Groggy and sated from the still-pulsing orgasm, she rose to her elbow to look at the bedside clock. She had two hours. Lots of time.

She stretched, still shaken by what she'd heard. This dream was different from her usually pleasant unfolding stories. She could hardly make sense of it.

The narrow, secret passageway ran between two bedrooms on the second floor. She'd been in there once. The peepholes were installed by the original madam who built the house. She and a troupe of intrepid women had come to Seattle from Butte, Montana. They'd operated an exclusive men's retreat that catered only to the very wealthy and powerful.

Retreat being a polite word for the country's most expensive whorehouse of the last century. Completed in 1911, Perdition House was now hers, left to her by her great-aunt, Mae Grantham, who in turn had inherited it from the original madam, Belle Grantham.

Faye had decided to sell and cash in on her inheritance.

The only obstacle to that decision—Belle still lived here, as did the original four prostitutes. Salacious spirits, the five of them wreaked havoc on Faye's libido.

Not that she minded all that much. What red-blooded woman wouldn't want three or four orgasms a day, she reasoned.

Faye had moved into the mansion and discovered Perdition House was a place of sin, sex, and secrets.

Faye loved every minute of living here.

Logic dictated that the screamer in this dream was one of the women who'd worked here. She hadn't recognized the woman, though, except that the color of her hair was so similar to Faye's.

She couldn't trust anything she'd seen in a dream anyway. Her great-aunt Belle would have done anything to keep Perdition House going when she was alive. Now she was dead, she was even more determined. Belle manipulated everyone who came here with sexual need and sleight-of-hand.

"Are you sure what you heard was a frightened scream? It might have just been a rapturous climax." Belle, her dead-for-decades great-great aunt, suggested.

For the moment, the beautiful spirit was perched on the staircase to the widow's walk, one of her favorite spots to sit.

"I don't know," Faye said, no longer fazed by speaking with a long-dead madam. "Maybe it was just a lusty come. Why not tell me what happened? Why the secrecy?"

Stupid question.